She buried h... ...ands and knew that she would never be as empty as she was at this moment, barren of everything in life that mattered.

No man, no child, no life except her own. Toni felt the tears on her face, and at that moment new determination was born. If the opportunity came to use Lane Monday to father her child, she would, and with no regrets. He'd made it perfectly clear that she wasn't his type, and that was okay. At least it would be when she could think of him without tears and anger. But she had two more nights to find a way to make it happen. God willing, the chance would come, and with the chance, the child.

It had to.

Dear Reader

Welcome to Silhouette Sensation® in the new millennium. As always we've got plenty of terrific reading for you, so come and forget the daily grind with us—indulge yourself!

Let's start with a very special man, January's **Heartbreaker** from Sharon Sala—*The Miracle Man*—he's the kind of guy most women would choose to father their child—if only they dared!

The Tough Guy and the Toddler by Diane Pershing pretty much speaks for itself, and *Like Father, Like Daughter* from Margaret Watson kicks off a set of linked books from this talented writer. Look for *For the Children* in March.

And last but never least, is favourite author Paula Detmer Riggs with a cracking read about a cop and his ex-wife whose son is abducted and how, once the boy is found, they become *Once More a Family*.

Enjoy!

The Editors

The Miracle Man

SHARON SALA

First published in Great Britain 2000
Silhouette Books, Eton House, 18-24 Paradise Road,
Richmond, Surrey TW9 1SR

© Sharon Sala 1995

ISBN 0 373 07650 9

18-0001

Printed and bound in Spain
by Litografia Rosés S.A., Barcelona

SHARON SALA

is a child of the country. As a farmer's daughter, her vivid imagination made solitude a thing to cherish. As a farmer's wife, she learned to take each day as it came without worrying about the next. After she and her husband, Bill, raised two children and too many crops to count, she went from clothesline to deadlines with a smile on her face. Writing is nothing more than the fulfilment of a lifelong habit of daydreaming. Giving birth to characters in her mind and then sharing them with those who like to read is the thing she loves best.

This book is dedicated to the belief in miracles and miracle workers everywhere. To the doctors, nurses, care givers and EMTs. To men and women of the cloth. To all the men in law enforcement who daily put their lives on the line, and to everyone who believes.

And especially to the miracle workers who have impacted upon my life: Dennis Dukes, EMT; Kathy Orr, EMT; RaeAnne Berry, EMT; Dr Frank Howard, Dr Robert L Talley, Dr Ross Pope, Dr Michael Goddard and Dr Don Mace. Also a belated thanks to retired doctors John G Rollins, MD, and Jake Jones, MD, and to the late Dr Ned Burleson, as well as the late Dr Kirk T Mosley, who was always there when I needed him.

Chapter 1

The small, twelve-seater airplane assigned to the United States Marshal's Office sat on a runway at the Tallahassee airport. As armed guards watched from the runway, a nondescript blue van pulled up and began emptying its deadly cargo.

Three men, marked by prison uniforms, leg irons and shackles, filed out of the van with little fuss. Hog-tied by more than the bonds of the criminal justice system, they had nowhere to go but up the ramp and into the waiting plane where they were placed in seats.

Emmit Rice muttered belligerently as he shifted his six-foot-five-inch, three-hundred-pound bulk toward two of the three seats at the front of the airplane.

Oversize handcuffs circled his massive wrists, and the shackles and leg irons, compliments of the Federal Correctional Institution in Tallahassee, Florida, rattled when he came to an abrupt stop at the seat and landed with a grunt. He glanced up and then glared at the marshal who was waiting patiently for him to settle.

"What the hell are you looking at?" he muttered.

For the past fifteen years, Lane Monday had served as a United States marshal. So a disgruntled prisoner, even one the size of a small tank, was nothing new to him.

Lane grinned, then ducked out of habit to keep from bumping his head as he maneuvered his own six feet six inches into the bulkhead of the plane. His answer, as well as the slow appraisal that he gave Emmit Rice, were telling.

"What am *I* looking at? Not much," he said, and stifled another grin when Emmit Rice's face flushed in anger. It was probably one of the few times in his life, Lane mused, that Emmit Rice had been reduced in size, as well as strength, by little more than a look.

Rice snorted and stretched his massive body into as much space as he possibly could. It was an intimidating gesture that he knew usually netted results. But the cool, assessing stare that the big marshal gave him was proof that intimidation was not going to work. Not on Lane Monday.

Monday was more than a match for him in height. And while he had nowhere near the bulk of Emmit Rice, he had a powerful body to back up the gun that he carried.

And it was Lane Monday's size alone that had been the reason for his recall from a much-needed vacation. Someone had to escort Emmit Rice from the Federal Correctional Institution in Tallahassee, Florida, to the one in Lexington, Kentucky. Who better than a man who could look Rice in the eye and come away grinning?

The last man to board the plane was the other marshal, Bob Tell. "Buckle up, boys. Better safe than sorry." Bob laughed at his own joke as he did a last-minute check of the prisoners and their restraints.

One of the prisoners laughed with him. The other two, Rice included, neither smiled nor looked at the man who thought he was a comic. Their eyes were fixed upon the mass of man who stood between them and freedom, wearing a cold blue stare and a gun on his hip.

"Time to check guns," Bob said, opening the lid of a strongbox and holding it toward Lane, while he kept an eye on the prisoners who were watching the proceedings with entirely too much interest.

Monday slid his weapon out of its holster and dropped it into the lockbox as Bob followed suit, pocketing the key before stowing the box in the cockpit.

It was standard procedure to check guns before taking off. The last thing a lawman wanted was to be overpowered by a prisoner and have his own weapon taken away and used on an innocent bystander—or on himself.

Finally the plane was airborne, and there was nowhere to go but down. It was then that the air within the cabin seemed to settle, and two of the prisoners even dozed while Bob sat watch.

But Rice didn't sleep. His small, green eyes were firmly fixed upon the marshal who'd had to turn sideways to get his shoulders through the door.

Lane Monday didn't budge from the position that he'd taken when the plane had lifted off. He knew all too well how desperate the man was he'd been assigned to transport.

Emmit Rice was a lawman's nightmare. He was a lifer with nothing to lose. Regardless of what else he might do, he'd already lost everything that mattered but his life. And the way he looked at living behind bars, his life was already lost.

And then they flew into the storm and everything changed, including the hand that fate had dealt them.

Although it was still hours before nightfall, the clouds that had arrived, seemingly from nowhere, were pitch-black. In the space of a heartbeat, the plane appeared to go from day into night as it flew right into the mouth of a storm. Lightning flashed outside the plane, momentarily illuminating the sky.

"Son of a bitch," one of the prisoners muttered, ducking his head from the brilliant flash of electrical energy.

In seconds, Bob was on his feet and heading for the cockpit while Monday stayed put, bracing himself against the bulkhead with both feet outspread and his arms above his head, riding out the air pockets with grim-lipped determination. He'd been in some bad spots before and gotten through them fine.

But something told him that this time might be a different story.

"We're gonna crash! We're gonna crash!"

Prisoner DeVon Randall was losing control. His voice had elevated three octaves as, wild-eyed, he stared around the cabin, trying to free himself from the seat in which he was bound.

Emmit Rice glared at Randall, hating him for verbalizing what they all felt. He would not have admitted his fear under penalty of death, but he was afraid the little man might be right.

"Calm down, Randall," Monday said.

His order to the prisoner went in one ear and out the other. The man was chained—and in hysterics. The combination could prove lethal for them all. Then Bob burst out of the cockpit and nearly ran Monday down.

"Damn, Monday. This is bad. We've got to prepare the men in case of—"

He never finished what he was saying. Blinding light, followed by a loud crack, sent both lawmen to their knees. The plane bucked and the cabin momentarily went dark. When the lights flickered back on, Bob was scrambling for the keys in his pocket and heading for the three prisoners, pinned in their seats by shackles and leg irons.

"Help me," Bob shouted. "We're going down, and they'll die for sure if they can't get out."

Monday hesitated for a moment. It was instinctive. Letting these three loose, even inside a plane in danger of crashing, was taking chances that he didn't want to consider. But leaving them as they were was the same as shooting them where they sat.

"I want my gun back," Monday growled. Bob nodded, hurrying to retrieve their weapons.

When his gun was safely back in its holster, Monday headed for Emmit Rice. He was, after all, the reason that he'd come.

Nearly nose to nose with the big marshal, Rice stared up into a cold blue gaze and swallowed. He wanted to be able to threaten him; he needed to reassert himself and his territory.

But he was too damned afraid of crashing and burning to give much thought to the hard warning that was evident in Monday's eyes.

"Don't even think about it, and assume the position," Monday warned as he put the flat of his hand squarely in the back of Rice's head and pushed.

Rice obliged by ducking his head between his knees. Not for the first time, he wished that he didn't have so much belly to get around. It would have been easier to brace himself for the crash if he could have gotten lower in the seat.

"Tell, buckle up!"

Monday's warning coincided with the second bolt of lightning that hit the plane. The sound of his voice was lost in the thunder and the second wave of darkness that ensued.

Monday felt the floor of the plane tilt. *Oh, hell, not down.*

But his plea went unanswered, and his heart followed the angle of the plane as he braced himself for the impact that was bound to come. Once again, lightning flashed, and he had a moment's impression of Emmit Rice lying unconscious against the bulkhead between the cockpit and the seating area.

"What the...?" Monday muttered as he staggered with the pitch of the plane.

When he'd last checked, Rice had been buckled in his seat. Now that he was out, Monday figured that Rice had been planning to try something. Although the man was obviously unconscious, he frowned at the thought of Rice on the loose and slipped a pair of handcuffs out of his pocket. If Rice tried to escape, the prisoner was going to have to take him along when he did it.

Purposefully, Monday fastened one bracelet of the handcuff around his own wrist, then waited for the plane to steady before heading for Rice. When Rice revived, he was going to have more company than he might have wanted. Being cuffed to a lawman was going to put a big kink in his plans for escape.

Bob Tell's expression, and those of the now-chained prisoners, became grotesquely illuminated from the blue-white flash of lightning, which gave them all a deathly appearance.

Monday grimaced and wondered if he looked the same. Then the plane lurched unexpectedly into a sharp downward angle, and everything, including his thoughts, went out like the lights as the plane hit the ground.

Blinding rain stung Lane's face and eyelids. It was his first indication that he was still alive. Thunder rumbled overhead, grinding through the air like a runaway train. He flinched at the sound, and then groaned when the small movement caused him pain.

The scent of fuel was strong. Even through the deluge, sparks arced from the wreckage with frightening irregularity. He knew that it was only a matter of time before what was left of the plane exploded.

"Bob? Bob? Where are you, man? Answer me!" Lane shouted, then waited, praying for his partner's voice to come out of the darkness. When he shouted again and still received no answer, he tried to get up, then cursed when he found himself unable to move.

My God, don't let me be trapped.

His stomach turned at the thought of surviving the crash, only to burn alive. If he was going to die, he would choose his own method of exit. A bullet was definitely an easier way to go than burning. His hand shook as he reached for his gun and then came away empty.

"Damn."

The gun was missing from its holster. When his panic had subsided, his training kicked in, and he began to assess where he was by feel alone.

It was with no small amount of relief that he realized he could feel his feet and legs. Even the sharp, burning pain up his thigh was a welcome antidote to his initial fear that he'd been paralyzed. At this point, pain was the lesser of two evils.

He tried, unsuccessfully, to move again, and only then did he realize his predicament as he felt fabric and metal beneath his fingertips. Something large and heavy had him pinned to the ground.

Lightning once again shattered the darkness, streaking across the night sky like a flame running up a fuse.

"Son of a…"

Lane inhaled and tried not to panic at what the momentary burst of light had revealed. At least now he knew why he hadn't been able to move. He was pinned in the wreckage by a section of seats…and DeVon Randall's body. Instinctively, he traced the shape of Randall's face down to his neck, searching for pulse. There was none.

Using his massive upper-body strength, Lane pushed until the seats gave. Randall's lifeless body followed, and finally Lane was free. He crawled to his feet in blinding pain, then staggered, losing his center of gravity as another streak of lightning flashed across the sky.

But this time, in the swift flash of light, in spite of his nausea and disorientation, he saw the rest of what there was to see. Bob Tell lay sprawled atop the other prisoners. Lane didn't have to touch them to know that they were all dead. It was a well-known fact that no one lived with their head on backward.

Rain continued to hammer down on Lane's face and body. Sparks continued to fly. The smell of burning fuel became stronger and stronger. *He had to get out. Now!* He turned, then staggered, and as he did, metal clanked against metal, and he felt the dangling handcuff at the end of his wrist.

It was then that he remembered Rice. He was the only prisoner as yet unaccounted for. The last time he'd seen him, Rice had been lying unconscious against the bulkhead of the plane.

But Emmit Rice was nowhere in sight, although Lane told himself that the man could easily be under any part of the wreckage. Lane tried to take another step, when a sharp pain rocketed through his leg, sending him to his knees. The plane was a time bomb waiting for the right spark, and he'd just realized that he couldn't walk. Never one to let a small thing stop him, he began to crawl, searching for a way out.

He was less than twenty yards from the plane when the first explosion came, rocking the ground on which he crawled and sending burning debris straight up into the air, only to shower back down around him like shrapnel. The empty holster around his waist hampered his movements, and he quickly unbuckled it and then continued to drag himself out of harm's way.

There was no time to worry about missing prisoners or burning bodies. All Lane could do was get as far away from the fire as possible.

Just when he thought he was out of danger, the ground gave way under him. He went headfirst off the ledge and into the flood-swollen waters of the ravine below. For the first time in his life, he wished that he'd been born a runt. Then he would never have been on this godforsaken flight.

A short time later in the fading light of dusk, he surfaced, gasping for air and cursing to keep from passing out from the pain. A log struck him in the back, and he bobbed with the impact, then turned and grasped it as if it were a long-lost lover. He was barely afloat. Barely alive.

Antonette Hatfield gave the new strand of wire on the north pasture fence a final twist, then cursed beneath her breath when the shiny barb poked her knuckle.

"If I had a man, *he* would be out here melting in this damned heat and I would be home doing something better. Like tending to a house and raising my babies."

But her complaint was an old one, said only out of habit and not real dismay.

Antonette had long ago given up expecting Mr. Right to appear on her doorstep. For some reason, she kept scaring the good ones away. It had occurred to her that her size, nearly six feet tall and generously proportioned with womanly curves and valleys, might have had something to do with it. That and the fact that she had no tolerance for fools seemed to send a lot of men packing.

The few who had lingered over those two hurdles had never made it past the knowledge that she had seven brothers who would take great pride in hurting them—badly—should they cross the line of proper behavior. Her brothers considered it their responsibility to see "Toni" suitably wed. Better, they thought, that she become an old maid, than bring someone into the family who didn't belong.

At her present age of twenty-nine, she had even given up her dream of marrying Mr. Wrong. What she wanted now— and what she would settle for at the drop of a hat—was a baby. Granted, it took one to get the other, but the way she looked at it, the mister could take himself off to greener pastures any old day, as long as he left her with child before he did it.

While she was daydreaming, a warning rumble of far-off thunder made her look up.

A storm was brewing.

Thankful that she had this job nearly finished, she leaned back against the seat of her all-terrain vehicle and pulled open the top of her water jug. The ice had melted long ago, but the water was wet and fairly cool, and for the time being settled the hungry grumble in her belly as it went down.

The sultry, late-evening air had already molded her clothes to her body. And while she'd started the day with her long hair twisted haphazardly on top of her head like a thick brown nest of curls, heat and work had sent it tumbling down around her face and neck.

Sweat stung her eyes. She absently swiped at it with the back of her forearm, then thought of iced tea and a clean change of clothes, and began gathering up leftover fencing material. Ignoring the impulse to return it as orderly as it had been loaded, she cast one last look at the gathering storm and began tossing the fence posts and wire into the back of the small, low-sided wagon she was pulling behind her ATV.

The thick Tennessee woods in which she lived had few paved roads, and even fewer that were graveled. Raising cows, corn and hay, with eight children thrown in for good measure, were all that Anton and Lissy Hatfield had ever done. But Lissy had been dead for years, and all seven of her sons had married and moved away from home. Four months ago, Anton Hatfield had joined Lissy, leaving their baby alone to care for the family farm.

That ''baby,'' Antonette, was stronger than most men, and

her being nearly six feet tall had little to do with it. She was still the youngest, and she bore, on a daily basis, the constant, unsolicited advice of her neighbor, Justin, who also happened to be her oldest brother.

Beyond the hills thunder rumbled. Toni looked up and frowned. She wanted a bath, all right, but not the kind that accompanied thunder and lightning. Anxious to beat the on-coming storm, she tossed the last of her tools into the wagon and jumped on the ATV.

She was miles from home. And pulling this load, it would take her a good twenty minutes to get to safety. She squinted, assessing the buildup of storm clouds now evident over the treetops, and made a bet with herself that she would be wet before she got home.

The ATV roared to life. Moments later, Toni was speeding past her new quarter mile of fence, racing storm clouds toward the home that sat high on a hill above Chaney Creek.

A couple of miles down the road, she came to a sliding halt in a cloud of dust. Some of her fence posts had bounced from the back of the wagon onto the ground, forcing her to stop and go back for them.

"I don't know why I'm hurrying," she grumbled to herself. "There's no one at home to care whether I'm late, wet, or both."

Feeling a little sorry for herself and aching through her shoulders from the long day of stringing barbed wire, she stomped back to her ATV and slipped it into gear. Rain or not, she would take her time about getting home.

By the time she reached Chaney Creek, the sky was as black as the inside of a devil's heart. Thunderheads rolled with in-creasing intensity as the wind within them continued to blow. The quickening breeze lifted the thick, loose hair from Toni's neck as she contemplated the load in her wagon against the steep hill ahead of her. She would have to go very slow to save what was left of her posts. Carrying them up the hill by the armload didn't appeal to her at all, not even if she were physically strong enough to do so.

Before she had made any decision, the rains came. All at

once and without the warning of a few early droplets to let a body know that it was time to run. Toni sighed and lifted her sweaty face to the torrent, letting Mother Nature cool her weary body.

She looked back at the wagon again and then once more at the steep path leading to her home. Her decision had just been made for her. She might succeed in getting the ATV up the hill, but in this downpour, she also might not. The hill was mostly red clay, and when it got wet, it was, as her brother Justin always said, "slick as snot."

She parked beneath the overhang of a large spreading oak just as a tremendous explosion rent the air. Stunned by the intensity of the sound, she jumped out from under the massive branches before a fork of lightning could find its way to this tree and fry her along with it. Squinting against the oncoming darkness and the downpour of rain in her face, she looked at the rim of the next hill and saw a huge, orange ball of fire spiral into the sky.

"Good Lord. Lightning must have struck something awfully big."

Reassured by the fact that her home was in the opposite direction, Toni started to run.

The path was slick, just as she feared it would be. Her shirt and jeans were plastered to her body. Had any of her past, fair-weather suitors gotten a glimpse of the generous curves she normally kept hidden beneath nondescript clothing, they might have been tempted to give her one more try. But they weren't and she was alone and running like hell in the near dark toward the hill above Chaney Creek.

Lightning flashed again. This time it was close. Too close. Toni froze in place. In shock over the near miss, and momentarily blinded by the flash, her vision cleared only to present her with another, more frightening dilemma than being caught in a storm. Someone had fallen into Chaney Creek and was being swept downstream.

"Oh, my God!" Toni pivoted on the path and ran down the hill toward the flooded waters of the creek, unable to believe her eyes. "Hey! Hey! I'm here! Swim this way! I'll help you."

But the man gave no indication of having heard her. And the closer he came, the more convinced she was of his distress. Only the upper portion of his body was above water. His arms were wrapped around a piece of log that bobbed in the foaming water like a float on a fishing line. It was all that kept him afloat. His eyes were closed. He moved only where the water took him. It was obvious to Toni that if he survived, it would not be under his own steam. With no thought for her own safety, she waded into Chaney Creek after him.

Normally, the creek would have had a hard time wetting her ankles, but the rains were heavy, and the runoff from the hills above had increased the trickle in the creek bed to a torrent. Now when she ran into the water, she was at once knee-deep in a current that nearly swept her off her feet. In spite of the rain that continued to pour, the roof of her mouth went dry from fear. One misstep and she would be as lost as the drifting man, unless she was careful.

Moving faster, but choosing her position with care, Toni waded into the path of the oncoming man and his half-submerged log, readying herself for the grab. It should have been simple, really, for a woman as strong as Toni Hatfield. Any one of her brothers would have bragged about her physical ability as they would of an equal's, but that bravado didn't take into account the now waist-high water, or the size of the man and the log.

With her arms outstretched and her legs braced against the impact, she caught both man and log and was instantly swept off her feet by the blow.

She went under as swiftly as she'd entered Chaney Creek. Water went up her nose and in her eyes as she struggled to right herself. She had strength and stubbornness on her side, not to mention the fact that she'd grown up playing in every twist and turn of this old creek. Water or no water, Toni Hatfield was in familiar territory. She reached up, connected with cold flesh and wet wood, then pulled herself from under the water by sheer determination.

It was almost completely dark. The only light that Toni could count on now was the intermittent flashes of lightning that briefly brightened the sky. But the man was too big to miss, and the water too deep and too swift to fight. And yet fight she did.

Unwilling to give up, Toni wrapped her arms around the man and the log and started treading water, riding with the current as she swiftly calculated how fast and how far they were being swept downstream. Lightning flashed again, and Toni went weak with relief. She recognized the huge, over-hanging limbs of the tree just ahead. It was the big willow above the outcrop of rock that she often stood upon to fish.

If she could only steer herself and her cargo toward the side, she might have a chance. The outcrop had to be just below the surface of the water. It would be the foothold that she needed to save them both.

Just when she thought she had made it, the log bobbed, then hit something with such force that Toni was almost thrown free.

"No, damn it, no!" she screamed. Frustration and fear were battling neck and neck as she struggled to stay afloat. But the moment she shouted, she instinctively shut her mouth before she swallowed too much water.

Sheer strength and muleheaded determination kept her from releasing the man and his buoy. But with the impact came the realization that she was holding on to more than a body. The groan that she'd heard had not been her own. He was still alive!

Toni reacted without taking time to think, aiming the log toward the bank. When the outcrop of rocks bumped her shins, sending shafts of pain rocketing to the roots of her teeth, misery had never been so welcome. She scrambled for a firm foothold, churning water and scraping what skin was left on her palms, as she grabbed at the low-hanging limbs with her right hand, while clutching the man with her left.

Lightning streaked across the sky. Thunder followed. Rain pelted her body, while the floodwaters once again rushed up her nose and into her throat.

"Turn it loose," she screamed, trying to make the man release the log that had kept him alive so far. He didn't respond; he had a death grip on the broken stub and was in no condition to think of alternatives.

Toni groaned as her wet hands kept slipping on his cold, slick clothes and skin. "Oh, my God, I'm going to lose him."

And then something floated past and blessedly jammed them both firmly against the creek bank. It was all the edge that Toni needed. She crawled onto the submerged ledge and slipped her hands beneath his armpits and pulled. It was the unexpected movement that slid the man's hand free of the stub.

With a grunt, Toni fell backward onto the bank with the man in her arms. Halfway out of the flooded creek, she lay unmoving, with the back of his head against her cheek. And when he groaned again, she started to shake.

Okay, mister, you're out. Now, what in the world am I going to do with you?

Only one thing came to mind. She had to find a way to get him up the hill and into her house, or he would drown faceup in the downpour as surely as he'd chanced drowning in the flood.

She rolled him over onto his belly and pulled him the rest of the way up the bank, then waited for the next lightning flash to tell her where she was.

When it came, she groaned. The water had taken her a good quarter of a mile from where she'd parked the ATV. Toni leaned down until her mouth was against the curl of his ear. "Don't move," she said, convincing herself that he could hear. "I'm going to get help."

She got to her feet. Ignoring the tremble in her legs, she navigated the trees along the bank. No more than five steps from where she'd started, she turned and looked back just to make sure he was still there. Even in the dark, even in the downpour, the size of him was impossible to overlook.

"My God," she muttered. "How did I just do that?"

But no one answered, and when she turned, her eyes were focused on the path in front of her.

Chapter 2

It was so dark beneath the trees that she could barely make out the path. Toni gripped the handlebars on the ATV with stubborn force and squinted, wishing that the headlights on her vehicle were brighter and stronger. Although she had lived here all of her life, she found herself now losing her bearings and knew that it was panic that had her so rattled. No one had ever depended upon her for their life, or on her ability to find her way through the woods at night.

It was only after the headlights on the ATV caught the shape of the man's body that Toni realized she'd been holding her breath.

"Thank God, he's still there," she muttered.

She slipped the vehicle into park, then left it running with the headlights centered on his body. Her legs shook as she dismounted the four-wheeler as she would a horse. The wagon she pulled was now empty; the fencing equipment had been left behind beneath the tree where she'd first parked.

Toni gauged the distance from the empty wagon to the man and groaned beneath her breath. She was going to have to drag him again, and as tired as she was, and as big as he appeared, even a yard would be too much. Her hair was matted and cold against the back of her neck, and her clothes stuck to her body with muddy persistence. But she knew her discomfort was nothing compared to his state. She'd come this far with him, it was too late to give up now.

The rain had all but stopped. The wild blast of wind from the passing storm was down to a mere whistle through the trees, but the roar of the flooded creek still echoed in Toni's ears. Lingering horse tails from the storm clouds drifted across the sky, baring the half-moon and its weak glow for added light by which to see. She knelt by the man she'd dragged from the water and ran her hand across his forehead, then gently down the side of his face. He was so cold and too still.

The features of his face were cast in repose as he lay flat on his back with his arms out, unmoving. Toni shuddered. It was too close to the expression that her father had worn just before they had shut the lid on his casket.

"Mister, can you hear me?"

No answer. Not even a groan. That fact alone was enough to send a shiver of worry across Toni's senses. There was no way of guessing how long he'd been in the water, or even how he'd gotten there. The blood on his face looked black in the moonlight, and seeped from a cut somewhere in his scalp, running down his forehead and across one closed eyelid. Even in this half-light, he looked blue with cold.

"Okay. I did this once, I can do it again."

She slid her hands beneath his armpits and started to pull him toward the now-empty wagon. Without the buoyancy of water to aid her in moving him, his deadweight was almost impossible to budge.

But Toni had been told all of her life that she was a "big girl," and that big girls didn't need any help, they could do anything. And so, because she believed that she could, she did.

She maneuvered what she could of him into the wagon, then collapsed in a heap upon the ground and contemplated the fact that while he *was* in the wagon, there was an awful lot of him left hanging over the sides. It seemed impossible to consider, but he looked even bigger in there than he had on the ground.

His shirt and jeans were torn, and only half of his jacket was still on his body. The backs of his knees lay across the wagon's shallow sides, leaving the lower half of his legs and his feet to dangle down to the ground. One of his arms was jammed against his side, but the other was over his head and limply aimed toward the ATV. Try as she might, there was no way that all of him was ever going to fit, and she had yet to negotiate the steep hill leading to her house. The thought made her shudder.

"Okay, mister. We're going to take a little ride. And while I'm a damned good driver, if I say so myself, I suggest you hang on. The first step is a doozy."

Her attempt at humor was lost upon the unconscious man. He didn't even flinch when she slipped the ATV in gear and began to wind her way back through the trees toward the path that led up to her house.

True to her fears, the "slick-as-snot" path had them moving sideways as often as moving forward, but eventually, Toni made it. When she reached the top of the hill and saw moonlight reflecting off the rooster weather vane on the roof of her house, she breathed a quiet sigh of relief.

The front porch of her house had two steps. Toni took the ATV and her wagonload of man straight up both.

Unloading the man was much easier than loading him had been. She simply unhooked the wagon and let it tilt. He rolled onto the porch without so much as a thump.

"Sorry," Toni muttered, although he didn't seem to hear or care whether she made an apology or not. She stepped over his prone body, opened the front door and turned on the lights. At least now she would have light by which to maneuver. Just a little farther, and she would have him safely inside, out of the night and the inclement weather.

Once again, Toni assumed the position and pulled. He slid easier on the porch planks than he had on the wet ground. Three hefts and one agonizing grunt and she had cleared his long legs of her front door before slamming it shut.

Moments later, Toni was on the phone in the hall, calling for help. Unfortunately, she didn't even have a dial tone with which to argue.

"I should have known." She replaced the receiver and hoped that the sinking feeling in the pit of her stomach had nothing to do with the man's ultimate destiny. The phones and electricity in the area always lost power during storms like this one. "But at least I have light."

No sooner had the words come out of her mouth than the lights flickered and died. If it hadn't been so tragic, she thought, it might have been funny. But Toni had no way of knowing how badly this man was hurt, and the last thing she wanted was to have dragged a dead man up the hill and now be stuck with him for the night.

Water squished in her tennis shoes as she felt her way along the hall toward the kitchen. With a flashlight and two candles in hand, Toni headed back to the living room and the man sprawled upon her floor.

Candlelight was supposed to be romantic, not traumatic, but that was exactly what Toni felt when she knelt at the big man's side.

"Please don't be dead," she begged.

Her voice was just above a whisper as she touched the side of his neck, searching for a pulse. When it jumped beneath her fingers, she fell back on her heels, sighing with relief.

She needed an extra pair of hands, another someone to hold the flashlight so that she could better see what she was feeling. And what she felt was man—a whole lot of man. From the breadth of his shoulders to the width of his chest. Hard and wide, but cold and wet.

When he shivered beneath the brush of her fingers, she breathed a littler easier. Any sign of life was better than the lack of response that she'd had from him so far.

"I should get a blanket," she told herself as she traced the length of his arms, telling herself it was to test for injuries, when she knew full well she was daunted by the man's size.

It was when she pushed his jacket aside to feel his rib cage for possible broken bones that she sensed his focus returning.

His head jerked, and he inhaled long and deep as his fingers clenched and reclenched in slow motion.

Toni shuddered, mesmerized by the latent power in him. It was like watching a volcano building for an eruption. He groaned, and lifted his left arm. Candlelight reflected off the circle of metal dangling from his wrist.

Handcuffs! She'd fished a man out of the flood who'd been handcuffed!

"Oh, Lord, what have I done?" Toni tumbled backward in shock. If she hadn't been so stunned, she might have crawled away in time to prevent what happened next. But she was and she didn't and it happened anyway.

Toni gasped. For a man who had been all but unconscious only moments ago, he moved awfully darned fast. Before she could blink, he grabbed her by the arm. Raising himself onto one elbow long enough to prove who was boss, he hit the open end of the handcuff against her wrist and squeezed.

The click was loud. Metallic. Ominous. Toni looked down in disbelief at what the man had done, then watched as he swayed precariously on his elbow before passing out with a thump.

"Oh, my God." Toni looked, but couldn't believe what she was seeing.

He'd handcuffed them together!

She yanked, and succeeded only in hurting her wrist. When she tried to crawl away from him, she went no farther than the length of his arm.

"Oh, my God!" Saying it a second time still had not conjured up any heavenly helpers. Her shock gave way to rage. "Damn you. Let me go! You repay me for saving your worthless life by doing this? Let me go!"

Not only didn't he answer, but she wasn't even sure he was still breathing. This was bad. Really bad. She was handcuffed to a man who could be anything—even dead.

Dismayed by the possibilities, Toni crawled as far away from him as possible, relishing the fact that his elbow thumped on the floor with a rather sharp thud when she gave the cuff a vicious yank.

She sneezed. Her lower lip quivered as she tried not to cry. Big girls didn't cry. But no girl, no matter how big or small, wanted to be bound to the unknown as Toni was. Either he came to and did her harm, or he died, and she found herself arm in arm with a corpse.

She stared, then glared. All of her compassion for him was gone. But as she watched him, to her utter dismay she saw a single tear roll out the side of his eye and down into the hairline above his ear.

"Ah, God, help me," Lane whispered, unaware that he'd even spoken.

The whisper was soft, almost inaudible. But Toni heard it just the same, and she bit her lip as she considered the fact that this man, whoever he was, had called on a higher power for help. That had to mean he was one of the good guys, didn't it?

She leaned forward. Just a little. It was a move that she shouldn't have made. As quickly as before, without opening his eyes, the man reached up, then pulled her down. Now, not only was she bound to him by a metal bracelet, but her neck was firmly caught between the crook of his elbow and the wall of his chest.

"Snufabch."

Toni's curse was muffled and as weak as the candle's glow above her head. She had a worm's-eye view of the floor, as well as the tear on his shirt pocket. From her new angle, she had only two options. Either she struggled until she hanged herself, or she lay still and hoped that he would turn her loose as suddenly as she'd been caught.

While she was cursing the mysteries of fate, wondering if she had enough guts to search his pockets for a key to unlock the cuffs, the candles had the grace to burn out. She was literally in the dark. What remained to be seen was whether it was man or monster that she had fished out of Chaney Creek.

Antonette Hatfield had wished all of her life for a man, one that would take her in his arms when they went to bed and only reluctantly turn her loose when it was time to get up.

This wasn't exactly what she'd had in mind.

The only thing pertinent to this mess with regard to her dream was the fact that he *was* a man. In every sense of the word.

During the long and miserable night, she had been under him, on top of him and beside him. And during that time, she'd learned a few facts about the fish that she'd landed, as well as some shocking facts about herself.

It felt as though he weighed a ton. After the initial shock of having his weight upon her body, and further adjusting her breathing to it so that she would not be smothered, she hadn't minded nearly as much as she knew she should. Without her assent, she'd been dragged on top of him in the most intimate of positions, under him in a frightening and demanding manner and beside him in an "up close and personal" view of his neck and chin. And in every possible, miserable position, the man held fast to her body.

Not only hadn't she been able to put an inch of distance between them, but even in semiconsciousness, he'd found a way to fit her curves to his valleys and vice versa, until Toni knew the man's shape as well as she knew her own. It was daunting to know that when they were body to body, face-to-face, the tips of her toes were still inches above the ankle area of his boots. She knew the size of…everything…about him. And yet, she didn't even know his name.

More than once during the night, when she should have been screaming in panic, she'd actually felt safe. As big as he was, she'd expected to be crushed bone by bone.

And she always knew when he slid from one dream into the next, because the texture of his touch would drastically change. He didn't actually hurt her, but if she survived this mess, she knew she would have bruises in places she couldn't even see.

Dawn broke over a calm sky. Toni awoke with a numb left arm, nose to nose with the bluest eyes that she'd ever seen. That they were wide and colored with pain and confusion didn't seem to matter, not when she wanted a bathroom and a change of clothes worse than anything she'd ever wanted in her life.

"Oh, my God, are you still here?" she muttered, halfway between hope and sleep that it had all been a bad dream.

But her disgust was nothing compared to the shock that Lane Monday felt when he had come to only moments earlier and found himself in possession of someone other than his prisoner, Emmit Rice.

That the someone was female and looked mad as hell, had yet to sink in. He was more amazed that he was still alive.

"Get off of me," Toni groaned, flexing the fingers in her lifeless hand and wondering if they would ever be the same.

Lane jerked in response to the demand, then gritted his teeth as the room rocked and pain left him flat on his back, too breathless to speak.

Toni sat up, staring coldly at her other half and willing herself to look formidable. But she felt like hell and suspected that formidable was too much to expect.

Lane groaned, then clasped his head with both hands. He wasn't prepared for the woman who came flying across his chest with the action.

"What in the hell are you trying to do, lady?"

If he didn't already have a dozen bumps and bruises and one particularly ugly-looking gash she could vaguely see through the tear in his jeans, she would have given him an answer he wouldn't have liked.

She rolled off of him, then held up her arm without speaking, letting the chain that bound them speak for itself.

Lane stared, first at the handcuffs that bound his wrist to hers, then up at the fury on her face.

"How…?"

"You did it." Her answer was starkly succinct.

"When…?"

"Last night."

Her chin jutted mutinously. Lane had seen mad on a woman plenty of times, but never quite this pronounced.

"Why did I…?"

"I've been asking myself that same question for hours,"

Toni said, then scooted back as far as she could before she continued. "What I came up with does not make me happy. I've been asking myself why a man would be wearing hand-cuffs to begin with," Toni muttered. She looked away, unwilling to let him see her fear.

Lane frowned, then winced as the motion sent pain all the way to his back teeth before he managed to speak.

"I'm a lawman. I've got a key."

Toni glared. "I would love to see it. I haven't gone to the bathroom since before eight o'clock yesterday evening."

Lane flushed, then forgot that they were still connected, once again yanking her on top of him when he started to dig through his pocket. But the only hand to get anywhere near his pockets—and his manly parts—was hers.

"Will you *please* quit doing that?"

The woman's voice was barely above a snarl. The hiss burned the side of his cheek as he stared up into eyes that reminded him of the underside of a burned cookie. They were dark, and brown, and looked hot as hell.

"Sorry," Lane said. "I can't reach that pocket with my free hand. You'll have to use yours."

Toni's eyebrows arched and her face flushed. She'd wanted a man. She'd even prayed more than once for one to be delivered unto her. But this was not what she'd had in mind.

"You want *me* to—"

The image of Bob Tell's broken neck, and the last sight he'd had of the plane and the prisoners, made his stomach roll. And because he was sick and in so much pain, his words were sharper than he'd intended.

"Damn it, woman, I don't know how this happened, but I have more things to worry about than your sense of propriety."

Toni jammed her hand into his front pocket, stuffing it as far as it would go. She ignored everything in her quest for the key that would get her out of this hellish mess. But there was too much of him to ignore, and the key was nowhere to be found.

"It isn't there," she hissed again.

"Oh, God." Lane's head dropped to the floor with a thump. "Try the other pocket, lady. Please. One of us has got to be a man about this, and I'm not in any position to volunteer for the job."

At that moment, Toni hated him. She didn't want to be a man about anything. But fate, and the fact that she was taller than most, hadn't given her much choice.

To her growing dismay, the other pocket yielded exactly what the first one had. Nothing.

"It's not there, either," she said, then yanked her arm up, ignoring the pain that racked his face when she did.

"It has to be," Lane said, closing his eyes, and trying not to think about turning her over his knee. Damn, he needed to get to a phone.

"Not if you never had one," Toni said. "Not if you were the prisoner instead of the lawman."

Lane grew still. For the first time since he'd awakened, he realized how frightened she must be. He opened his eyes and stared up into her face. His voice was low, but the promise was there if she would only hear it.

"Lady, I swear to God, I am not a criminal. I am a United States marshal. And I need like hell to get us loose." The walls tilted, and he closed his eyes to keep from getting sick by the motion.

Toni sighed. She had no other choice. Whether she believed him or not was moot. They were connected in body, if not in spirit.

"Good grief," she mumbled. "Like I don't need it as badly as you?" She crawled to her knees and leaned over him. "If I helped you, could you stand?"

Lane sighed, then inhaled slowly. He couldn't remember the last time someone had offered him a shoulder, or anything else to lean on.

"I don't know, lady, but I'm damn sure willing to try."

Because of their combined size, going through doorways side by side was impossible. And as luck had it, there were two doors between them and the kitchen. By the time they staggered into the room, both of them were reeling from the effort.

Lane felt sick down to the toes of his boots. The room kept spinning. Pain racked him. More than once, he'd felt his leg buckle and knew that it was solely due to this woman's gutsy determination that he did not fall flat on his face.

"Just a little farther," Toni coaxed. "I need to get to my tool drawer."

Lane gritted his teeth and complied, his left leg dragging with every step.

A few minutes later, he was seated at a table, his forehead resting in the crook of his free arm, hoping that the room would stand still. But he feared that wasn't going to happen as long as this damnable woman kept hammering on the hand-cuff chain with muleheaded determination.

With each blow of the tool, his ears buzzed and his head pounded. She might as well be using the hammer on him, instead. It couldn't possibly hurt any worse.

"Oh, shoot," Toni muttered beneath her breath. "It keeps slipping."

Lane reacted before thinking. He yanked the hammer from her hand and tried not to see the fear that spread across her face when he raised it above his head. She looked as if she expected him to hurt her with it right there and then.

He pulled until the chain that bound them was on the edge of the table. "Don't move," he warned, swinging the hammer with every ounce of strength he had left.

The chain and the table broke simultaneously. Frozen by the image of what lay before her, Toni gawked at her table lying broken on the floor, its legs upturned like a dead possum, then she staggered backward in shock.

To hell with the table, she thought. She and the man were no longer bound. She bolted from the room. Seconds later, she'd shut herself in the bathroom, leaving the man with the hammer to his own devices.

Relief came as she quickly washed her face and swiped her hair from her face. She would kill for a bath and a change of clothes, but first things first. There was a big, strange man in her house. If he was a criminal, she would know soon enough.

Toni came out of the bathroom much slower than the way she'd gone in. When she walked back into the kitchen, the man was nowhere in sight.

"Hey?" she called, then waited for an answer that didn't come.

She found him in the hall, using the wall for a leaning post and wearing a disoriented expression on his face as he kept trying to talk into a phone that had no power.

Toni took it from his hand and listened, then replaced it on the cradle.

"Phone's still out," she said.

"Ah, damn."

The soft complaint put her off guard. But when he turned and started toward her with the hammer still clutched tightly in his other fist, she screamed, then bolted for the living room.

Oh, my God, I was right. He's going to kill me!

The front door was stuck. Tight. It had been sticking every time it rained for more than twenty-nine years, but that was not a fact that Toni was ready to deal with right now. She was just at the point of going headfirst out a window and taking chances on cutting her own throat, when he staggered into the room with a blank look on his face.

"What the hell is wrong with you?" Lane growled, and then slid down the side of the wall because he could no longer stand.

Toni saw her chance and yanked open the closet near the front door. It had once served as a closet for all the Hatfield children's coats and hats. Now it was simply full of junk.

"Oh, God, oh, God! It's here somewhere, I just know it," Toni muttered, digging through the mess with shaking hands.

When her fingers closed around the cool metal barrels of her daddy's double-barreled shotgun, she yanked it free, spun around and aimed as smoothly as if she'd done it a thousand times.

"Drop that hammer," she ordered from across the room. When he did not comply, she came a little closer, thinking she could intimidate him with the yawning holes of the twin barrels.

Lane blinked. Once. Twice. His vision cleared enough to see that she had drawn down on him. In spite of his misery and pain, he started to grin.

Toni froze. The small smile had done things to his face that she hadn't expected. There were matching grooves on either side of his mouth that she knew, in his youth, had been dimples. The twinkle in his eyes was obvious, even through the misery of his drawl.

"If you're gonna shoot, you might want to knock the mud daubers' nests out of the barrels first, or it could blow up in your face."

She gawked at him, then turned the barrels up. Both were plugged tighter than her daddy's jug of whiskey.

"Oh, for Pete's sake," she said, and turned the gun down toward the floor.

"No, lady, for mine. Please get me to a phone. I have to report a plane crash and too damn many victims."

The misery in his voice was impossible to miss. A flashback of the explosion that she'd witnessed just as the storm hit last night made her shudder. Had that been his plane going down? Dear Lord, had she been an unwitting witness to people's deaths?

"Oh, no," Toni whispered. "I'm sorry. So sorry."

The gun slid out of her hands and onto the floor. She kicked it aside as she knelt at his feet. Gingerly, she took the hammer from his hand and saw the shock on his face when he realized he still held it.

"You *are* for real, aren't you?" Toni asked.

Lane groaned. "I'm about as real as it gets, lady. Now help me up again. We've got to get to a phone."

Toni shook her head. "If what you say is true, you're not moving unless it's in an ambulance. I can't carry you to my pickup, and you can't walk. Besides, your leg is bleeding badly. I need to get it stopped before I go for help."

She got to her feet.

"Where are you going?" Lane asked.

"To get some scissors and cut those clothes off of you. I can't fix your injuries unless I can see where they are."

Lane gritted his teeth once again. But this time, there was force in his words as well as his grip when he stopped her departure by grabbing her ankle.

"Lady, you would be well-advised not to cut anything off of me, unless you don't mind seeing me buck naked."

Toni shook off his hand and took several hesitant steps back. "I don't get it," she said.

Lane swallowed a rush of water that bubbled up his throat. If he didn't lie down somewhere fast, he was going to either throw up or pass out.

"Look at me. I'm willing to bet that there aren't four clothing stores in the state that would have clothes to fit me. If you want something off, I'll help. But for God's sake, don't tear up any more of it than has already been."

"Oh."

If Toni had been in a mind to doubt, the width of his shoulders and the length of his legs were a vivid reminder of the truth of his words.

Long minutes later, Toni had all but dragged him into her father's room just off the hallway and was helping him off with his clothes.

"Damn, damn, damn."

It was all Lane was able to say as Toni pulled off his other boot. His head hurt like the devil, and his leg was a mess. He just hoped to hell that nothing was broken. There was a long rip in the leg of his Levi's and blood all over the place. Whatever was down there couldn't be good.

"I'm sorry," Toni muttered.

Lane blinked. It was the only indication that he acknowledged her apology. "I'll unbuckle and unzip. You pull."

His order went in one ear and out the other when his hands went to the belt at his waist, then unzipped the fly of his Levi's. Toni's mind boggled at what he was about to reveal.

After last night, she'd already felt every bulge and bone on his body. But feeling was one thing, seeing was another.

"Pull, damn it. I'm so close to passing out, it doesn't even matter,'' Lane said, his voice breaking on the last word. Sweat beaded across his upper lip as the room spun again.

Refusing to admit how intimidating he was, Toni grabbed hold of the cuffs of his jeans. As best he could, Lane lifted himself from the bed when she pulled. The jeans slid down his hips and legs without a hitch, leaving him bare below the waist, except for a very revealing pair of cotton briefs.

I won't look. Good Lord, what's wrong with me? The man is in pain and all I can do is stare at his…

''Oh, my God, your leg.''

Lane cursed beneath his breath. Hearing the shock in her voice made him almost afraid to look, but he did. Expecting to see bone sticking out of flesh, or at the least, a knot beneath the muscles that bespoke fractures, he was faintly relieved to see that it was only a gash. Granted, the wound ran from the middle of his upper thigh to just below his knee.

''It's just a cut. Give me something to make a pressure bandage, then go for help,'' he said.

''What if you pass out? You could bleed to death before I get back,'' Toni countered.

''Lady, if you don't quit talking and start moving, I'm going to bleed to death, anyway.''

She flushed. Once again, her lower lip slid slightly out of position. Her brother Justin called it a pout. Toni considered it nothing more than an expression of disgust.

She packed his wound with all the bandages that she had, then after fastening them on his leg with several white towels, she leaned back and sighed. There was nothing else she could do for him here. If he bled through these towels, then nothing was going to stop the flow.

He was so pale around the mouth, and he'd grown so quiet that Toni feared he might have lost consciousness again. Before she thought, she brushed a lock of thick black hair away from his forehead and leaned over to whisper in his ear. ''I'll hurry,'' she said. ''Don't give up.''

She hadn't expected him to answer, let alone hear her. But before she could straighten up, she found herself staring down into a well of blue so pure it almost made her cry.

''Lady, I don't know the meaning of the word.''

She gasped and straightened, then an odd thing happened. For the first time since she'd fished him out of Chaney Creek, they connected. She smiled. And he smiled back.

Chapter 3

Minutes were precious, but she wasted no more than necessary as she changed her shoes. Her clothes she could bear, but the sand in her wet sneakers was rubbing her feet raw.

Anxiety for the man in her bed gave way to relief as she saw the new red pickup pulling off the road and into her driveway.

"It's Justin. Thank God," she muttered, and ran out the door to meet him.

"You won't believe what I did last night," she said, waving her arms above her head and talking with every step. "And I need to borrow your truck."

"I came to see how you weathered the storm," he said. "And I don't mind if you borrow my truck, but what's wrong with yours?"

Before she had time to answer, Toni saw the smile slide off of her brother's face.

Justin looked over his baby sister's shoulder to the porch beyond. He grabbed Toni by the arm and yanked her around to face him, his eyes blazing. "Antonette Hatfield, just what the hell *did* you do last night?"

His question coincided with the discovery of the handcuff that was still locked around her wrist. If she hadn't been in such a panic, she might have considered getting nervous.

Toni groaned beneath her breath as her brother yanked her about. She didn't have to ask what had sparked his fury, she could see for herself. Her "fish" was standing on the front porch, and except for the "brief" cotton briefs and the matching half of her handcuff, he was as bare as God had made him.

"You wouldn't believe it if I told you," she said, and spun out of his hands. "Stay with him. For God's sake, put that bandage back on his leg before he bleeds to death. My phone is out, so I'm going into Chaney for an ambulance."

Toni grabbed the pickup keys from Justin's hand and, moments later, was on her way to the neighboring town, leaving Justin to deal with the stranger she'd left behind.

Then anger slid out of Justin Hatfield as quickly as it had come, as he took a longer look at the big man on the porch. He saw beyond the obvious to the bruises and the horrible cuts that had started to weep a steady stream of red.

"Hey, buddy." Justin caught Lane just before he staggered off the porch. "Let's get you back inside. Then you can explain why you're naked as a jaybird in front of Antonette."

Everything was confusion inside Lane's head, but one thing had connected. Now he had a name to go with that mule-headed woman and her big dark eyes. Her name was Antonette.

"My head hurts," he muttered, vaguely remembering being put to bed. He didn't remember getting out of it, but when he found himself in the hallway of a strange house, trying to find a door, instinct had led him toward the sounds of voices. "I was a…I need to…to make a call."

Justin grunted with effort as he tried to navigate the staggering man back through the doorway. "Come on, big fellow. As soon as I get you back in bed, you can call everyone in town."

Lane shuddered as darkness began to envelop him. He never even felt the softness of the mattress at his back, or the gentle way in which Justin Hatfield replaced the bandages that he'd mindlessly removed. Blessedly, he was out for the count.

Toni sat in the hallway near the emergency room of Chaney Clinic and listened to the low rumble of voices beyond the curtains. She would give ten good acres of land to know what they were saying, but she knew that wasn't going to happen. She was a woman. It didn't matter that he was *her* piece of Chaney Creek flotsam, or that she'd fished him out of the flood with great danger to herself. All of a sudden, she didn't belong.

"So, what else is new," Toni muttered to herself. She'd spent her entire life knowing that she didn't quite fit in.

Loose hair tickled the back of her neck, and she remembered that she had yet to brush it. Grooming would have to wait, but she *could* redo the clasp holding it away from her face. With that thought in mind, she lifted her hands toward the back of her neck, and in doing so, caught the dangling edge of the handcuff chain in her hair.

"Good grief."

When she tried to free herself, she succeeded only in tangling it more. From the way that it felt, she would have to pull the spot bald to get herself loose.

"Damn," she muttered, and wondered how long she could fake holding her head without looking ridiculous.

"Here now, Toni girl. Let me do that."

Sheriff Dan Holley's voice was familiar, but she hadn't been expecting him. Then she remembered the stranger's claim about being a lawman and wondered if he might have been telling the truth.

"Don't fidget, girl, just be still, and I'll have you loose in a jiffy."

Toni gritted her teeth and closed her eyes. It would seem that she was doomed to experience humiliation upon humiliation.

To her great relief, the sheriff easily freed the chain from her tangles, then unlocked the cuff that encircled her wrist.

"Thank you, Dan," she said, and was equally grateful that

he hadn't bothered to ask her how she'd come to have it on there in the first place.

When the handcuff fell loose in her lap, the emotion that swamped her should have been relief, but that wasn't what she felt as her last link to the man behind the curtain had been severed. It was loss.

"What are you doing here?" Toni asked.

"Got a fax this morning. You know, those things are a real wonder, and that's a fact. You get hooked up to a phone just right, and you can get everything over them things, even pictures."

Toni sighed. It took Dan Holley forever to get to the point.

"What does that have to do with why you're here?"

"Oh, that. Well, it seems a U.S. marshal's plane went down somewhere over the Smokies."

"What was it carrying?" Toni held her breath, waiting for the answer.

"Two marshals, three prisoners and two pilots." Dan Holley slid a finger beneath his hat and scratched, then settled the hat back in place without mussing his hair. "Don't suppose that fellow you brought in had any ID on him?"

Toni shook her head.

Dan Holley grinned. "Didn't think so. Heard he didn't have on much of anything when the ambulance got to your house." He glanced down at the handcuff, then back up at her. He'd made his point.

Toni flushed and then glared. It was hell living in the same town in which you'd been born. Everyone knew everyone else's business.

"He's been hurt pretty bad," she said, ignoring his teasing. "He has lots of bad cuts and bruises. Something could even be broken. It's all he can do just to stand up."

"Heard he's big. Real big," the sheriff said.

Toni rolled her eyes. "You aren't telling me anything new. I didn't think I would ever get him out of the water, let alone myself."

Holley frowned. He picked up Toni's hands and turned

them palms up, then whistled slowly at the raw, chafed areas across the center.

"What do you mean you pulled him out of the water? What in blazes were you doing in there to begin with? Chaney Creek is still in flood stage."

Toni shrugged. "I went in after him."

Dan Holley's mouth dropped. Before he had time to respond, the curtain parted and the attending physician in charge came out.

Toni caught a glimpse of bare leg, bare torso, a curve of stubborn chin, and then the curtain fell back in place. She shuddered. There had been an awful lot of gauze and bandage on what little of him that she'd seen.

"How's he doing, Doc?" Holley asked.

Dr. Bennett saw the handcuff lying in Toni's lap. "If you don't mind, Sheriff, I would appreciate your removing the other half of that thing from my patient."

The sheriff slipped through the curtain with the key in hand. Because of his occupation, he'd often used his voice authoritatively. It carried well. Toni listened intently, hoping to finally hear something important regarding her stranger's condition, but she heard nothing beyond a soft chuckle and the sound of metal falling onto tiled floor.

Moments later, Dan Holley came out and dropped the other half into her lap. He grinned. "Want a souvenir?"

"I want some answers," Toni grumbled. "Was he able to tell you his name?"

"He didn't have to," Holley said. "Along with that fax, we got pictures of all who were aboard. There were two men of nearly equal size on that plane. One was Emmit Rice, a criminal bound for the federal correctional facility in Lexington, Kentucky. The other was U.S. Marshal Lane Monday. You got lucky, girl."

Toni felt herself going limp. "Are you saying he's the marshal?"

Dan Holley nodded. "Got himself quite a reputation as a hard-nose, too. But I guess that's what it takes to get his kind of job done."

"Oh, my." It was all Toni could think to say. But her thoughts were another thing altogether. *His name is Lane. Lane Monday.*

Then the curtain parted, and Toni stood. The air stilled around her. Voices and people faded until she forgot that they were there. She forgot everything, and everyone, except the man lying on the bed. His eyes were closed, his face in repose. She started toward him, and when she did, his eyes popped open as if he sensed the approach of someone new, and Toni found herself staring down into pain-filled eyes that were so blue they looked translucent.

"How are you feeling?"

Lane started to nod, and then reconsidered the movement when pain rocked the back of his neck. He licked his lips and decided that it would hurt less to talk.

"Better."

Sheriff Holley gave Toni's shoulder a companionable thump as Justin moved to the foot of the bed.

"You've got Toni to thank for pulling you out of that flood," Dan said. "I still don't know how it was accomplished. You're a big ol' boy, and that's a plain fact."

Justin's laugh was short. "Shoot, nothing's too big for Toni. She can take care of herself and anything else that comes along. She's as strong as an ox."

Lane blinked. *She?* He was getting confused. And when the woman he knew as Antonette paled and turned away, he knew that somehow the words had hurt her. Maybe this Tony fellow meant something to her.

Toni's voice was a couple of octaves below shrill. "Thank you for reminding me, Justin. You really know how to make a woman feel special."

Disgusted with herself for letting them know that the words had hurt, she hunched her shoulders against the humiliation she felt, and stalked away from the bed and out into the hallway while blinking back tears.

Why did her brothers see fit to remind her on at least a weekly basis that, as a woman, she was too tall, too strong and altogether too capable for a man to feel needed? She sighed, then leaned against the wall and contemplated her shoes. If that was what people who loved her really thought, then it was no wonder she was close to being an old maid. To a stranger, she must be just shy of a geek.

"What the hell did I say?" Justin asked as he watched Toni's angry flight, and ran a hand through his hair.

Sheriff Holley shrugged. "You sort of belittled her part in saving this man's life, that's what you did," Holley growled. "Damn it, Justin, she didn't just throw some rope around him and haul him out of the water as if she were landing a damned fish. She told me that she went into the flood after him. Hell's bells, you fool, your sister could have drowned trying to save this man."

Justin paled, but it was nothing to the shot of adrenaline that raced through Lane's system. Before the sheriff could think to move, Lane had him by the wrist.

"I thought you told me someone named Tony pulled me out of the water."

The sheriff nodded. "I did. That's Toni with an *i,* not a *y.*" He pointed over his shoulder with his thumb. "Antonette Hatfield might be on her birth certificate, but she's been Toni as long as I've known her."

"My sweet Lord." Lane couldn't believe what he was hearing. Unaware of the sheet he was wadding in both hands, he stared out the doorway through which the woman had disappeared. "That little bitty thing pulled me out of a flood?"

Justin grinned. "Oh, Lord, you really did get a lump on your head. You've got to be seeing things to think Toni is little."

Lane almost glared at the smirk on the man's face. "Mister, I don't remember your name, but I do remember who and what I am. I'm six inches over six feet tall. The last time I weighed myself, the scales only went up to two-fifty, and the needle went off the mark. You add that to deadweight and the force of a flood, and I don't know how the hell she did it. From where I stand, when I'm standing, she doesn't look that big to me."

In the hallway, Toni gasped. She'd left the room, but she

hadn't gone so far as to be unable to hear what was being said. If she hadn't overheard it with her own ears, she wouldn't have believed it was true.

Lane Monday had stood up for her. He'd even chastised Justin for making fun of her size. No one had ever done that for her. Suddenly the experience became too much to bear. She hid her face in her hands and bolted for the ladies' room. There was no way on earth she wanted anyone to see her cry.

Minutes later, while drying her hands and face, she heard Justin's voice outside the ladies' room door.

"Toni, Toni, are you in there?"

She yanked open the door and gave him what she hoped was a cool, disdainful stare, noting with some satisfaction that he seemed worried.

"What do you want?"

"I'm sorry, honey."

Toni refused to relent. "For what?" she asked. "For thinking I'd spent a wild night in handcuffs with a naked man, or for calling me a moose in front of God and everyone, then laughing about it? Exactly which *thing* are you apologizing for?"

"Well, hell. I damn sure didn't call you a moose."

Toni rolled her eyes. "Your apologies stink, Justin. I hope you're better at telling your wife you're sorry than you are at telling me."

Before he could answer, Toni stalked away, her head held high, her shoulders straight.

"Damn woman," he muttered dryly.

Toni returned to the emergency room just as the doctor was issuing orders that Lane Monday didn't seem to like.

"Look, Mr. Monday, I know, as you just reminded me, that nothing is broken and that your concussion is mild, but you have numerous stitches in several places. They have to be tended. And you strained ligaments in your knee. At this point, you cannot take care of yourself without help. You really should be admitted to a hospital, at least for a few days. I recommend the one in Knoxville. It's closest and will give your leg time to heal."

Lane's chin jutted mutinously. "I lost a good friend in that crash, as well as two, maybe three, prisoners who'd been given over to our care. Until I know that Emmit Rice is dead, I won't rest. I'm praying that the S.O.B. burned with the plane, or is floating facedown somewhere in a river, but we have no way of knowing that until the bodies at the crash site are identified. I'm not lying flat on my back while people do my job for me, and that's a damned fact."

"He can stay with me."

It was hard to say who was most shocked, Toni for saying it, Justin for hearing it, or Lane for considering the offer.

"Now see here, Toni—"

"Shut up, Justin. You've already said enough to me and about me for one day. Look at him, for God's sake. He's flat on his back and in pain. And look at me! I'm the *moose* who can take care of herself, remember? Exactly when do you expect him to jump my bones, while he's crawling from his bed to mine, bleeding all the way?"

Justin flushed.

Dan Holley reentered the room and walked unwittingly into the argument. "I just got off the phone with your superiors," he told Lane. "They said to tell you they're real sorry about Bob Tell, and very glad that you're all right, and not to worry about anything except getting better. They're sending people to go over the crash site. They'll coordinate with the FAA, and we'll have this wrapped up in no time."

"I may be missing a prisoner," Lane warned. "He was the only one I didn't see before I got out of the wreckage. Emmit Rice is dangerous. If you find him alive, don't assume he'll go quietly. He'll die before he's recaptured, and he'll take someone with him when he goes."

Holley frowned. "His rap sheet is on my desk. I know the type."

"You don't know Emmit Rice. He doesn't take hostages, and he leaves his victims in pieces."

"Oh, my God." Toni felt the room beginning to spin.

"Grab her," Justin shouted. "She's going to faint."

The help came from an unexpected source. Lane rose onto his elbow and caught Toni as she staggered.

"Hey, lady, don't go out on me now," he said gently.

With the low rumble of his voice, the room settled, along with Toni's stomach. His hand was warm, his grip firm. She stared first at it, then at him, then swallowed twice before she could speak.

"I don't faint."

He smiled, and Toni's heart fell all the way to her toes.

"I imagine I knew that," Lane said.

Toni took a deep breath. "Well, are you going to take me up on my offer, or do you want to recuperate here?"

"I think that if you're willing to take me and all this on, then I would rather be with you." When he realized how that sounded, he felt obliged to add, "It would put me closer to the on-site investigation."

Toni nodded. She'd known what he meant. At this point in her life, there was no way she would assume a man could possibly have a romantic interest in her. Besides, she reminded herself, she wasn't looking for romance, not anymore. What she wanted was a family. It took a man to get a baby, and there was a lot of man on the bed.

She gave him a long look. Now that she knew he was a socially acceptable person and not the missing prisoner, he might be the answer to her prayers. That is, if he had no personal attachments....

Then she heard herself asking, "Do you want us to notify your wife, or significant other?"

Toni's question was simple, and not entirely unexpected. Yet somehow, Lane sensed a desperation in the polite request. Answering her question hurt. Saying aloud a truth that he had spent five years trying to accept wasn't easy. He lay back on the bed and looked up at the ceiling. If he didn't have to see their faces, maybe it wouldn't be so hard to say.

"I don't have a wife. Not anymore. And there are no others, significant or otherwise."

It took all she had not to smile. Her relief was so overwhelming that she missed the grimness around his mouth as he spoke.

"Well, then that's that." She gave the doctor a straightforward look. "You'll have to give me instructions for his care. What I can't do, Justin can."

Justin didn't waver under her look. "Sure thing," he said. "Always ready to help a good man out."

With this act, Antonette Hatfield's fate was set in motion.

By the morning of the next day, the Hatfield farm was crawling with police, FAA investigators, men with bloodhounds and several local hunters who were familiar with every nook and cranny of the Smoky Mountains surrounding Toni's home.

She went about her chores as if there were no one there. But when she went inside her home, there was no way to ignore the man whose presence permeated every inch of space.

She came in the back door and winced as it slammed behind her, hoping that Lane hadn't been asleep. If he had, he probably wasn't now. The sound was still echoing through the house.

"Shoot," she muttered as she went to the kitchen sink to wash her face and hands. "Only four months since Daddy died, and I've already lost all of my manners. Momma would have had my hide for slamming doors."

The water ran swift and cool beneath her fingers as it sluiced her heated skin. For early May it was very hot and the day was so humid that her clothing had become stuck to her body in the first five minutes she'd been outside. Unaware of how revealing the damp clothes were against her skin, she washed, then dried her hands, while absently considering what she might fix Lane to eat.

The crutches thumped with every swing of his arms, but Lane's socks-clad feet made no sound as he moved from the bedroom where he'd been resting, in search of Toni. She didn't seem like a stranger, and he wondered if it was because of the life-and-death situation in which they'd become entwined. Then he knew that was a foolish thought, because he had little to no memory of anything except waking up in the wreckage and then crawling off the edge of a cliff. What he did remember vividly was waking up handcuffed to a mad-as-hell woman.

He still wondered how that had happened, and stifled a smile. Man alive, but his Toni could work up a snit faster than anyone he'd ever known. When he realized he'd just thought of her as *his,* he staggered into a wall and bumped everything that hurt.

"Oh, damn," he groaned, and propped himself up with the crutches until the stars dancing beneath his eyelids stopped spinning.

Toni heard him coming up the hallway, followed by the groan and the curse. She was out of the kitchen before he could think to hide his pain.

"What do you think you're doing? You already broke my table and now you're aiming at my walls." She slipped an arm beneath his shoulder and let him rest upon her instead of on the awkward crutch.

When Lane was able to talk, he looked down to speak, but got lost instead in the study of her face. Apart, not one of her features was particularly unique. But the accumulation of them upon her face, coupled with her statuesque body and fiery temperament, made her unforgettable.

Her eyes were so dark that he had to strain to discern the pupils from the irises. Her nose was not too long and not too short, a perfectly straight nose for a straightforward woman. But there were freckles scattered across the bridge that he suspected she would not like to be reminded of. Her eyebrows and lashes were dark, a perfect match to the thick, almost chocolate-colored hair, and her mouth was full, just shy of voluptuous. Just like her body. At that thought, he shuddered. There was quite a lot of woman in his arms.

"I'm sorry," he said, unable to think of anything else to say.

"You know that you shouldn't be up," she reminded him.

"You've been up since daybreak," he countered.

"That's different. I wasn't in a plane crash. I didn't try to drown myself in Chaney Creek. I didn't—"

Lane put a finger across her lips, shocking himself as much as her by his action. "Oh, but, lady, I think you did just that," he said softly. "You saved my life, at great risk to your own, I might add. How do you think that makes me feel?"

Toni could only shake her head. She had no idea how he felt. But at that moment, she could have given lessons on lust. Everywhere she touched, she felt muscle. Everywhere she looked, she saw a brown, firm expanse of skin. And beyond the obvious attraction of so much man and so little time, Toni felt a sense of loss. She wished those clear blue eyes were darkening with passion for her, and not his own pain.

"I think you probably feel like hell," Toni said.

"I think you're right," Lane replied, then sighed.

"Do you want to lie back down?"

"No. In fact, hell, no," Lane growled. "What were you about to do?"

"Fix us some lunch."

"Can I watch? You can tell me what's going on outside. It makes me crazy knowing that everyone is involved in my business except me."

For a long moment, they stood arm in arm within the confines of the cool, dark hallway, assessing the possibilities that lay between them. But when it came down to fact, there was nothing between them. Not really. Two days ago, neither of them had known the other existed. Today, one of them had the other to thank for a life.

"Come with me," Toni said. "You can sit in Daddy's chair. He used to watch me work before he got so sick he couldn't sit up anymore."

As she helped him down the hall and into the kitchen, Lane silently absorbed the textures of her sadness, and wondered how long she'd been alone here on her farm.

Pillowed by the old recliner in the corner of the kitchen, he was forced to let her help him. It disgusted him greatly that he couldn't even lift his own leg onto the extended footrest.

As she cradled his foot, the muscles in her bare arms corded, and for the first time he was forced to consider her strength. She wasn't bulky like a man would be, but when she moved, the muscles rippled delicately beneath her skin like ribbons upon water. He liked how it made her look. He liked how she made him feel. If only they had met under different circumstances—when he was strong on two feet and not flat on his back—he might like to test the waters between them in other ways.

But he lived in Florida, and she was here in Tennessee. The city in which he lived was hectic, and his job was often a reflection of the uglier side of humanity. On the farm, her life was simple, almost sedate. Fate had thrown two people from two different worlds together. There was no way a relationship between them would ever work, and he had no will to even attempt one. He thought of Sharla, and the image of her petite features and short, flyaway blond hair came and went within his mind's eye. He thought of his wife's smile—and then of the pain that she had endured before she died.

Forget it all, he told himself. *Toni has no place in my life.*

With that thought firmly settled in his mind, Lane looked out the window at the circus of vehicles and people beyond the walls of her house.

"Is this making you nuts?" He meant the mess outside, but she'd taken it another way.

Toni turned. "What? Having you here? Of course not. I'm glad for the company."

The moment she'd said it, she wished that she hadn't. It made her sound pitiful, and she wasn't a pitiful sort of person. She was resourceful. She should know; she'd been told so by her family all of her life.

"How long since your father died?"

Toni's hand stilled on the potatoes that she'd been peeling. Her emotions were well in hand by the time she turned to answer.

"Just over four months. Sometimes it seems like only yesterday, other times…" She shrugged. "Other times it seems like I've been by myself forever."

"I know there must be times when you're lonely, but don't you ever feel afraid?"

The smile on her face was too wide, the glitter in her eyes too bright. "Of what? In case you haven't noticed, I'm a very big girl. I can take care of myself."

Lane frowned. This wasn't the first time that he'd heard her put herself down. He sighed. Hell, from what he'd heard out of her brother Justin, her family had probably been doing it to her for years. She was simply echoing what she'd heard all of her life.

"You may be taller than some, but I don't know where you get off thinking that makes you less of a woman, lady. From where I sit, it only makes you more."

Toni's eyes widened and her mouth went slack. A faint flush slid across her cheeks and up into her hairline. She could feel the heat of her blush under her skin, as surely as the man on the other side of the room who was already under it. Then she eyed his bandages and the gray pallor on his face and knew that he was way too hurt and sick for what she was thinking.

"It's time for your medicine."

The minute she said it, Toni knew how inane she must have sounded. He'd paid her a dazzling compliment, and all she wanted to do was knock him out with pain pills. She needed more than her head examined.

Lane grinned. "Doping me up won't change a thing, Antonette."

She glared. "If it will shut you up for a while, it's worth it." She ignored his smirk and turned with relief as Justin entered the kitchen with a bang.

"I just talked to Dan Holley," he said.

"Who?" Lane asked, certain that the name was one he should remember, yet unable to think where he'd heard it.

"The sheriff," Toni said. "He took the handcuff off of you in the hospital, remember?"

Lane nodded, then hid a grin when he saw Toni's blush. He would give a lot to know exactly how that had occurred, and what exactly had happened afterward.

Justin frowned and got back to the story that he'd been about to tell. "Sheriff Holley says that old Sam Sumter left home again. I swear, that sorry excuse for a man leaves every time his wife has another baby. Their latest can't be more than a month or two old. If he doesn't like to feed them, why in hell do they keep having them?"

Toni frowned. It wasn't right. People like Livvie Sumter had babies they didn't want, and she wanted one she couldn't have. The world was not a fair place.

"Where does he go?" Lane asked.

Toni shrugged. "Who knows? The pitiful thing is that he always comes back, and Livvie Sumter keeps having babies."

Justin snorted. "Right. But while he's gone, every farmer within ten miles of the Sumter place will come up short on anything that isn't tied down."

Lane frowned. "Why?"

"Because Samuel Sumter has eleven, maybe twelve, children and they're hungry," Toni said. "Sometimes, they take something they can sell for money to buy food. Other times, they steal the food outright. About a year before Daddy died, we lost a cow. Never did find it. We figured that the Sumter boys took it for the milk. I didn't have the heart to send Dan Holley out to check."

Outside, a car horn honked as a man shouted. Justin frowned. "I haven't seen such a mess outside since the day of Momma's funeral," he grumbled.

Toni sniffed, then turned back to her potatoes. "It's not on your front porch, so I don't see why you're squawking."

Justin glared. "Even if you hated it, you wouldn't tell me so because then you wouldn't be able to argue about it."

Lane grinned. Although brother and sister seemed in constant disagreement, it was obvious that they were close. It was especially obvious to Lane when Justin gave him a long, assessing look.

"So, feeling any better?" he asked. "I see you're able to get about."

"A couple of other marshals will be spending the night here for a while, Justin," Toni stated. "They've already been here with their luggage, so you can wipe that look off of your face. God forbid that I might spend the night alone with a man.''

''Well, hell, Toni, I don't remember hearing myself say anything about where you spend your nights, or who with.''

She turned away from the conversation and dumped the potatoes into the sink, then washed and cut them up before dropping them into a pan to boil. While both men tried not to look at her, or at each other, Toni got Lane's medicine.

She didn't speak as she dropped the pills into his hand, then shoved a glass of water beneath his nose.

''What's that?'' Justin asked as the lawman made a face.

''Knockout pills. She's trying to shut me up,'' Lane said, and stifled a grin by tossing the pills to the back of his throat and chasing them with the drink of water.

''I hate both of you,'' Toni said mildly, and walked out of the kitchen before she said anything else that she would later regret.

Justin looked miffed. Lane grinned. It was an odd ending to a hell of a day.

Chapter 4

Toni stared down the long garden rows and stretched the aching muscles in her back, wishing that she'd had the foresight not to plant so many rows of peas. But the long pods of purple-hulls had been her father's favorite.

"I don't know what I was thinking." She had planted them long after her father's death.

Even if she ate peas all year long, she would never be able to eat them all. The only thing she could do was call upon her two brothers who lived nearby. Their wives would be glad for the chance to pick the patch; feeding their hungry families was a never-ending job.

The muted sounds of voices carried over the evening air, permeating her solitude. She sighed. This was the third day since the crash, and the authorities still weren't finished with the investigation. It was getting late. They must be quitting for the day, she thought.

She glanced at her watch. Nearly four and a half hours had passed since everyone from the FAA to the coroner's office had filed through her front yard. The crash had been ruled an accident due to the weather. Surely this investigation would end soon.

She thought of Lane and wondered where he was. He'd been resting when she left the house. But if she knew Lane Monday, he wouldn't be flat on his back when they brought what was left of his friend out of the hills.

She hefted the bushel basket of peas onto her hip and started toward the house. Minutes later, with the peas sitting in the shade of the back porch, she entered the kitchen, pausing only long enough to wash the purple stain from the pea pods off of her fingertips.

"Lane?"

Her voice rang clear throughout the house, but an echo was her only answer. Where had he gone? She began drying her hands on her denim shorts as she headed toward the front door.

She looked out and could see him at the far end of the yard, and in the thick of things, right where she'd expected him to be. All she could see was his back, but she could tell by the set of his shoulders and the stillness with which he stood, that the impact of what was taking place had hit him hard.

His crutches were by the steps where he'd obviously dumped them in frustration. They were too short for his height, but they were the longest ones in town that had been available for rent. The jeans he was wearing were the ones that he'd had on when she found him. They had been laundered, but Toni had purposely not mended the tear in the left leg of his Levi's to accommodate the bandages over his stitches.

As she stared across the yard, she couldn't help noticing that blue jeans suited him better than most of the men she'd known and decided that it had something to do with his long legs and the way the fabric cupped his backside. His blue, long-sleeved shirt hung loose upon his shoulders. Untucked and unbuttoned, the tail flapped gently in the hot summer breeze as he watched the proceedings going on before him.

Toni frowned as he wiped a hand across his face. She hoped that he was only sweating. If she saw him cry, she would not be able to keep her heart at the distance it needed to stay. Already, she had become more emotionally involved with him than she'd intended. It wouldn't pay to care for the man she'd chosen as a means to an end.

He turned at the sound of her footsteps crunching on the graveled path, and the last straw in her resistance crumbled. She'd never seen so much pain on a man's face in her life.

When he saw who it was, he turned away without speaking, yet Toni knew that it wasn't because he hadn't cared about his partner, but because he cared too much.

She stood beside him without speaking, resisting the urge to hold his hand as the search crew carried what was left of five men through the clearing toward the waiting vehicles from the coroner's office.

One black bag followed another, pitifully small and weightless. Somewhere within them were the remnants of two prisoners, two pilots and one good cop. Yet, after crashing, then burning, what more would there be?

It was impossible for Lane to put into words what he felt. He sensed Toni's concern, and while he appreciated her presence, he could not trust himself to speak. His shoulders hunched against the sight of the five black bags. *Why wasn't I killed, too?* he wondered.

Therein lay the crux of his misery. He hadn't been able to get beyond that question. One thought after another had followed it, but it always came back without an answer.

The worst of it was that there was no reason for his survival. Upon impact, he and Emmit Rice had not even been strapped into a seat. By every rule and caution known to man, they should have been the first to die.

There should have been one more body at the crash site. And because there wasn't, Lane would not rest until Emmit Rice was found. Officially, Rice was listed as missing and presumed dead.

Hell, they are all dead…except me.

"Your leg is bleeding."

Lane jerked, startled by the sound of a human voice, after he'd been so lost in watching the parade of death passing by. He'd actually forgotten that she was still beside him. Toni's quiet voice held no censure, only compassion, but his bitterness had to go somewhere, and because she was the only one around, it fell to her to suffer his rage.

"Tell it to them," he said harshly, and pointed toward the body bags before he turned and stalked back toward the house.

Tears blurred her sight, but not so much that she couldn't see him dragging his injured leg as he hobbled over the graveled path on his bare feet.

Knowing that he wasn't ready to hear it, Toni waited until he was out of earshot before she muttered, "It's not your fault, you know."

She ignored the impetus to follow and assure him further. Instead, she turned away, unable to watch him leave. She didn't want to feel compassion, or give in to the urge to throw her arms around him and comfort him. She needed to feel separate from him in order to do what she'd decided upon.

Last night, in the midst of a sleepless and lonely vigil, Toni Hatfield had come to a life-altering conclusion. She didn't know how, and she didn't know when, but she wanted Lane Monday to be the father of the child she so longed to bear. And she kept telling her heart that she didn't care that he would come and go in her life without notice. What he left behind would, for her, suffice. If she wasn't destined to know the love of a good man, so be it. But there was no handwriting on the wall that said she couldn't have a good man's child.

That was what Toni kept telling herself as she watched the last vehicle drive away. A stray lock of her hair slipped out of its clip. Toni gave it a halfhearted swipe as she turned toward the house, ignoring a painful shaft of conscience. She couldn't afford to care about a man who would be leaving in a matter of days. She had the rest of her life to live without him when he was gone. With that thought in mind, she started up the hill.

"Miss Hatfield, wait up," a voice said.

Toni turned and looked back down the hill. Coming toward her were the two other men from Lane's office who had arrived the night before to coordinate the investigation. Along with a stack of papers and an armful of cameras, they had brought a suitcase full of Lane's clothes. Someone had had the foresight to recognize the situation that a man his size would be in.

Bill Reese and Chuck Palmer were ordinary-looking men. The only thing that set them apart from just anybody on the street were the U.S. marshals' badges that they carried. From the looks on their faces, they had been affected by the situation as deeply as Lane had been.

"You both look as if you would trade your last dollar for a bath and something cold to drink. Am I right?" she asked.

The men looked at Toni, then at each other. Chuck Palmer managed an uneasy chuckle as Bill Reese spoke.

"Yesterday when you offered to let us stay here with Lane, I knew you were one-in-a-million. Now we find out you're a mind reader, as well. Just lead the way, pretty lady. We're right behind you."

Toni flushed. Pretty lady, indeed.

"Lane's not in a very good mood," she warned as they neared the porch. "He's fighting a lot of hurt from both directions. Right now, I would hate to guess what hurts more, his heart or his leg."

Reese sighed. "Coming up a body short in the investigation doesn't sit well with us, either. We've got searchers and dogs in the hills, checking for any sign of Rice, but we're pretty sure that he drowned in the same flood that nearly got Lane. It's simply a matter of waiting for the body to surface, and it will. As for Lane being sad, well, he and Bob Tell were real close friends and had been ever since Lane's wife died," he said.

Toni stumbled and paled, but the men behind her never noticed.

"Watch that first step, it's loose," she muttered, and hoped that it covered her shock.

Lane had told her that he'd been married, but she'd assumed he was divorced. Knowing that his wife had died instead changed a lot of things. He might not be as receptive to what she'd planned as she'd hoped. What if he was still grieving? What if the idea of making love with another woman was repugnant to him?

"How long has he been a...when did she die?" Toni asked.

Reese frowned thoughtfully and then looked at Palmer for assistance. "At least four or five years, don't you think?"

Palmer nodded. "At least. Monday's two years younger than I am, and I just turned forty. He was in his early thirties when it happened. Yeah, that would be about right."

Toni nodded while she made mental calculations. Four or five years. Surely he'd passed the celibate part of grief by now. If he hadn't, all of her plans would be futile. The cold, abstract calculation of what she was planning made her feel guilty as hell. But the last man she'd counted on had broken her heart. She'd long since given up on being loved by a man. She was past counting on anyone but herself.

"When you're ready, supper will be waiting," Toni said.

Both men hurried past her on their way to their rooms, anxious to remove the stench of death from their clothes and their memory.

Lane heard them come into the house. Their voices carried down the hall and into his room. He rolled over on his back and closed his eyes, hating himself for the way that he'd lashed out at Toni. It was a miserable thing to do to the woman who'd saved his life.

And yet, he couldn't get the sight of those body bags out of his mind.

"Damn it, Tell, that wasn't the way it was supposed to happen," he groaned.

His stomach lurched as he fought back a wave of emotion. Like Bob Tell, Lane had contained no illusions about his job. Being a sheriff had always held more than the normal share of risks. Every lawman faced the possibility of being shot in the line of duty, maybe even dying in such a manner. But the senseless act of nature had been unexpected, and because of that, oddly more difficult to accept.

Outside his door, the sound of Toni's laughter was soft, but unmistakable. One of the men, probably Reese, had obviously cracked a joke. Lane knew Reese was good at making strangers feel comfortable.

He wondered if Toni's eyes had crinkled at the corners as

he'd seen them do before. Or if she'd turned away to return to her work with a lingering smile on her face. And the moment he thought it, he wondered why he cared. What was happening to him? Why was he becoming so fixated upon Toni Hatfield's every movement? She was a good woman, maybe even a special woman. But that was as far as it went.

He rolled to the side of the bed and sat up, trying to make sense out of what he was feeling.

"This connection I feel with her must be because she saved my life." He combed his fingers through his hair in frustration and wished for things he could not have. "That's got to be what it is. I don't have a personal desire to get mixed up with a woman again. Damn it, I don't!"

Yeah, Monday, say it often enough and you might even convince yourself, he thought, pulling himself to his feet.

The stitches in his leg pulled as his muscles contracted. He winced, savoring the pain; he felt he deserved that and much more. What was a little pain compared to the devastating sense of loss that the families of those crash victims would suffer? His pain would pass, but their loss would be with them forever. And Lane knew about loss in a big way.

When Sharla had died, he'd wanted to die with her. Month after month, he'd waited for the breath to leave his body as ruthlessly as it had left hers. But it hadn't, and over time, the feeling had passed. He was proof that life did go on, maybe not as fulfilled as before, but breath was drawn, years passed and the pain faded, leaving a void where his heart had once been. That void was not going to be filled, not if Lane had anything to say about it. He had loved once. He wasn't about to go through the pain of loving and losing again.

But while he wasn't ready for emotional entanglements, the apology he owed Toni was past due. He'd had no reason to lash out at her when it had been himself with whom he'd been angry. Shame sent him out of his room and in search of the woman who had borne the brunt of his pain.

He found her on the back porch. He stood in the kitchen and looked out the screen door, absorbing the serenity of the scene before him.

The evening shadows that stretched across the yard were long and pencil thin, a reminder that the day was near its end. The porch-swing chain gave an occasional squeak, warning its occupant not to fall asleep. A half-empty basket of peas sat nearby, while Toni shelled from the bowl in her lap.

Toni's repose as she worked was so much a part of the scene that Lane hesitated to interrupt. Her long, nimble fingers bent, stripped, then emptied the supple, purple pods of their bounty, spilling the dark-eyed little peas into the bowl with constant regularity. Her purple-tinged fingertips bore the mark of her labor, while a small pile of empty pods accumulated at her feet.

The screen door squeaked as Lane pushed it open. Startled, Toni turned sharply at the sound, causing a dark abundance of curls to spill from her loose topknot of hair. The tendrils fell against the back of her neck, then fluttered in the soft evening breeze, giving her face an unusually fragile, feminine look. Lane saw beyond the richness of her hair to the shadows in her eyes, and hated himself for being the cause.

"If it didn't hurt so much to bend, I would kneel at your feet," he said.

Her pulse jerked, then steadied. From the tone in his voice, she guessed that he'd come to apologize.

"I would settle for a helping hand instead," she said, and gave him a judging glance before scooting over on the porch swing to make room.

Lane sighed as his guilt lifted. Just that small, telling look and a gentle smile from a woman he hardly knew, and the knot in his belly was gone. He wondered what else she might remove if given half a chance, and then the minute he thought it, he willed the thought back to hell where it belonged. He didn't need this kind of trouble. But, if he was going to help shell peas, he did need a bowl. When she handed him hers, he wondered if she also read minds.

Blue was her favorite color, but Toni wondered if she would ever again be able to see it and not think of Lane Monday's eyes. She looked at him and forgot what she'd been about to say, so she handed him the bowl in her lap instead.

Reflex made him grab for it, and when their hands touched, Toni jerked back and then jumped to her feet, suddenly anxious to put some space between herself and the future father of her child.

"Do you know how?" she asked.

Lane grinned. That was a loaded question if he'd ever heard one. And being the man that he was, he couldn't resist the urge to taunt.

"Do you really want me to answer that, lady?"

The flush on Toni's face went from pink to red before she found her voice. "I meant shelling peas, and you know it."

She glared as he grinned.

"Maybe you'd better demonstrate," Lane said. "Do a couple for me. I'll watch and learn." And when Toni bent over to do just that, his deep voice rumbled in her ear. "I'm a quick study and really good at just about everything."

Her hands trembled, but she wouldn't have bolted for all the trees in Tennessee. This was her land, her home, her back porch, for Pete's sake. Why should she let some overgrown oaf make her act like a silly schoolgirl?

"Maybe so," Toni said shortly. "But you don't float worth a darn."

Lane couldn't think of a thing to say in response to her less-than-subtle reminder that she'd saved him from drowning. He looked down at the bowl in his lap, then at her long, slender hands deftly working their magic on the pea pods, and he tried to imagine them holding his head above water, and pulling his limp and all-but-lifeless body from the flood.

"You aren't paying attention," she warned, and was rewarded by a grin before he refocused on what she was doing.

It looked as simple as unzipping a zipper, but something told him that it had probably taken her years to perfect the skill. And when she laughed at his effort, he knew he'd been right.

"You'll get the hang of it...eventually," she said. "You're a quick study. Remember?"

Not wanting her to leave, Lane caught her hand, then turned

it over palm up, and studied the perfect shape and hidden strength.

Toni's stomach tilted, and her pulse raced as she looked down. As big as she was, his hand dwarfed her own. Just thinking about his body covering hers in the same manner made her sick with guilt, and she realized that what she was planning to do might be too cold-blooded to consider.

No matter how badly she wanted a child, she was finding it more and more difficult to face the idea of lying down with this man and taking something from him that he might not be willing to give.

There's always artificial insemination. Her stomach turned at the thought. Now she was back to square one and a lonely, empty life unless she was able to talk this man into her bed.

The ball of his thumb traced the center of her wrist, testing the pulse that pounded beneath.

"Toni, I'm sorry about this afternoon. I hated not being a part of the search team, and I wanted someone to tell me they found Emmit Rice's body in the wreckage. Watching them carry Bob Tell out instead was hard. I took my hurt out on you. It was uncalled-for, and unforgivable, especially after all you've done for me, but I'm asking you to forgive me all the same."

The blue in his eyes had softened to a dusky gray. The tone of his voice had gone from sexy to serious. Resisting him was impossible; giving up her dream even more so. She wondered if it could be done. She pulled back her hand, unwilling to let him learn too much about how she felt.

"I knew why you said it," Toni said. "I didn't take it personally." And then she grinned, unaware that bitterness colored her smile, as well as the rest of her response. "I learned that lesson the hard way a long time ago. A man rarely means what he says, at least not to me."

She stood abruptly, causing the porch swing to tilt. "Supper in thirty minutes. I'll finish the peas later. Go visit with your friends or something. You don't owe me anything, Lane Monday. I did what I did because I don't think before I act, not because I wanted something in return. And don't you ever say I did.''

The back door slammed as she disappeared into the house, and he wondered where the hell that had come from. All he'd done was try to apologize for being rude and offer to shell a few peas.

He sighed. *Try to figure out what goes on in a woman's head and a man will go crazy.*

He looked down at the bowl in his lap, then frowned and picked up a pea. By God, he wasn't going anywhere until he'd shelled this bowl of peas first.

The night air still held the heat of the day. Although the air conditioners hummed softly inside the house, Toni couldn't bear another minute of being cooped up within these walls. Lane had his friends to keep him company, she'd already changed the bandages on his leg, and the last pea had been shelled and stored in the cooler. There should be no further need of her services from anyone or anything, at least not today. She slipped out the back door, careful not to let the hinges squeak. She was tired of pretending that she didn't care.

Just when she'd gotten used to being unneeded, all of this had happened. When everyone left, she would have to adjust to loneliness all over again. But tonight, she wished for something more than a job to keep her busy. She wished for companionship, even for love. But because there was no one there to hold her, she hugged the porch post instead, closing her eyes and leaning her forehead against the cool, smooth wood in weary defeat.

It smelled of paint and the fainter, but more enticing, scent of wisteria. The vine was nearby, running up the trellis and falling down around the edge of the back porch like a lavender ruffle. The thick, sweet scent made Toni think of her mother. Next to her eight children, the vine had been her mother's pride and joy.

Toni opened her eyes and lifted her head, gazing intently into the dark, cloudless sky. The new moon gave off no glow, and the stars seemed too far away to even twinkle. She had more company inside her house tonight than she'd had since the day of her father's funeral. But she'd never felt so alone…or so lonely.

"Toni."

Startled by the sound of Lane's voice, she caught her breath, thankful that the night hid her face from his all-seeing eyes. "What?"

"Are you all right?" he asked softly.

"Of course. Was there anything you needed?"

Her answer was casual, but the tone of her voice was not. During the day, something had changed between them, and although Lane wasn't in the habit of trying to placate a woman's whims, something about this one kept getting under his skin. Maybe it was because she tried so hard not to need anyone. And maybe it was something else he wasn't ready to face. Whatever it was, Lane couldn't leave her, or well enough, alone.

"Why do you keep answering a question with a question?" he asked.

Because it's safer. Because you won't want to hear what I really want to say.

"Sorry. I wasn't aware I did that. I suppose that's what comes of answering to no one but myself."

Lane shoved his hands into his pockets and ignored the thrust of pain to his thigh.

"All through supper, you seemed…bothered. If it's something we've done, I wish you would say so. This whole business has probably uprooted every routine you ever had. It won't be long before we're out of here, and then your life can get back to normal."

Normal? My life will never be the same.

Toni laughed, but there was no joy in the sound. Lane didn't have to look to know that there were tears in her eyes.

"You're probably right," Toni said. "I never did get through fixing that north fence." She started past him into the house. "I'll see if the men want any more cobbler. It's never as good the second—"

"Toni…"

She paused. A faint light from within the house cast shadows on his face, once again reminding her that this man was only passing through her life. She sighed and swallowed a lump in her throat.

"Don't," she said softly. "In a few days, you'll be gone. Whatever it is you're about to say, you would later regret."

She walked away, leaving Lane alone on the porch with the night and his thoughts.

I may have some regrets, lady, but they won't include you. Never you.

He followed her into the house. Without thinking, he locked the door behind him, as if it were his own house. Like the woman, the farm had already claimed its place in his heart. What, he wondered, would his apartment in Tallahassee be like when he returned? Would his footsteps echo from room to room? Would he pace the floor at night, longing for the sound of her voice and a sight of her smile, or would she fade with the memory of it all?

"Hellfire," Lane muttered, and bypassed the trio in the kitchen who were sharing the last of supper's dessert. "You know where you belong, Toni Hatfield. You're as much a part of these Tennessee hills as the trees that cover them. If I could be as certain as that, I would know more than I do right now."

Breakfast was on the table when Justin Hatfield walked into the house without knocking, just as he'd done for all the years that he'd lived there. "I see you finally got the table fixed," he said, eyeing the crack on the top and the edges of plywood showing on the sides that Toni had used as patches.

Toni cocked an eyebrow as a greeting. Her brother acted as if he owned the place. As the eldest in the family, she supposed it was his right, although he'd married and moved away years ago.

"Have a biscuit and a cup of coffee, Justin. Maybe they'll give your mouth something else to do besides yap."

Justin grinned.

Lane eyed Toni's brother, then the table, and shrugged. He still didn't remember a damn thing about the whole episode except waking up handcuffed to the maddest woman he'd ever seen. Already a veteran of several meals at the patched-up table, he wisely shifted his plate to the end that didn't rock and slid into the nearest chair before someone else beat him to it.

Reese and Palmer took one look at the steaming plates of eggs and sausage, the basket of hot biscuits and the jars of jelly, and groaned.

"I may never go home again," Reese said. "Toni girl, you're going to make some lucky man the best darned wife in the state."

The smile was halfway to ready on Toni's face when Justin snorted, and then laughed aloud.

"She would make a better man," he said. "Say, Toni, that reminds me of why I came. Someone knocked down your mailbox. You better put it back up before the mail carrier comes around."

Toni froze. It was nothing more than what she'd heard from her brothers nearly all of her life, but to have it thrown in her face in front of three near strangers was almost more than she could bear. Her shoulders were stiff, her expression blank as she set the coffeepot on the table.

"Eat while it's hot," she said softly. "I'll be back later." Without looking back, she walked out of the room.

Lane froze. He couldn't believe what he'd just heard. Reese and Palmer took one look at their buddy's face and started talking at once, obviously aware that if someone didn't change the subject, Justin Hatfield might find himself on the outside looking in.

"I can't believe you said that," Lane said.

Justin froze, the biscuit halfway in his mouth.

"Said what?" he mumbled around a mouthful of buttery crumbs.

"You know what," Lane said, dragging himself to his feet, then leaning across the table until he was only inches away from Justin's nose. "You don't want to make me hurt you, do you?"

The biscuit broke into pieces and fell from his fingers as

Justin stared back. "Hell, no," Justin said, leaning forward until they were nose to nose. "But I would like to know why you're so damned mad before we start throwing punches."

Lane inhaled. He couldn't believe it, but it seemed as if Justin really didn't get it.

"You've got about three seconds to clear out of this kitchen and go fix what you sent your sister to do, or so help me God, I'll…"

Justin gawked, then jerked as if he'd actually been punched. "But Toni always fixes the—"

"She shouldn't have to," Lane said. "She's a woman, for God's sake. Doesn't anyone around here see that besides me?"

Reese and Palmer stared regretfully at their plates of sausage and biscuits and got to their feet. "We'll do it," they said in unison.

"It's the least we can do for our room and board," Reese added.

Lane's eyes never left Justin's face, and the longer he looked at him the colder they got. Finally, he shook his head once and grinned. It was enough.

"No, boys, finish your breakfast like Toni said. I think Justin was already on his way out the door, weren't you, buddy?"

Justin gave Lane a considering look and then nodded. "I think you may be right," Justin said, and took a biscuit with him as he left.

Lane dropped into the chair and shifted his leg so that he didn't have to bend it to reach his plate.

"Reese, pass the eggs, please, and don't eat all of the biscuits. Save Toni some. She should be here any minute."

Less than five minutes later, Lane's prophecy was proven true as Toni entered the kitchen. As usual, her unruly curls were already on the move. A slight smudge of dust shadowed the upper thrust of her right breast, and she wore a matching handprint on the thigh of her blue jeans. Her eyes were wide and slightly shell-shocked as she went to the sink to wash up.

She would have given a year of her life to know what had been said after she'd left. But whatever it was, Lane's expression was as unreadable as Justin's had been when he'd taken the posthole digger from her hands and sent her back to the house with a terse command.

She slid into the empty chair and picked up her fork before she had the guts to look up at the men who were staring at her, waiting for her to make the first move.

Thankfully, Lane took the initiative. "Want some eggs, Antonette?"

Toni took the bowl that Lane offered and spooned clumps of fluffy yellow egg onto her plate without thought.

"How about some sausage, and maybe a biscuit?" Reese added, and elbowed Palmer to pass Toni the jam.

She took what was offered, then stared down at her plate, unable to take a bite. Shame and embarrassment overwhelmed her. What must they be thinking?

"Like the man said, you'll make a hell of a wife."

Lane's voice echoed over and over in her ears, drowning out everything except the hammer of her heartbeat.

Chapter 5

By noon Toni's embarrassment had eased, but she still couldn't bring herself to ask Lane what he'd said that had sent Justin to the mailbox and her back to the house. And she hadn't received any information from Justin, either. When the mailbox was fixed, he'd crawled into his truck and driven away without further explanation, leaving no clue to his unusual behavior except for the telling glance he'd given Lane Monday before he'd left.

Now, with lunch out of the way and Reese and Palmer checking on the searchers who were dragging the river downstream for Rice's body, Toni had hours before supper and plenty to do. If it rained again, the grass might green up in the lower pasture, and she could end one chore by not having to hay. But except for the thunderstorm several days earlier, the spring had been unusually dry, and hay still had to be fed to the cows.

Toni headed for the barn with work gloves in her hand, wishing instead that she were going to the creek to swim. But while the water was slowly receding, it was still unfit for any recreational dip. In any case, she had no desire to prance around on the creek bank in front of a dozen strangers.

So work it would have to be. She backed her pickup truck toward the hay bales stacked at the north end of the barn, then got out and started tossing them, one after the other, into the bed of the truck.

A half hour later, she shifted the last bale into place, then jumped down, tossing her work gloves into the driver's seat as she walked past. Her blue jeans stuck to her legs, and her old long-sleeved shirt was thin from years of wear. Although she knew that T-shirts and shorts would have been cooler apparel, she also knew that handling hay would have been impossible against all that bare skin. She would trade hot for scratched and itchy any day.

Before she drove up to the pasture to feed the cows, she wanted to check on Lane and get herself a drink. She came out of the barn on a run, and ran face first into the second button down on Lane Monday's shirt.

"Oh!" She grabbed her nose and staggered, seeing stars as the unexpected thump brought tears to her eyes. If it weren't for Lane's quick reaction, she would have fallen backward in the dust.

He caught her as she stumbled, but the grin that he'd been wearing died as she tore out of his arms and pushed him away.

"Don't touch me," she grumbled, still holding her nose, and then couldn't believed what she'd said.

Her shock was nothing compared to the anger that swamped him. He cursed beneath his breath to keep from shouting.

"You can get that indignant expression off of your face right now, lady. I was only trying to keep you from falling on your butt," he said, then started back to the house, forgetting as he did, why he'd come in search of her in the first place.

"Oh, good grief, why did I do that?" Toni moaned. She was shocked by her own behavior and by what she'd said. "Lane! Please wait."

Her shout stopped his progress, but the touch of her hand on his arm was the magnet that turned him around.

"What?" he muttered. "And don't tell me you left something out, because you were pretty damned clear to me."

"I'm sorry," she said. "I didn't mean to react like some stupid, fainting female. You just startled me, that's all."

"Females who faint aren't necessarily stupid, Antonette," he said shortly. "And I came to tell you that Justin called. He wants you to call him back as soon as possible."

Choosing to ignore his assessment of womanly attributes, she frowned at the message instead. "Did he say why?"

Lane shrugged. "Just something about missing chickens and dead dogs."

"Good Lord," she said, more than a little startled, and looked toward the barn. The hay would have to wait. This definitely took precedence over her chores.

They started toward the house together, and Lane could tell that she was torn between trying to slow her gait to his and the need to find out what was wrong at her brother's place.

"Don't wait on me," Lane said. "I'll get there when I get there."

She went from walk to run in three seconds flat, and when her long, shapely legs went from step to stride, Lane forgot to follow. He was too lost in watching the beauty of her body as it moved. She was as graceful and lithe as a gazelle, and in spite of her aggressive, independent tendencies, about as shy. He'd already noticed that when Toni got nervous, she slipped into a bossy mode that could make a man nuts.

"What am I thinking?" he muttered. "She's already made me nuts, and I've only been here four days."

With that thought came the knowledge that soon he would have to leave. As easy as it would be to stay in the quiet and comfort of these green Tennessee hills, he couldn't stay here forever. He had a job, friends, people who counted on him. And as soon as he thought it, he knew that when it came time to go, he would be leaving a part of himself behind that had nothing to do with gratitude for his life being saved. Toni Hatfield and her Smoky Mountains had insinuated themselves into his heart as quietly as a sigh in the wind.

He entered the house in time to see Toni drop into a chair,

the phone pressed against her ear like the lifeline that it was to the world outside her home. And then he frowned in response to the growing expressions on her face that looked to be a mixture of dismay and despair.

"How many?" Toni asked, and missed seeing Lane's frown deepen. "When did it happen? Is that Bobby crying?"

She bit her lip and pressed her hand to her belly in response to the shaft of sympathetic pain. She could hear the child's sobs, even though Justin had claimed that the boy was in another room. Her heart ached for the child's sorrow, and she wished that she were there to give him a hug.

Without thinking, Lane walked up behind her and slipped a hand across her shoulder. It was instinctive, just a comforting gesture he might have given to anyone in a similar situation. But the moment he touched her, Lane felt her tense like a skittish colt. He sighed, then moved away, wondering as he did, how this woman had ever gotten a date. And then he turned back and stared.

She was twenty-nine. He knew, because she'd announced it one morning at the table as firmly as if she'd asked him to pass the salt. Remembering, he could almost say that she'd thrown the information out like a gauntlet, as if daring him to make something of the fact that she was alone and unmarried and, to all intents and purposes, well on her way to being an old maid.

He snorted beneath his breath. Antonette Hatfield was as unlikely an old-maid prospect as the possibility of his becoming a midget. But something told him that if he was a betting man, he could make money guessing the number of times this woman had gone out with a man who was not her kin.

"Oh, Lord, Justin, I'm sorry," Toni said. "Yes, thanks for calling. I'll be careful, but I got rid of the chickens when Daddy died, remember? And I'll keep watch on the livestock." She sighed, then hung up the phone.

"Honey, what's wrong?"

Lane was so fixed upon seeing a smile come back into those dark chocolate eyes that he hadn't even heard himself call her by an endearment.

But Toni heard. She saw and took note of everything concerning this man who'd washed down Chaney Creek and into her life. And she knew that if she wasn't careful, he would take the heart out of her when he went home. She shrugged and spread her hands in a defeated gesture as if she couldn't believe what she was about to say.

"This morning, while Justin was over here, something or someone got into their chickens. He thinks it might have been the Sumters stealing food."

Lane frowned, but thought little of it. This was, after all, mountain country. Keeping animals was bound to hold some risks, even from ne'er-do-well neighbors.

"That's too bad," he said. "Is Bobby one of Justin's boys? I heard you ask why he was crying. Were some of the chickens his pets?"

Toni looked up, then quickly away. She didn't want to see his sympathy.

"Yes, he's Justin's oldest. He's just past ten. And no, they weren't his pets."

She frowned, then walked to the window overlooking her front yard, parting the curtains to glance out before she spoke again. Her voice trembled and her stomach kept rolling. But not in disgust. It was fear that held her thoughts. In all the years that thefts had been blamed on Sumters, not once had anything like this ever happened. She could hardly bring herself to say it.

"Something killed Bobby's dog, too."

She spun, and the lace curtains fell into place behind her like a bridal veil. As he stared at her, Lane caught his breath and then forget to take another, so shocked was he by the image that flashed through his mind. But it wasn't Toni that he'd seen when she'd turned around. Just for a moment, he would have sworn that it was Sharla's face that he saw— Sharla, silhouetted by the lace. It took everything he had to get back to the conversation and away from the vision that Toni had unwittingly inspired.

He inhaled slowly, relishing the burst of oxygen into his

starving lungs, then wiped a shaky hand across his eyes. He had to get back to the matter at hand.

"Would those Sumter kids do something like that?" Lane asked.

Toni frowned, then shook her head. "Justin thinks so, but for some reason, I don't."

"Why not?" he asked.

"Brownie was a redbone." When she saw the puzzled expression on his face, she added, "That's a breed of hunting dog, and the Sumters live for hunting and dogs. I don't think they would randomly kill one like that."

"They would have taken it with them, right?"

She nodded. "I would have guessed it was some animal that killed Brownie, but Justin said that there was hardly any blood on or around the dog, and no footprints that he could see. A wildcat would have cut a dog that big to shreds before it died, the same way a wolf would have done. There would at least have been wounds from a fight. And, the chickens were out and running all over the yard. Justin didn't even know how many were missing until he began to put them up."

Something within Lane started to surface. His lawman instincts had kicked in. There were some more questions he wanted to ask. "Surely the missing chickens are out there. Maybe they just flew off and are somewhere up a tree."

"Maybe," Toni said, "but chickens can't fly far, usually no more than a few yards." She shrugged and looked away.

Lane could see that she didn't buy his theory, either, and truth be known, he didn't think much of it himself.

"So how did the dog actually die?" Lane asked.

Toni turned. Lane felt her fear from across the room.

"A broken neck."

"Well, damn," he whispered, and this time the thought bubbled again. A little harder. A little longer.

"I've got to go feed the livestock," she said, starting out the door. "If you want to watch television or read, feel free to look through Daddy's things. I haven't been able to pack them away." Her lip quivered. "At least not yet."

"Where were you going?" Lane asked, remembering the pickup with its load of hay.

"To the back forty. I have ten, cow and calf pairs. I like to feed the mamas more when they're nursing than the cows that range. It's been so dry this spring that the grass is short. I've been supplementing their pasture grass with hay."

"I'm going with you."

Toni looked startled. She knew her mouth was open, but she couldn't seem to help it. The last time someone had followed her at work, it had been her father. And he'd simply been telling her what to do, not actually helping to get it done.

"I don't need any help," she said. "You can't lift because of your stitches and bad knee, and I'm strong as an—"

"Antonette, in spite of my aches and pains, I am not the man with whom you should be arguing strength."

She couldn't help it, but her gaze went straight to his broad shoulders and massive chest beneath the soft plaid shirt he was wearing. Finally, she looked up and caught his cold, blue glare as he continued.

"I said, I'm going with you. You have no business roaming all over these damned mountains alone, especially after what happened at Justin's. What if it's a bear that's the culprit, for God's sake? Do you want one to walk up on you while you're babying those cows?"

She paled. She hadn't thought of that possibility. There *were* still places in the mountains that were wild and unfettered. And something big *had* broken the dog's neck. A swipe of a bear paw would just about fill that bill.

Determined not to show how deeply his warning had affected her, Toni shrugged. "Okay, okay. I'm sure it's no big deal, but you can come if you promise not to be a back-seat driver. I don't like to be told what to do."

Lane grinned. "Now why am I not surprised?" he drawled, and pulled a piece of straw out of her ponytail as she started past him.

Toni glared, then stomped out the door, refusing to admit, even to herself, that she was darned glad he was behind her all the way.

* * *

She fed the cows without incident, and with little argument from Lane, other than his telling her she shouldn't be lifting all that weight. She'd made fun of his concerns, but secretly cherished the thought that he believed she could actually have a fragile bone in her body. If she had one, she had yet to discover its location. But for the time being, she was perfectly willing to let Lane keep his fantasies about her. If he thought she looked weak and helpless, then God love him for being a fool. He was the first man who had ever told her she was too little to do something.

It was when they started back to the house that Lane's perception of Toni took a sharp right into shock.

"I need to stop here a minute," Toni said, parking beneath the trees that lined the dirt path. "I'm missing a good hammer and I think I may have lost it the night of the flood."

Lane's attention piqued. That would be the night she'd pulled him out of Chaney Creek. "Where are you going to look? There has got to be at least a thousand trees between here and the house."

The pickup door slammed behind her as she started down the incline.

"Oh, I know where to look," she said over her shoulder. "It's either where I dumped the fencing materials when I went back for you, or where I loaded you onto the wagon."

"I want to see."

She paused and turned. The expression on his face made her shiver, but not with fear. Anticipation threaded through her system, reminding her that the tension between them did not run on anger, but on interest.

"So come," she said. "But watch where you walk. It's downhill most of the way. You don't want to pull out your stitches."

No, I damn sure don't, he thought, and then sighed when he saw that she was waiting on the path for him to catch up. He should have known that she would be ready, if necessary, to offer another shoulder to lean on.

Toni girl, how am I going to manage the rest of my days

*without you telling me what to do? And without you to catch
me if I fall?*

"It's not here," she said after carefully searching beneath
the trees where she'd parked the night she'd seen him caught
in the flood. "I'm going farther downhill. You may want to
wait here. It's almost a quarter of a…" His glare ended her
advice and sent her down the hill with him only steps behind.

"Tell me," Lane said when he figured she'd cooled down
enough to talk to him again.

"Tell you what?" she asked.

"About that night."

She shrugged. "What's to tell? You already know I'd been
fixing my fence. I was on the ATV, and luckily for you, pulling a wagon." She paused and looked back. "You know, the
one that's in the backyard near the garden."

Lane nodded.

"When I saw the storm coming, I tried to hurry. But the
wagon was full of posts and wire, and the mud was too thick
to get up much speed. By the time I got to the foot of the hill,
it was raining pretty hard. I left the ATV because I was afraid
I might get stuck going up the hill. I would rather be wet than
stuck in red clay, any day."

"And…" He urged her to continue.

"And…I heard an explosion and thought lightning had
struck something and set it on fire." She paused, then turned
to look at him when she continued. "I still can't believe that
what I saw was you…falling out of the sky…and men dying.
It still gives me nightmares just thinking about it."

Lane was surprised. "I didn't know that you saw the plane
crash," he said.

"Well, I didn't know what I saw, either, until you told me
differently. All I saw was an orange ball of fire above the
trees." She shuddered, then looked away as she resumed her
walk, afraid that he'd seen too much.

"So, what did you do then?" he urged.

"I started to run. I didn't want the lightning to strike me,
too. That's when…"

She got quiet. Lane knew what came next. But he hadn't

heard it from her. The sheriff had volunteered that information and everything else he'd learned about Toni's part in saving his life.

Lane caught up with her, and when she wouldn't stop, he grabbed her by the arm. She had no choice but to give in to his silent demand. She turned and looked up at him.

"Why did you go in after me?" he asked.

She swallowed around a lump in her throat. It was hard to look at the face of a man who had come to mean far too much to her for her own peace of mind.

"Because you couldn't get out any other way," she said. "Come on. It's going to get dark unless we hurry. I won't be able to look for the hammer."

Because I couldn't get out any other way.

The simple statement was deceiving. What she'd done had taken more than nerve. It had taken a stronger spirit and a braver heart than most men would have had.

Lane started walking, one foot in front of the other, barely noticing his sore leg. Going down was easy; coming up was going to be hell. But he wouldn't have missed this trip with Toni Hatfield for anything.

A few minutes later, she stopped and started walking in a circle, her eyes down to the ground as she searched for the missing hammer. Lane kept walking until he came to the edge of the hill overlooking the ravine and stared down into the steadily flowing stream that was Chaney Creek.

Debris from the flood was still caught in the tree roots that sprouted from the creek bank high above the water. A watermark was still visible, and would be for several days until the heat had dried it back to its normal shade of dirty red. A couple of feet from where he was standing, a sharp overhang of rock shaded several square feet of creek beneath. Lane stared, unable to fathom what had happened here…in a storm…in the dark.

"It's not here, either," Toni muttered, stomping to the edge of the ravine, then absently staring over to the other side. She pointed. "Look. That side of Chaney Creek is the back edge of Justin's place. He bought it right after—"

"My God!"

Lane took her by the shoulders and made her look at him. He couldn't get past the thought of what she'd done. His fingers dug into the soft skin of her shoulders until he felt muscle and bone, and still she seemed too fragile to have pulled them both out of a flood.

"What's wrong?" Toni asked. "Did you hurt your leg?" She started to kneel to see if blood had seeped through the bandage and into the denim of his jeans. "I knew this was too far for you to—"

He yanked her to her feet. "Don't kneel at any man's feet, Antonette. If there's any kneeling to be done, I should be the one doing it. This has to be where it happened, but I've got to know. How in hell did you get us out?"

He turned her toward the creek, and then couldn't make himself let her go. It was as if he was suddenly afraid she might fall. And as he held her close against him, she felt his body pressing against her backside like a wall.

She closed her eyes to see more clearly within her mind the night…and the storm.

"I think it was all due to a streak of lightning and a big streak of luck." She leaned over and pointed to the rock below. "I knew that outcrop of rock was there, and I counted on being able to get a foothold." She turned and laughed, remembering what had come next. "Even with that, we still almost drowned. I couldn't get you to turn loose of that log you were holding."

Her chuckle seemed out of place next to his shock. How could she laugh at nearly losing her life to save his?

He lifted her hands and turned them palms up, rubbing a thumb in the center of each as if testing their strength. Unable to voice his thoughts, all Lane could do was lift them reverently to his face.

He pressed one, then the other to his lips, and when he did, Toni Hatfield forgot the promises she'd made to herself about not caring for this man. She forgot that she'd all but given up thoughts of babies and motherhood. And when he wrapped his arms around her and held her clasped against his chest, Toni wanted to cry.

Why did I have to meet you when it's too late for you to care? she thought.

One big hand cradled her head, while the other rested low around her waist. She was trapped as neatly as if she were in a vise, and yet she had never felt this cared for or this safe in her life.

"As long as I live, I will never be able to say thank you enough," Lane said softly, and cupped her face with his hands. "You, Toni Hatfield, are one hell of a woman."

He leaned down.

Toni saw his intent. She could have objected. She could have moved. She did neither. Instead, she stood and waited for the world to stop, and when his mouth slid across her lips, then centered perfectly on hers, she found that it was her heart that had stopped.

Lane expected her to resist, and when she didn't, he was not prepared for the soft, open invitation she made when their lips connected.

He felt her tremble and heard her sigh, but when she shifted slightly beneath his touch and then slipped her hands onto his waist to steady herself, he lost sight of what he'd started to do.

It was supposed to be a simple thank-you, accompanied by a light, friendly kiss. But the woman who stood within the circle of his arms was accepting more than he'd meant to give.

Lane groaned, and when Toni took one step forward, his hands slid off of her shoulders and down her back, drawing her deeper into the kiss of no return. He vaguely remembered thinking that this couldn't go on, then Toni's arms slid around his waist and locked behind his back.

He remembered little of what came afterward beyond a few undeniable facts. Her skin was softer than he'd expected. Her breasts fit his body contours to perfection, and he'd never wanted to be inside a woman this badly in his entire life. But that wasn't going to happen, not if he had anything to do with it. He couldn't repay a lady like Antonette by using her body in a fit of lust. Not even if she seemed willing.

He gave up their connection with painful regret as he tore his mouth from hers; then he closed his eyes and rested his chin on the crest of her head.

"Ah, damn," he said softly as he rubbed his hands up and down the middle of her back in a gentling motion. "I'm sorry, Toni. I didn't mean to let that go so far."

Toni's heart shattered. He was sorry? It was the last thing she'd wanted to hear him say. She ducked her head and tried to laugh as she pushed herself out of his arms. In her mind, things hadn't gone nearly far enough.

"Forget it," she said shortly, and hated herself for the bitterness that she heard in her voice. "It was just a kiss. And you're not the first man I've known who's handed one out, then moved on to something better."

"That's not what I…"

He could have saved his excuse for Sunday morning, because Toni was already walking away. And, if he read her reaction correctly, she thought that he'd quit from lack of passion. Guilt overwhelmed him. He'd known her self-esteem was low, but this was ridiculous.

She thinks I stopped because I got bored? Lord have mercy. What does that woman see when she looks in a mirror? Doesn't she know that she's beautiful?

He groaned and started uphill, telling himself that he deserved every ache that came with the trip. He hadn't gotten himself into this kind of condition with no chance of relief since high school. And, to be honest, he wasn't sure how it had happened from just one kiss. As a rule, he had more control over his emotions than this. But that was before he'd taken the back door into Tennessee, and then been fished out of Chaney Creek like a sack of unwanted pups.

He ate supper alone, standing at the counter and chewing his sandwich while he watched her from the kitchen window as she worked. The weeds in her garden were suffering the consequences of what had transpired between them. She wielded the hoe with frightening irregularity, as if one false swipe and someone's head might fall instead of the uprooted weed.

"My stitches will be out in two more days and then I'm gone. How do I make this right before I go?" Lane muttered to himself as he gave up pretending to eat. Toni wouldn't even look at him, never mind talk to him. He didn't know how to make things right between them again.

But Lane had a streak of stubbornness that was almost as big as he was. He dumped his sandwich on the counter and headed for the door. "Damn her hide, she's going to listen to me or else."

He stomped outside and never realized that his leg hardly hurt at all. He was healing, and at the same time, still suffering from an attack of misplaced indignity.

"Antonette!"

Toni paused and turned. From the look on Lane's face as he came toward her, the massacre of weeds would have to wait. She'd seen mad on her brothers' faces so often that she recognized anger on sight. It had something to do with the jut of male chin, lower lip and a glower across the forehead. She sighed. As tired as she was, dealing with a wounded ego was going to play hell with her manners.

"You shouted?"

He flushed, then made an effort to lower his voice several octaves before he spoke again. "I've already said I'm sorry that I overstepped the bounds of friendship you've shown me. I wish to hell that it hadn't happened. I like watching you smile. I like sharing a meal with you. But I don't like feeling like Jack the damn Ripper. Can't we please go back to square one?"

A rush of pleasure came and went so fast that she almost forgot it had ever happened. It was what he'd said after "sorry" that had hurt the most. And it was because he would soon be gone that she had the nerve to say what was in her heart.

"That's just fine, Mr. Monday. I'm glad I give good service. I'm glad you find my manners pleasing to your taste. And while I don't feel threatened by your presence in any way, shape or form like I might with Jack the damn Ripper, I do resent the hell out of hearing that you wished you hadn't kissed me.''

Unintentionally, she leaned closer. Lane was stunned by the depth of anger in her eyes.

"I, personally, was enjoying it when you got an attack of conscience, or guilt or whatever men call it when they don't want to leave any strings behind.''

"I didn't mean that I didn't—''

"Didn't you just say you wished it hadn't happened?''

He swallowed and nodded. At this point, answering her was impossible. He might be bigger, but she could outbalk a mule.

"And you want to go back to square one?'' she asked.

He sighed and nodded again. Finally they were getting somewhere.

She smirked. "I hope that doesn't include the handcuffs. I would hate like hell to spend another night on the floor tied to you.'' She handed him the hoe. "Oh, and I don't think my table is up to another parting of the ways, so let's just agree to disagree on this, and drop the subject altogether. What do you say?''

"I give up.''

"What?''

Lane sighed and shrugged, then used the hoe for a cane as he started trudging up the row toward the house.

"I can't outtalk you, Antonette. And half the time, I don't know what you're thinking, so I give up. I hurt your feelings and didn't mean to. I'm sorry. I'm sorry. I'm sorry.''

"Apology accepted,'' she said softly, and anxiously awaited his reaction.

He hadn't expected an answer, so when it came, he wasn't ready for the flash of relief that settled in the pit of his stomach. He stopped, looked down at the dirt beneath his feet and grinned wryly before wiping the smile off of his face. He turned to face her.

"You're a hard woman, Antonette Hatfield.''

She nodded. "It's a hard life, Mr. Monday.''

"That it is, lady. That it is."

He held out a hand. Moments later, Toni's fingers slid across his palm and threaded through his. She looked up, gauging his reaction to their reluctant connection.

"It's getting dark," she said.

He lifted his head and smelled the air, then squinted toward the blaze of colors on the horizon. "Want to sit on the porch for a while and watch the sunset?"

Toni was thankful for the shades of dusk that hid her sudden tears. She would give a year of her life to be able to spend the rest of it with this man...on some porch...watching life and sunsets pass them by. But she was going to have to settle for a couple of days' worth instead.

"I suppose," she said. "At least we don't have to shell any more peas. Justin's wife, Judy, and my brother David's wife, Laura, will be over tomorrow to pick the patch."

Lane rolled his eyes and pulled her gently out of the garden. "More family?"

She nodded.

He grinned. "Reese and Palmer won't be back until late tonight, so let's get dibs on the swing before company comes."

His smile was easy, his tone of voice gentle. The lines on either side of his cheeks deepened from the smile. It made him seem younger, more innocent. At that moment, Toni forgot everything ugly that had happened during the day, including the harsh words that had come between them.

Toni's steps were lighter as she followed in his wake, their hands still connected in a way that their bodies could not.

"You don't have to hurry," she told him. "The porch swing isn't going anywhere. Besides, it's a long time until morning."

The blue in his eyes turned black with emotion. Her warning put thoughts in his mind that had no business being there. He could think of several good ways to get through a night, and all of them needed a woman like Toni to make them work. But they weren't going to happen. Toni kept herself and her emotions as distant as the state in which he lived, and considering all of the facts, that was as it should be.

"Don't remind me," Lane said, pulling her up the steps and into the swing. Before Toni had time to make something more out of what he'd said, he added, "My stitches come out the day after tomorrow."

"It will be all right," she assured him. "I'll go with you." Absently, she reached over and patted his uninjured thigh, before closing her eyes and letting the swing take her places her thoughts dared not go.

Lane couldn't look at her. And he damn sure wouldn't touch her. If he did, he would ruin everything that he'd spent the afternoon trying to fix. But he couldn't get over her easy, gentle assurance that he would not suffer alone.

Dear God, if only I dared hope that might be true, I would never leave this woman.

But old wounds and painful losses kept Lane's thoughts and wants to himself, just as Toni cherished her dreams to herself. And because of those reasons, the two of them watched the sunset in silence, wishing for things that couldn't be.

Chapter 6

Kids ran wild across the yard, climbing trees, running down hills and adding high-pitched shrieks of delight to the hysteria brought on by being together. While their mothers picked the bounteous overflow from her garden, Toni sat on the front-porch swing. She kept one eye on her nieces and nephews' riotous behavior, and another on the youngest member of the Hatfield clan, three-month-old Lucy, who belonged to Justin and Judy.

The baby's tiny head was covered with a downy layer of soft, brown curls. Her small nose wrinkled in sleep, and her rosebud lips pouted, then sucked in a reflex motion as Toni shifted her from one shoulder to the other.

Toni inhaled the sweet scent of baby powder and line-dried clothes as she patted Lucy's diapered bottom in rhythm to the rocking of the swing. With children in the yard, and one in her arms, her life seemed nearly complete.

And then, Lane Monday walked out of the barn and started toward the house. The absence of a limp was noticeable, as was the length and breadth of the man himself. Toni clutched

Lucy a little tighter and tried not to notice, or even care, that his big body moved like a well-oiled machine.

A ball rolled near Lane's feet. He laughed, and tossed it back to the children at play, and for a moment, Toni pretended that this was her world, and the man coming toward her was a permanent fixture in it.

The baby whimpered, and without missing a beat, Toni set the swing back in motion with the tip of her toe, pushing off like a bird taking flight.

Pat, pat on the baby's bottom. Back and forth in the old porch swing. The rhythm felt right, and as old as Time. A mother rocking a child to sleep.

And then Judy Hatfield came around the house with a weary smile and a bushel of peas, and set it near the porch. Her sister-in-law, Laura, followed with her bushel.

"We're through," Laura called. "Hey, kids, put away the toys and go wash. We've got to go home."

Grumbles and groans could be heard all around, but the children did as they were told.

"Bet you thought I would never get done," Judy said, and lifted the baby from Toni's arms, missing the empty look that swept over Toni's face as she did. "The peas are great. I'll put the kids to shelling when we get home, and Justin can baby-sit later while I put them up."

Toni's heart felt as empty as her arms. She looked down at the sleeping baby and wanted to cry. "I could keep Lucy longer if you needed to—"

"No way," Judy said. "Laura and I have already imposed upon you long enough by asking you to watch this wild bunch."

"It wasn't an imposition," Toni said softly, unaware that Lane saw all of what she felt and was trying to hide. "I like taking care of the kids, especially the babies," she said, and brushed a baby curl behind Lucy's ear, just so she could feel the silky softness one more time.

"Judy's right," Laura said. "Every time we have a family get-together, you wind up playing nursemaid to all the little Hatfields, instead of enjoying the day with the rest of us."

Then she groaned and rolled her neck. "Tonight, I will ache in places I didn't know I had."

Laura batted her eyes and giggled as she tucked a loose blond curl beneath her headband where it belonged. She was small and plump and David Hatfield doted on her.

You don't understand what a real ache is, Toni thought. *The children are why I enjoy the day.* But she kept the thought to herself, as she did everything that was dear to her heart.

Lane stood to one side and watched. He didn't understand Toni's pain, but it was obvious to him that she was hurting. And because it hurt him to see her sad, he took the opportunity to break into the conversation.

"Ladies, if you would tell me where to put your baskets, I'll set them in your cars."

Judy and Laura gave Lane a considering look, as if trying to imagine this man and their socially inept sister-in-law together.

"I'll get them," Toni said, and ran to the edge of the house where the women had set them down.

She picked one up and was about to drag the other, when Lane walked up behind her, took them out of her arms and hefted one onto each hip.

"No you don't. You do too much and lift too much as it is. I'll do it," Lane said, and ignored Toni's frown.

Two at one time would have been more than a normal-size man could have handled. Lane had them balanced on his hips, one beneath each long arm as if they were nothing.

"If you can find an empty spot in the car, you can put mine anywhere," Laura said, giggling, and headed for her car to open the trunk with Lane right behind her. Her less-than-subtle reference pointed to the fact that four of the six children loading into cars were hers.

"Be careful," Toni called. "Remember your stitches."

Lane loaded the baskets, then turned. There was a soft smile on his face and a deeper one in his eyes. "My hands and arms do not have stitches, Antonette. And after tomorrow, neither will my leg. You fuss too much. I'm fine."

Toni was at a loss for what to do or say while he loaded

the baskets into the cars. All she could do was watch while
the joy in her morning disappeared.

Because Lane and the children had otherwise occupied her
thoughts, she missed seeing the all-knowing look that Judy
and Laura exchanged. It was an ''Aha!'' look if ever there
was one.

As Lane deposited the last basket in her car, Judy apolo-
gized. ''Toni is right. We forgot that you've been through so
much. You seem so strong and healthy, we just—''

''I'm fine,'' Lane said. ''Toni's just trying to keep me in
one piece long enough to ship me out.''

''Oh, wait,'' Toni said, then darted back into the house.
Seconds later she was back with a half-empty bottle in her
hand. ''Lucy's milk. She went to sleep before she finished it
all.''

Judy smiled as Toni stuck the bottle into the baby's bag.
''The little squirt's been doing that lately, then waking up an
hour or so later squawking for more. I swear she's going to
be as hardheaded as her daddy.''

''We're off. Thanks for the peas,'' Laura shouted, waving
as she drove away.

Judy echoed the sentiment, then drove away, leaving Toni
and Lane alone in the yard.

''I always feel like I've been in the eye of a whirlwind when
the kids leave,'' Toni said, and didn't know that her chin quivered as she watched them drive away. ''But I wouldn't trade
them for anything. I would keep them all if their mothers
would let me.''

''Toni?''

''What?'' she asked, still lost in the memory of what it had
felt like to hold the baby against her breast.

''Why aren't you married?''

Pain, followed by anger, made her lash out. ''Why aren't
you?'' she countered, satisfied by the startled expression on
his face.

''*I* was,'' Lane said, and wished he'd never started this.

''Don't you ever want to remarry? Maybe raise a family?''
The expression on Lane's face went blank. Toni didn't

know what she'd said, but something had struck a serious nerve in him.

"I will not father any children, and that's a damned fact," he said bitterly.

Toni was shocked. She would never have believed Lane to be the type to dislike children. Matching his defiant answer with a defiance of her own, she spoke before she thought. "If I could, I would have a hundred. Children are wonderful. They're the most loving, honest people I know."

Lane grew cold, from the inside out. He didn't see the angry tears in her eyes, or hear the tremble in her voice. Memories as painful as the wounds healing on his body were making him sick. He saw nothing but the memory of Sharla in a pool of blood and the way she'd looked when the life had gone out of her eyes.

"Then you should have gotten married and had a dozen," he muttered, wishing to hell that this conversation had never started.

Hurt and angry at learning that he held disdain for what she most wanted out of life, she spoke the truth before she thought. "No one ever asked me," she said, and then paled and walked away before she saw the sympathy on his face, hating him for making her admit the fact.

The shock of her statement yanked him out of his bitter memories. He knew by the set of her shoulders that his thoughtless statement had hurt her as deeply as if he'd struck a blow to her heart. He would give anything to be able to take back what he'd said. But it was too late. The damage had already been done.

"What in hell is wrong with the men around here, anyway?" he muttered, and followed her into the house, unwilling to let what he'd said fester between them. "Toni?"

He was not surprised when she didn't answer. She'd probably had enough of men and their stupidity to last her a lifetime. But Lane wasn't the type to give up, so he went from room to room until he found her in the kitchen…ignoring him.

It took everything he had not to focus on her long bare legs and shapely backside, encased in frayed denim cutoffs. Her pink T-shirt was soft and old, and he knew that if she turned around, the outline of her bra and the defiant push of her breasts beneath could make a man forget his manners. And while he would have liked to undo her braid and dig his fingers into the tangles so deep that he would be forever caught, he knew that it wasn't smart to let lust get in the way of why he'd come in search of her.

"Look," he began, "I've never been good at saying I'm sorry, but that doesn't mean I can't admit when I'm wrong. I was way out of line out there. I would like to think you'll forgive me and just chalk it up to a bad day."

Toni turned. His apology was welcome, and oddly, unexpected. She should have been happy to know that he'd cared about her enough to at least clear the air between them. But she was too upset about something else to do much more than nod.

"It's fine," she said. "Forget it."

Lane took a deep breath and resisted the urge to shake her. "It's not fine, Antonette, and we both know it. I said some things I shouldn't have and I—"

"My pie is gone."

Her remark was so unexpected that Lane forgot what he'd been about to say. "What do you mean, your pie is gone?"

She shrugged and pointed. "Just what I mean. I took an apple pie out of the oven just before Judy and Laura arrived, and put it out back to cool. It's gone." She sighed. "The boys probably took it and ate it while their mothers weren't looking. I don't really care, but I would like to know where my pie pan is. It's one of my favorites."

"I could look around for you," Lane offered. "They couldn't have gone far with it. Maybe it's in the barn or out behind your machine shed."

Toni sighed and dropped into a chair. "It doesn't matter to me," she said. "It's just that you won't have dessert today, and I would lay odds that three little boys will have a belly-ache before the afternoon is over."

Lane grinned, aware that what he was about to say would get a rise out of Toni. "I can give up dessert for a day, even several if I have to, but why are you blaming the boys? There were several little girls out there, too.''

"Because the girls don't like to get dirty. They wouldn't have eaten a pie with their fingers even if someone had tried to make them. I know my nieces…and my nephews. Believe me, it was the boys."

"Are you going to call their mothers?" Lane asked.

Toni looked up, then quickly away. There was too much tenderness in his expression to face. "No way. Favorite aunties do not snitch. At least, not over missing pies."

Lane bent down and covered her hands with his own. "Toni, look at me."

The touch of his hands was bittersweet. He gave so little, and she wanted so much more. But she bit her lip and complied. She had, after all, no other choice. There was no way she could let him know how much she'd come to count on his daily presence in her life.

"What?"

Lane sighed. Her name was Antonette, but someone should have called her Defiance instead. "Are you going to say it?" he asked.

"Say what?" It was a dumb question. She knew what he wanted to hear. It was just so hard to say the words, because acknowledging what he'd said about children was like the death of a dream.

"That I'm forgiven for hurting your feelings."

Toni sighed. "You're forgiven."

Lane laughed, but it was a harsh, unhappy sound. "Damn, Toni, don't overdo the sentimentality on my account."

Her gaze was level, her voice calm. "I can't afford sentimentality, Lane. I am a self-assured woman, remember?"

What I remember is the pain in your voice, lady. I hear what you say. But do you hear yourself saying it?

The thought was impossible to voice, because however badly he might wish to do so, he was in no position to change one single aspect of Toni Hatfield's personal life. He'd already given happiness a try and been cut off at the heart for the effort. He didn't have enough guts to repeat the pain.

''So, what are you going to do?'' he asked.

Toni pushed herself up from the chair. ''Call the doctor and confirm your appointment.''

''Appointment?''

''You've got a checkup coming and stitches to be removed.''

''Trying to get rid of me, are you?'' It was a poor joke that fell flat between them.

Toni paused in the doorway, looking strangely elegant in spite of her T-shirt and shorts. Her chin tilted and her eyes darkened with defiance.

''Does that mean you're not anxious to leave?'' she asked.

He flushed. How could he answer that and not hurt her worse than he'd already done? He chose to remain silent.

Unbeknownst to him, his silence hurt her even more. But she would be damned if she let him know that.

''That's what I thought,'' Toni said. ''There's a casserole in the refrigerator. Heat what you want in the microwave. I'm not hungry anymore.''

All six feet six inches of his body went numb. He knew he kept breathing, though, because the pain around his heart had not gone away. But he couldn't have moved or spoken to save his life. If he didn't get the hell out of Tennessee soon, he was going to ruin both their lives.

There was a note on the table, and Toni was nowhere to be found. If he hadn't sat down on that sofa, he wouldn't have dozed off. He hated this lingering weakness and would be heartily glad when his full strength finally returned.

''How could she disappear without my hearing her leave?'' Lane muttered, picking up the note and then frowning. ''Eleven o'clock tomorrow. Not even a 'Dear Sir' or 'go to hell.'''

He tossed the note back onto the table. That, he supposed, was the confirmation of his appointment time; the lack of everything else had to be the sum of what his departure meant to her. Absolutely nothing.

He sighed and ran a hand through his hair in frustration.

How did she expect him to act? They'd known each other less than a week. Granted, the circumstances surrounding their meeting had been more dramatic than most. And it was true that you get to know a person real fast when you spend the night handcuffed together. That was a fact that Toni could claim. His situation was a little bit different, though. He had the feeling that if he could remember it, too, then he would be a lot better off.

How, he wondered, did that old Chinese proverb go? If you save a man's life, then he will be in your debt forever?

That didn't help his guilt. So he owed her his life, but that didn't mean he had to give up the rest of it for her, did it? Surely she hadn't expected him to just toss off fifteen years of law enforcement and try farming, Tennessee-style.

"What the hell am I doing?" Lane asked himself. "She hasn't asked a damned thing of me. Why am I reading so much into what she doesn't say?" But there were no answers forthcoming, and no tall, dark-eyed woman to deny what he thought.

Lane walked outside to the back porch and looked up into the hills beyond the house. A haze hung above the treetops, filtering the heat of the sun just enough to give the less cautious a dangerous burn. He stood at the edge of the top step, gazing intently into the tree line, watching for something, anything, that might tell him where Toni had gone. He heard nothing, and saw nothing but a lone turkey buzzard riding the air currents far above the house.

As he watched, it dawned on him that this was part of her everyday life. She came and went to suit herself, and she knew that when she came home, no one would be standing on the porch watching and waiting for her to arrive.

A slow, sick feeling settled near the center of his belly. Now that he'd met her, how could he leave, knowing that she would be alone? He'd seen the longing in her eyes for more than life had seen fit to give her. He'd sensed the emptiness with which she lived, although she would have been the first to deny it, especially to him.

"Ah, lady, why did this have to happen? You deserve a whole man, not one who's been crippled by life."

But admitting that he wanted to stay would be admitting the reason why. And Lane Monday wasn't ready to face the fact that he was falling for the woman who had saved his life.

"I'll get back to Tallahassee and this *thing* that I feel between us will fade," he told himself.

Relieved to see her coming out of the trees, Lane knew that he'd been lying. To himself, and to her, ever since the day that they'd met. He didn't want to leave Toni Hatfield, but he would. And it would be one of the hardest things he'd ever had to do. Maybe even harder than the day he'd buried his wife.

And then he realized that Toni was running and he forgot to breathe. He could tell by the way she was moving that something was wrong.

The last thing Toni had expected to find when she left the house was a dead calf. And she knew that she wouldn't have found it for days if the mama cow had not kept bawling.

She'd heard it earlier when Laura and Judy were in the garden and she was on the porch with the baby, but she'd thought little of it. Cows bawled all the time.

But later, after confirming Lane's appointment, she'd stepped outside to get a breath of fresh air, hoping to clear away the misery of knowing that he would soon be gone. The first thing she'd noticed was the distant, but steady, bawl of a cow. Without thought, she'd struck out across the back lot, heading for the repetitive sound.

She'd gone farther than she'd meant to on foot. If she'd known she was going to go this far away from the house, she would have taken the ATV. But the longer she'd walked, the sillier it would have been to turn around and go back to get the vehicle. Any minute now, she expected to find the cow and see that she'd worried for nothing.

But that hadn't been the case.

When she walked into the clearing and saw the cow in the corral on the opposite side, she sighed.

"Well, bossy, how did you get yourself stuck in there?" she muttered.

And then the cow lifted her head and bawled again. Toni could see that her udder was tight and swollen with milk. It was clear that the calf hadn't nursed at all during the day. It was then that Toni had started to worry. It was odd that the cow had gotten herself caught inside the corral, but even stranger that the calf was not right there, on the other side of the fence, bawling to get in to its mama.

"I'm coming, girl," Toni said softly, and started walking across the pasture.

The cow lowed again. Toni imagined she heard sadness in the cry, although she knew that it was just her sympathetic heart working overtime again.

"Do you hurt, girl?" Toni asked as she neared the cow. "It'll be all right. We'll get you out of there and find your baby for you, and you'll be good as gold."

Her hand was on the gate when she saw the calf at the edge of the trees. She'd expected it to be nearby. But she hadn't expected to find it dead, or in its present condition.

The left hind leg was gone from the carcass. She knelt and held her breath against the gory sight, needing to see, yet unwilling to touch.

It hadn't been dead for long. The blood was still red and fairly fresh, although the edges of the wound were already starting to curl and dry. If she could only see the...

"Oh, God!"

She jumped to her feet and staggered backward before slowly turning in place. She searched the surrounding tree line with a sharp gaze. The calf's throat had been cut. Someone, rather than something, had killed it. And it was then that she realized the leg hadn't been torn from the body; it had been butchered instead.

"Damn, damn, damn," she muttered, thinking of the Sumter family and the missing father. This was worse than before. She could understand starvation, but she could not suffer wanton waste. If they were hungry, then why on earth hadn't they taken the entire calf?

A sense of profound violation crept into her soul. Someone had come onto her property and taken something belonging to her, something that had depended upon her for food and care. Rage for that injustice overwhelmed her. She doubled her fists and resisted the urge to scream. And the moment she thought it, she felt a different sense of urgency. What if they were still here? That might explain why the calf was dismembered. Maybe they'd heard her coming and been frightened away from finishing the job.

The cow lowed and moved toward the back of its pen. Toni paused in the act of turning around and cocked her head just a bit toward the tree line.

But she saw and heard nothing. And that was when her anxiety turned to fear. Subconsciously, she'd noticed what her conscious self had not; there was a complete and overwhelming absence of sound. Not a bird. Not a bug. Not one thing was moving, not even the cow she'd just put in the pen. It stood, with its head lifted and ears up, looking into the woods behind her. The flesh crawled beneath her hair. It felt as though someone were blowing on her neck. She shuddered and clenched her fists, trying to regain some of her earlier anger.

She told herself that she was imagining things. Then something popped behind her, a familiar sound she'd heard all of her life. It was the sound of twigs breaking beneath the steps of someone's feet.

"Oh, no, they're still here," she gasped, and remembered that Samuel Sumter's three oldest boys were in their twenties and nearly as big and worthless as their daddy.

She turned in the direction of her house. Lane was near. Only minutes away. But she had the terrible feeling that he would still be too far to help her.

Without looking back, she bolted from the corral, ran across the clearing and deeper into the woods, dodging trees and jumping rocks as if her life depended upon it, certain that they were coming after her.

She ran until her legs were shaking and her heart hammered in her eardrums. She ran until the stitch in her side was in danger of becoming a real pain, and she never looked back to see if she was being followed.

She was out of the trees and coming down the hillside toward the house when she saw Lane moving toward her. Unaware that he'd already sensed she was in trouble, Toni wanted to shout, to somehow warn him that someone might be in pursuit, but there was no breath left in her body to talk, only enough to run. Until she ran straight into his arms.

Lane caught her in midstep, bracing himself against the impact of her flight. He wrapped his arms around her shoulders and held her fast against him. Even through the pounding of his heart, he felt her trembling and heard her trying to catch her breath enough to speak.

"Back there…in the woods…dead."

"Shh," he whispered, soothing her gently with the touch of his hand until he sensed that she was calm enough to make sense.

And then he realized what she'd said. Dead!

"Toni, calm down, honey. I've got you. Whatever it is, you're safe now. Take deep breaths and calm down so you can tell me what's wrong."

The pain in her side ripped across her belly. "Oh, Lord," she moaned, and jerked out of his arms before she doubled over, grasping her knees to keep from passing out.

Seeing her in this condition made him crazy. He needed to know what was wrong, and she was in such bad shape that she could scarcely breathe, let alone talk.

"Are you all right?"

She groaned and nodded, and as she realized that she really was all right, she began to feel foolish. She'd reacted like a silly female, jumping to conclusions just because she *might* have heard footsteps in the woods. She hadn't even looked to see. She'd simply assumed. Embarrassed by her behavior, there was no way she could tell Lane what she'd feared.

"Thank God," Lane muttered. Ignoring the dry pull of healing stitches beneath his blue jeans, he knelt at her side and cupped her face, brushing her hair away from her forehead and out of her eyes with one hand, while he cradled the back of her head with the other. The sight of tiny scratches swiftly turning red across her cheeks angered him. "Toni, sweetheart, listen to me. Did someone try to hurt you?"

"No," she gasped, leaning her forehead on her knees, intent on not passing out. "Just mad," she said, and then motioned for him to be patient. When she could, she would get it all out.

But Lane was not a patient man. "Mad at who?"

She shrugged. How could she say who when she hadn't really seen anyone, only heard what she thought to be footsteps in the woods behind her?

"Wait. Wait a minute. Then I'll talk," she said, still gasping.

Lane had no choice but to wait, all the while seething at the thought of what had made Toni so angry.

Chapter 7

When she could talk without gasping, Toni groaned and then held up her hand. "Help me up," she said, wincing as Lane pulled her to her feet. "Good grief, I won't be able to walk tomorrow."

"Damn it, lady, I've run out of patience. Start talking. What happened up there?"

Toni sighed. All things considered, it seemed silly. She suspected that she'd scared herself more than anything.

"I went to check on a cow," she told him. "All afternoon I kept hearing her bawl. I thought maybe she'd lost her calf."

Lane frowned. "Why didn't you tell me where you'd gone? I was worried." The look she gave him was measured and cool, almost as if to ask, why should you care?

"I was fine. I'm always fine."

He resisted the urge to shake some sense into her and wisely kept his mouth shut, waiting for her to continue.

"Anyway, I found the cow locked in the corral up in the back pasture. I thought she'd accidentally shut herself in until I found the calf. Someone had killed it. I think they were butchering it when I came up."

Lane grabbed her by the shoulders, pinning her in place with his grip and the blaze in his eyes. His voice was barely above a whisper. "Are you telling me that you walked up on someone out there in the woods?"

She shrugged. "Not exactly. I thought I heard something in the woods and when I saw the calf, I just assumed it was the Sumters."

"Even so," Lane said, "thieves don't like witnesses, Toni. The crime they're committing is called rustling. I don't know what the penalty is for that in Tennessee, but I would venture to say it's more than the thief is willing to pay."

She shivered, then tried to laugh. "I made a big deal out of nothing, Lane. It's not like this hasn't happened before. But damn it, if they were hungry, why didn't they take the whole calf? Why were they hacking it up piece by piece instead of carrying it off before they butchered it?" She frowned, and kicked the dirt with the toe of her shoe. "Even if they were hungry, I hate waste."

Lane spun around and headed for the house.

"Where are you going?" Toni asked. When he didn't answer, she ran to catch up.

"Hey! I asked you where you're going."

"I can't believe you even have to ask," he muttered, and hit the back door with the flat of his hand, pushing it open as if it were nothing more than a piece of paper.

Toni followed him into the hallway, and when he picked up the phone and asked the operator to connect him with the sheriff's office in Chaney, she took the phone from his hand.

"I can do that myself," she said, and turned her back on him so that he couldn't see the nervousness on her face when she retold her story.

Even now, she could feel the danger that she'd sensed, and she wondered why her reaction had been so strong. The Sumters were capable of stealing, but nothing else—of that she was certain. Then why, she asked herself, if I'm so right, do I feel certain that I just outran the Grim Reaper?

Lane paced, waiting for Dan Holley to arrive. Toni tried to pretend all was well, but it was extremely difficult to concentrate on the mending she had in her lap when her fingers kept trembling too much to hold the needle.

"When he gets here, I'm going out to the hills with you," Lane said.

Toni frowned. "It's a long way from the house. Are you sure your leg is up to it?"

Lane spun around. "Stop it!" he said, hating the fact that he was shouting at her. "Stop using my welfare to dodge the issue we have here, lady. My leg is fine. If it hurts tonight, then it hurts. It's not going to fall off just because I walked too far."

"You don't have to yell," she muttered. "I'm not deaf."

"Maybe not, but you're the most muleheaded woman I've ever known."

Toni's lower lip jutted mutinously. She glared, and received a similar look in return. The situation was saved by Sheriff Holley's arrival. When Justin pulled in behind him and parked, Toni could do nothing but mutter. "Oh, good grief, just what I need, more men to tell me what to do."

She inhaled, then counted to ten before opening the door. There was no other way to get through what was about to occur.

Lane heard what she'd said, although he was pretty certain that she hadn't meant him to. He considered her quiet complaint and then frowned.

Looking at the situation from her point of view, it probably did seem unfair. On the one hand, everyone assumed she could take care of herself and left her alone without help or company to do just that. On the other hand, let some trouble occur, and advice came from every corner, telling her how to mind her own business.

Hindsight was sometimes an unfortunate thing. It left a person with the memory of having made a big error in judgment, and no way of changing the past. Lane knew now that he should have asked Toni what she intended to do, instead of charging to the rescue. But taking over was a habit too deeply ingrained within him for him to stop without a reason.

However, he reminded himself, there was always tomorrow, then he stopped short at the thought. Tomorrow he would get his stitches out. The day after that, he would be gone. For him, there was no tomorrow. At least not where Toni was concerned.

"Damn it to hell," Lane muttered, jamming his hands into his pockets to keep himself from putting them through a wall.

But cursing gave him no satisfaction or relief. There was nothing he could do but play out the hand that life kept dealing; right now, that meant retracing Toni's steps into the hills. And, he reminded himself, taking backup.

He'd lost his gun during the plane crash, but thanks to Reese and Palmer, he now had another one. He'd never been on duty without one, and so he wore the gun out of habit. When he stepped out onto the porch and unconsciously took a stand behind the woman on the steps, it felt right to be armed. Without knowing, his heart had done what his mind had refused to accept. He was already behind her…all the way.

Toni leaned against the corral and watched the men combing the area where she'd found the calf.

The animal was gone now. Somehow, she wasn't surprised. *I knew there was someone in the woods, and I was right. It had to be the Sumters after something to eat.*

"Calf's gone," Justin reaffirmed, then leaned against the corral beside his sister. "Damn those Sumters, anyway. Someone ought to run them plumb out of the country, or lock them up for life, whichever comes first."

Toni frowned. Men's attitudes about things differed greatly from women's. There was no doubt about it. The way she looked at it, using energy on hate was wasted when a more viable solution to the Sumter problem could be found, such as relocating Samuel's family to a city where the younger children could go to school regularly, and where the older ones could find work. However, logic and reasoning did not necessarily go hand in hand with Justin's sense of justice.

"Yes, Justin. I know that the calf is gone."

"Are you going to press charges?" he asked.

"Against whom? I didn't see anyone. I can't blame some-one on suspicion alone."

He hit the post with the flat of his hand. "That's stupid," he said. "You know who did it. You're just too damned soft-hearted to say so."

Toni leaned forward until she and Justin were eye to eye. "That's just it, Justin, I don't know who did it. No more than you know what happened to your chickens and Bobby's dog. Did you press charges against the Sumters for that?"

He flushed and looked away. "Judy wouldn't let me."

She rolled her eyes. "Thank God for the sanity of women. She saved you from making a bigger fool of yourself than normal."

Before more than words could fly, Lane stepped between the two and put his hand on Toni's shoulder. "You were right about being followed out of here. We saw a set of footprints that ran parallel to yours. Whoever it was didn't follow you long, but he did follow you."

Toni shuddered. The thought of being pursued made her sick.

"Thank God those young whelps of Sumter's changed their minds," Justin said. "If you hadn't come up here by yourself, none of this would have happened."

Toni snorted softly. "What on earth is wrong with you, Justin? The calf was still dead, whether I found it or not. At least I saved the cow and called the law, which is more than you did when your dog was killed."

Sheriff Holley walked up in time to hear the last of what Toni had just said. He frowned as he poked his notebook into his shirt pocket. "What's this, Justin? Someone killed your dog?"

"And made off with some of his chickens," Lane added, then walked out of the argument to stare thoughtfully into the tree line, trying to imagine someone watching Toni from some concealed vantage point.

Something about this didn't feel right. And he thought of his missing prisoner. Even though they claimed that the Sum-ters were just harmless and hungry, the fact that Toni had been followed was contrary to someone's simply thieving. Stalking a victim was the approach an attacker would take. Someone who intended further harm would follow, whereas a sneak thief would run in the opposite direction in frantic flight, hoping to get away from the scene of the crime. Surely, he thought, Dan Holley could check this out and warn the Sumter family against further trespassing. He needed assurance that it was actually the Sumters who were responsible.

"We're ready to go," Toni said.

The sound of her voice startled Lane. He hadn't even heard her walk up. He turned, and when he saw the weariness in her eyes, he reached out and took her hand in his.

"You got lucky today, honey," he said softly. "Please don't take any more unnecessary chances. Until this mess with your neighbors is put to rest, don't go anywhere on foot, okay?" When she frowned and started to argue, Lane's voice softened. "I'm not telling you, I'm asking. Okay? I don't want to get a phone call from someone one day telling me that you've disappeared."

Her eyes widened as she worried the edge of her lower lip between her teeth. Lane hated seeing the look of shock on her face, knowing that he'd been the one to put it there.

"I didn't mean to scare you. I just want you to be careful. I care about your welfare, Toni Hatfield, just like you cared about mine. Understand?"

She nodded. *Oh, Lane, I understand all too well. You feel an obligation, and I want a commitment instead.*

"Come on," he said, giving her hand a tug. "Let's get back to the house. Reese and Palmer should be back by now. I want to talk to them before they leave tomorrow. Maybe they have news about the search for Emmit Rice's body. That's one identification I would willingly make."

She nodded, and for the moment she was willing to let someone else make some decisions. The day had gotten seriously on her nerves.

"Toni, I'm going to talk to Livvie Sumter," the sheriff said. "I know you're not pressing charges, but she's still got to know that I won't stand for any more of this going on in my county.''

Lane and Toni walked hand in hand out of the clearing, leaving Sheriff Holley and Justin to follow close behind. Once they arrived at their vehicles, the sheriff and Justin drove off. But not before Toni caught the scowl her brother sent her as he directed his gaze to her and Lane's clasped hands.

Within a few minutes of returning to the house, Toni found herself alone with Lane. Reese and Palmer had not returned. Memories of her flight into Lane's arms, and the way that he'd held her, kept colliding with the facts. And the facts were that he'd simply acted the way a friend would have by comforting her in a time of stress and that he'd meant nothing by it. Acceptance of that truth was what would get her past the next few days. She looked everywhere and at everything except him, and hated that she felt out of place in her own home.

Lane didn't know what was wrong, but if history had anything to do with it, it was bound to be something that he'd done.

''Lady, if you don't stop fiddling and pacing, you're going to run us both up a wall.''

She blushed and looked away, then without thinking took down her hair, intent on putting it back up again, only in a more sedate fashion. The trek up the hill, then back down again, had played havoc with her constantly unruly curls.

With her arms raised above her head, the thrust of her breasts against her shirt was unmistakable and impossible to ignore. Lane gritted his teeth and told himself to look away. And he might have been able to do that if she hadn't dropped the elastic band for her hair on the ground.

''Shoot,'' she muttered, then bent over to look at the floor, trying to locate the band that seemed lost against the pattern on the rug.

Lane would have offered to help, but he couldn't find the will to move away from the sight of all that hair falling down around her shoulders, or the way her jean shorts had suddenly conformed to her rear when she'd bent down. He had a sudden wish to see her standing before him wearing nothing but the smile on her face, and then he shuddered and walked out of the room before his body gave him away.

When she wandered through the kitchen moments later, he had his lust well under control. It had even crossed his mind to offer to help her fix the evening meal, until he turned, looked into her eyes and got lost in the memory all over again.

He was staring, and it made her nervous. In the past, when men had looked at her too long, they'd inevitably found fault with something about her. Because of that, she turned away and missed seeing the blatant look of want that spread across Lane Monday's face.

"I'm going to fix pork chops," she said. "If you have an objection, speak now or forever hold your peace."

"Whatever you fix will be fine," he said. "I'm going to go outside now."

He walked out after that odd remark, leaving Toni standing in the kitchen with no explanation for his behavior other than what she'd already assumed.

I must look awful, she thought. *And earlier, I clung to him like cockleburs. He probably thinks I'm going to do it all over again and embarrass him.* She'd made him uncomfortable. That had to be it.

Tears pricked at the backs of her eyes. But Toni swiped them away and headed for the cabinet to take down a bowl. Crying over impossibilities was a waste of time and effort. Why should she care what Lane Monday thought about her? In two days he would be gone.

But the longer she peeled and stirred and cooked, the louder the voice inside her cried out. *When he leaves, it will be too late to try having a baby. Do something, Toni, before it's too late.*

"But how?" she moaned. "How do I entice a man to make love with me when he can't even stand the sight of my face?"

"Those sure are good pork chops, Toni," Reese said as he helped himself to another without waiting for an invitation.

"They're going to keep dragging the river, aren't they?" Lane asked. The need to hear positive information about the fate of Emmit Rice was eating Lane up. He had no interest in food.

"We're dragging everything, including our tails between our legs," Palmer replied, and dipped a second helping of mashed potatoes onto his plate before passing the bowl to Reese.

Toni propped her elbows on the table and rested her chin in the palms of her hands. Her dark eyes went from one man to the other, gauging their interest in what was going on at the table as opposed to what had gone on during the continuing search. Lane hadn't eaten anything, and the other two men couldn't talk for eating. What a day this had been.

"Hell, Lane." Reese flushed as he remembered the lady's presence and grinned at Toni before continuing. "Excuse my language, but we may never find Emmit Rice, and you know it. That was a hell of big flood, and that creek empties out into one long river."

Lane stared down at the half-eaten food on his plate and tried to imagine never knowing Emmit Rice's fate. It didn't sit well with him at all.

"Okay," he muttered, tracing a pattern on the tablecloth that Toni had spread to hide her patchwork on the broken table. "I know that, but I don't like it. How about if we call back the men and the dogs and have them take a second run-through in the hills. Maybe see if they can come up with any new—"

"What the hell's wrong with you?" Reese dropped his fork in his plate and leaned back in the chair, his expression just shy of disbelief. "If the searchers came up empty three days ago, why would you think they would find something now? What is it you're not saying?"

Lane couldn't look at Toni when he said it, but he couldn't live with himself unless it was out in the open. He had to admit his worst fear aloud.

"I'm not saying anything specific," Lane told him. "But until I see Emmit Rice's body, I'm not going to believe that he's dead."

"Why not?" Palmer asked, sounding stunned. "It's nothing

short of a miracle that you survived. There is no earthly indication that Emmit Rice crawled out of that plane ahead of you. Damn it, Monday, you heard me tell you yesterday that they're not even sure who's in what bag. They're still trying to make positive identifications.''

Toni's chin slipped from her hand as her eyes grew rounder. Her mouth slackened, and her slow, unsteady gasp was all the indication they needed that this conversation should have been saved for somewhere other than the dinner table.

She knew the men were staring at her; she could feel their sympathetic looks. They'd spoken about human beings as if their remains were just pieces of meat. With that thought, she looked down at the pork chops, then back up at the men, and knew that she was going to have to leave the table. She held her breath and got to her feet. She needed some air. Now. The images that Chuck Palmer had just conjured were too vivid to ignore.

"Well, hell, Palmer. While you were at it, why didn't you just pass around the pictures you took at the scene for our viewing enjoyment?'' Lane growled, then watched with regret as Toni slipped from the room.

Palmer shrugged. "Sorry. I didn't think. I sometimes forget that she's not one of us. Besides, she's so competent and cool, I didn't figure it would bother her.''

Lane pushed back his chair and stood. "Why the hell not? She's a woman, and a civilian, to boot. The ordinary housewife is not usually faced with this sort of conversation.''

"She's not a housewife,'' Palmer muttered.

And she'll never be ordinary, Lane thought. *But she damn sure ought to be someone's wife.* He left Reese and Palmer and went to find Toni.

Someone's wife. Someone's wife...but not mine. "Oh, damn,'' Lane muttered.

Caring wasn't part of the plan. It was supposed to be: Remove stitches. *Find a way to say goodbye to Toni Hatfield.* Pack my bag. *Remember why loving the second time around isn't wise.* Get on the plane. *Don't think about the woman I'm leaving behind.* Put the episode behind me. *But not in this lifetime.*

He caught her on her way out the front door. "Toni, I'm sorry we upset you."

She turned. Framed by the doorway and the dusky evening shadows in the yard behind her, she watched as Lane moved toward her from across the room, and felt the world growing smaller with every heartbeat. He was so big that he dwarfed everything and everyone around him. And yet the look on his face was full of regret and tenderness. Her breath caught on a sob. That tenderness was going to be her undoing.

Lane heard the catch in her breath, and regretted the fact that, once again, they had caused her distress.

"Palmer wasn't thinking." He shrugged. "Or better yet, that's exactly what he was doing, thinking aloud. Only not about your feelings. He should have been more careful."

His hand cupped her face, intending to give comfort. But when her fingers traced the shape of his hand, he forgot what he'd been about to say. All he saw was the look of horror in her eyes.

She didn't mean to, but when he'd touched her, instinctively she'd returned the gesture. They had talked about death in the same breath as they'd complimented her on the pork chops, allowing no more consequence for one than the other. She didn't understand how they could separate their feelings from their work. Something like that would destroy her, just like the crash that had nearly destroyed Lane Monday. It was that thought which made her reach out, needing to feel proof of the life he'd come so close to losing.

And what better way to feel life than to touch the center of its existence. Toni's fingers went from his hand toward his chest. Her gaze was centered on the place above his rib cage where she knew his heart continued to beat. Her fingers shook, her legs trembled, but she needed to feel the life he'd so nearly lost.

"It could have been you." Toni closed her eyes and sighed as the rock-hard rhythm of his heart vibrated against the palm of her hand. "Thank God that it wasn't."

Lane almost didn't hear her words. Her voice seemed broken, barely above a whisper. And when her hand flattened against the wall of his chest, splaying across his heart, the look on her face nearly broke his heart.

He wanted to hold her but knew that would be a mistake. He needed to take away her pain, but instead he faced the fact that he would not always be around for her next pain, or the next.

"Have mercy," he groaned, unable to move.

Toni blinked, then shuddered and looked up. The muscles in his face appeared to have been chiseled from stone. His mouth was grim; his eyes narrowed against revealing too much emotion. She felt the heat from his body on her palm, and knew a sense of loss so profound that she could not speak. Instead, she simply dropped her hand, shook her head and walked out the door, leaving Lane to do as he chose.

What he wanted to do was follow her into the night and claim the woman and her heart without further delay. What he did was walk away. He'd seen too much of the woman she was to be able to hold her, then let her go. And let her go he must. For there was a line in their relationship that he must not cross...could not cross...and still hope to survive.

Toni knew when she walked off the porch steps that Lane would not follow. She'd seen the expression on his face go blank and felt him shut off his emotions as plainly as if she'd been slapped.

"Why can't I get this right?" she muttered, unaware of the tears streaming down her cheeks. "Why am I so stupid? I know I disgust him, and yet I keep setting myself up for these falls."

She laughed, but stopped when it came out a sob. Instead, she lifted her face to the starlit sky. "Help me," she whispered. "Just until he's gone. Then I promise I will help myself."

A breeze lifted the curls from her neck, then cupped the fabric of her shirt to her body like a jealous lover. Crickets sounded in the nearby grass while a whippoorwill cried in a nearby tree. Down the ravine she heard a cow bawl, then a calf answer. Weak yellow light spilled out in squares from the curtained windows of her house and onto the dark ground below it like butter on burned toast. Familiar sights, familiar sounds. And Toni felt as if she were dying.

She buried her face in her hands and knew that she would never feel as empty as she felt at this moment, barren of everything in life that mattered. No man, no child, no life except her own. She felt the tears on her face, and at that moment, hated as she'd never hated before.

She hated herself for having been born, and every male that she'd ever known for not being man enough to see past the surface to the woman she was beneath.

"That does it," she muttered, and swiped angrily at the tear tracks. "I've never been a weak, sobbing female, and I'm not going to start now. Especially over a man. But, by God, I will take from him what I can get."

In that moment, new determination was born. If the opportunity came to use Lane Monday to father her child, she would—with no regrets. He'd made it perfectly clear that she wasn't his type, and that was okay. At least, it would be when she could think of him without tears and anger. But she had two more nights to find a way to make this happen, to find a way to make him want her. God willing, the chance would come, and with the chance, the child.

It had to.

Chapter 8

"Well, Mr. Monday, I'd say you're as good as new. Your bruises are nearly gone and your leg is healing on schedule. I'd say you're about ready to fly the coop."

"Oh, hell, Doc. Smile when you say the word *fly,*" Lane said, and surprised himself by being able to poke fun at what had happened to him.

From her seat in the waiting room, Toni heard Lane's laughter. She didn't know what had amused him, because nothing was funny to her. The loss of his stitches had finally cut the strings connecting him to her. Now there was no longer a reason for him to stay, and facing that fact was getting harder and harder for Toni to accept.

Why did I have to like him? Toni thought, and blinked back tears as she looked at her lap rather than let anyone see how she felt. *It isn't fair.*

She sighed. Her dream of having Lane's child was exactly that, a dream. How was she possibly going to set her plan in motion? *All I have is tonight. Short of throwing myself into his bed like a fool, it's over.*

The weight around her heart settled a little heavier. She

knew that he was anxious to get home, and why shouldn't he be? He'd left his home over a week ago, expecting to be back that same day, and instead, wound up the sole survivor of a devastating plane crash.

While she was trying to regain a sense of self and dignity, the door to the examining room opened, and Toni instinctively looked up as Lane and Dr. Bennett emerged.

All they had done was remove some stitches, but Lane Monday walked out as if someone had removed the weight of the world from his shoulders. He moved with the confidence of a man who could whip snakes, fight bears and love a woman to the point of insanity. At that moment, Toni hated him for not loving her.

The smile on Lane's face froze as he looked at Toni. Her eyes were shimmering with unshed tears.

All of his joy at being pronounced fit and whole slowly died as he realized it also meant leaving her. Yes, he wanted to be well. And yes, he needed to be back in full swing in the department. He was good at what he did and took pride in that fact. But he hadn't counted on becoming attracted to the woman who had saved his life. Grateful, yes. In lust and near love, no.

"Take care, Mr. Monday," Dr. Bennett said, shaking Lane's hand.

"If you're ever in Tallahassee, give me a call. I'll save you a place beneath a palm tree and an extra-cold long-neck to go with it," Lane told the man.

The doctor grinned and gave him a thumbs-up before disappearing into the next examining room as Lane turned back to Toni. She looked like a child ready to cry. He would have liked nothing better than to put his arms around her and hug the sadness away, but the little he knew about women told him not to react to her mood unless she gave him permission.

"I'm ready when you are," he said.

Toni stood. *Ready? I will never be ready to tell you goodbye.*

When she walked past him and out the door without giving him time to play the gentleman, Lane suffered the slight in quiet. If he wasn't mistaken, he'd just received permission to react. He caught the door before it slammed shut in his face.

"Just what I like, a woman who speaks her mind," he said under his breath, and followed her to the sidewalk.

"Do you want to talk about it?" he asked as they neared her pickup.

When she would have ignored him, he grabbed her arm and then stopped, halting her momentum while he waited patiently for her to respond. Finally she had nowhere to look but at him.

"About what?" she asked.

"About whatever it is that's bothering you."

"Why, Marshal, whatever makes you think anything is bothering me?"

The sarcasm in her voice was impossible to miss. If he let himself, he could remember other times during the past week when he knew she would have let their relationship go farther than friendship. Lane had always been the one to call a halt, or refuse to take the next step toward changing it. And yet, for him, there was no other way. If Toni was resentful, he would have to live with that fact, because he couldn't live with himself knowing that he'd lied to a good woman by making promises he had no intention of keeping. And that was what moving their relationship beyond friendship would be. A lie.

"I don't know," he drawled. "Maybe it was the frown on your face, or it could have been the tears in your eyes that gave you away."

If someone had dropped a rock down her throat and into her stomach, it wouldn't have made any bigger impact than his accusation had.

"I wasn't crying," she muttered, and yanked her arm from his grasp.

"I didn't say you were crying, Antonette. I said that you had tears in your eyes. If you want, we can pretend they were never there."

She looked up at him and smiled wryly. "Just like a man.

It's easier to ignore things than to confront them, isn't it, Lane?''

Oh, damn, I think that I was right. She does hold it against me for being the one to hold back. But before he could think of how to respond, Sheriff Holley shouted at them from across the street.

''Hey, you two, wait up.''

Toni sighed, uncertain whether she felt relief or aggravation for the interruption. It was probably just as well that they'd been interrupted. Their conversation had nowhere to go but down.

''Don't think you're off the hook. This isn't finished between us,'' Lane growled as the sheriff jumped the curb and came huffing to a halt in front of them.

Finished? That's where you're wrong, Lane Monday. You can't finish something that never got started.

Toni did the best she could to hide her despair, but it was difficult. The feeling she had of impending doom was overwhelming. She wasn't off the hook and knew that better than he did. She was intent upon taking a part of this man from him, and keeping it when he left. That thought, and the fact that she didn't know how to make it happen, were killing her. She was dying by degrees; she just didn't know it yet.

And then the sheriff spoke up and ended her mental suicide. ''Hey, Toni, I'm glad I saw you two coming out of the doctor's office,'' he said. ''It saves me a trip out to your place.''

''Why?'' she asked. ''Have you learned something new about my calf?''

Holley shrugged. ''It's all in how you want to look at it.''

''How about from every angle?'' Lane said, then knew when Toni glared at him that he'd probably overstepped his bounds by insinuating that the sheriff hadn't done a thorough job.

Holley responded with a whoop of laughter. ''Man, I like your style,'' he said. ''You don't mess around, do you, boy?''

Lane had to grin. It had been years since anyone had had the nerve to call him boy. He'd outgrown the title long before he should have, simply because of his size.

"No, sir, I don't suppose I do," he replied. "So, what's up? Why were you coming to Toni's?"

It might have been the way Dan Holley didn't quite look her in the eye when he spoke, but Toni got the distinct impression that he wasn't entirely comfortable with what he was about to say.

"I talked to Livvie Sumter about her boys."

Before Toni could comment, Lane, as usual, took over the conversation and set her impatience on simmer all over again.

"Well, thank God," Lane muttered. "I hope to hell you told her to keep them off of other people's property, and I hope you told them the next time they think about frightening someone like they did Toni, they'll have to answer to an authority other than their mother."

Dan pursed his mouth as he worried the day-old whiskers on his chin. "That's just it," he said. "Those three oldest boys of hers, the ones who usually commit all the thievery, are gone. Livvie says they're in Nashville on a construction job." He shrugged, then looked Lane straight in the eye. "That part of her story checks out."

Toni watched a nerve jumping in Lane's cheek. Why did he keep worrying this thing to death? Unfortunately for all concerned, Samuel Sumter's children were not the only ones in the area capable of stealing.

"And?" Lane urged.

"She says Samuel's missing."

This time, Toni took the lead in the conversation and threw her hands up in disgust. "But, Dan, that's not news. He leaves her each time she has a baby, and we all know it. So it was probably Samuel who killed my calf, and not his boys. I'll bet if you look real hard, you'll find where he's camping. He's probably sulking because Livvie has to devote her attention to a new baby and not him. I think the man's a skunk."

Dan grinned. "I know what you think, Toni. You've made that perfectly clear more than once to anyone who will listen."

Her eyes flashed, then darkened, while the sheriff smiled. Above everything else, she despised condescension. And when Lane's hand slid across her shoulder in companionable silence, he might as well have patted her on the head and said "good dog," while he was at it, because that was exactly how she took it. It was, for Toni, the spark that lit her fuse.

"What's that for?" she said, pushing his hand from her shoulder. "And don't pretend to be on my side about anything, okay? I don't need to be babied. I can take care of myself. If I tell you Samuel Sumter probably stole my calf, then why can't I be right? Do you have any other suggestions that make more sense?"

His surprise turned to hurt, but was hidden by the lowering of his lashes. Then a flash of how unfair she was being to him turned it all to anger as he resisted the urge to shake her silly.

"Damn it, Toni, there is no my side or your side. You're the most aggravating, irritable female I've met in years. You would fry the hair off a cat and then wonder where it had gone. I touched your shoulder, not your butt. And believe me, it won't happen again."

He turned away without giving her time to argue as he re-focused his attention on the sheriff.

Toni was furious with herself and with Lane. She was taking all of her disappointment out on a man who didn't deserve it, but for the life of her, she couldn't seem to stop.

"Darn man," she muttered. Unwilling to stay and listen while they continued to ignore her presence, she went to the pickup and missed hearing the rest of the conversation.

Lane heard her mumble, and would have liked nothing better than to bend her over his knee. It took everything he had to concentrate on what he needed to ask. He wouldn't—couldn't—leave Toni alone on her farm without knowing all there was to know.

It was that instinct alone that made him a good lawman and a formidable enemy. Willing himself not to watch her walk away, he gave the sheriff his full attention.

"Reese and Palmer left this morning, so I'm out of touch with the downriver search for Emmit Rice's body. Are there any reports?" Lane asked.

Holley frowned. "No. But I assure you that when and if I get one, you'll be one of the first to know what it says." He squinted slightly as he tilted his head to get a better look at Lane's face. "You know what?"

"What?" Lane asked.

"I think something's going through that bulldog mind of yours that you aren't telling me. Are you of a mind to share?"

Lane shrugged. Saying anything before all the facts were in was not his way. "There's nothing to tell," he said. "I'm just checking every aspect of this mess before I leave."

"And when would that be?" he asked.

"Tomorrow," Lane said, squinting his eyes to gaze at the jet trail in the sky overhead. It was easier than facing what he'd just said.

"So if you hear anything, give me a call," Lane continued. "You have my number at the office."

"I'll do just that," the sheriff said, then walked away.

Lane crawled into the passenger side of the pickup and slammed the door behind him. A long, silent minute passed without any sound or movement from either one of them. And then they both chose the same instant to say their piece.

"I'm sorry…"

They spoke in unison, then stopped at the same time. The coincidence of their mutual apology was too odd to ignore. Toni sighed and leaned back in the seat while Lane grinned.

"You first," she said, and tried to ignore how small the interior of the cab felt with him taking up over half the seat.

"Lady, you won't catch me in that again," Lane told her with a chuckle. "No way. Ladies first."

She grinned in spite of her determination not to give him an inch. *Oh, damn you, Lane Monday. How can I stay mad and protect my heart if you keep behaving like this?*

"I overreacted. I'm sorry," she said, and knew it sounded grudging, but it was the best that she could do without throwing her arms around him and begging him to stay.

"Apology accepted," he replied, wanting her to look at him, but he could tell by the way she kept biting her lower lip that she wasn't about to do that. "I shouldn't have yelled at you. And I didn't mean to hurt your feelings about anything."

Toni wanted to cry. Her feelings were so miserable that an apology was never going to be enough to take away the pain. But from Lane, it was all she was going to get.

"You're forgiven, too," she said.

"Well, thank God," Lane muttered, and tried not to resent her halfhearted apology. That was his thanks for behaving like a gentleman, a sore-as-a-boil woman who wouldn't give him the time of day.

But when she neither moved nor made an effort to start the engine, he didn't have the guts to ask her why. If she had another purpose for coming to town besides bringing him to see the doctor, she was going to have to reveal it herself.

Toni was sick with anxiety. The thought of tomorrow was agonizing. Lane had consumed exactly seven days of her life, and when he left, he would be taking her heart with him. And while she had faced his rejection too many times to hope that he might actually care for her, she was having difficulty giving up her dream of bearing this man's child.

How do I ask him? How does a woman say...sleep with me and give me a baby.

Toni groaned, then hit the steering wheel with the flat of her hand, aware that as she did, Lane visibly jerked in reflex to the action.

"So, how does your leg feel?" she asked as if she hadn't just made her frustration clear.

Lane gawked. That was, without doubt, the most inane question she'd asked him since they'd met. He knew good and well that the state of his leg was not what was on her mind at the moment.

"It feels fine," he said. *Unlike you, I might add.* But he wisely kept the postscript to himself.

She gritted her teeth, then nodded. "Good. That's really good, I'm glad."

Lane turned to face her. "Toni..."

It was more a warning than a question. She knew he wasn't buying her conversational feint any more than she was.

"If you're through here, we may as well head back home. I've got all sorts of chores," she told him.

He sighed, then turned to look out the window. She wouldn't say what she was thinking, and he'd already made up his mind to keep his feelings for her to himself, so there was no point in dwelling on what each of them was unwilling to say.

"Fine. It'll give me time to pack," he said. "I hope when Reese and Palmer took off this morning, they left me their rental car as they'd promised. Otherwise, I'll have to beg another ride from you tomorrow when it's time for me to leave."

It was the wrong thing for him to have said.

Damn you! Damn you, Lane Monday. All you can think about is leaving!

With an angry twist of her wrist, Toni turned the ignition key and brought the engine to life, gunning it, backing up and then slamming the gears into drive before Lane had time to react. When they turned the corner that led out of town on less than four wheels, he braced himself with his hands against the dashboard and growled.

"I hadn't planned on being airborne quite this soon."

Toni reacted, but not in the way he'd expected. No sooner had he said the words than her foot hit the brake. She pulled over to the side of the road, got out of the pickup and walked around to the passenger's side without looking up. She opened his door.

"You drive," she said quietly. "I don't think I feel so good."

"Damn it, Antonette, don't do this. Not to me, or to yourself."

It was then that she looked up. Her expression was bland, her voice low and controlled. Only her eyes, dark and nearly blinded from pain, gave her away.

"I don't know what the hell you're talking about," she said quietly. "I'm doing nothing except asking you to drive."

He swore and scooted across the seat. When she crawled into the spot he'd just vacated, he would have sworn that he saw her hand linger on the place where he'd just sat. But when he looked again, he decided he must have been mistaken. She was busy buckling up her seat belt and digging into her purse.

They made the rest of the drive home in total silence.

Toni went about her chores like a woman in mourning. Lane watched from a distance as she checked on the livestock, then wisely gave her space when they'd returned to the house. While he suspected that she harbored feelings for him, he had no way of knowing that.

And that was the death of her dream for a child. It was, for Toni, over. She didn't know how to flirt, and she knew that she didn't have the guts to just ask him for sex. There would be no time left for happenstance to intervene because tomorrow he would be gone.

By nightfall, she had slipped into an "ignore the devastation and it will go away" mood.

She might be fooling herself, but she wasn't fooling Lane. Her misery, like his, was visible. One had only to look at the set of her jaw, or the stance that she took when she believed no one was around, as if she were bracing herself for a mortal blow, to know that she was hurting.

As for Lane, his agony was of a different sort. He'd already faced the fact that he was drawn by more than debt to the woman who'd saved his life. He'd held her and kissed her. He'd tasted woman and wanted more.

Tonight would be their last night together. While it was only their second night alone in the old farmhouse, it was going to be the longest eight hours of his life.

Sleeping wasn't an option. He needed to maintain his determination to leave her as intact as the day that they had met. The thought of pursuing intimacy with her was overshadowed by his admiration for her as a woman. He could not take what she offered and give nothing back. And nothing was all that he had to give.

And so they sidestepped each other all evening, and laughed uneasily at things that were not funny, and when it came time to go to bed, they parted without saying good-night. It was far too close to saying goodbye.

* * *

Toni lay on her side, dry-eyed and aching, and clutched the sheet beneath her chin as she rolled herself into a ball.

I will not cry. I will not cry.

When she tried to smooth out the sheet and get some sleep, she realized that it was nothing but a wad, and yanked it off of the bed in a fit of anger, throwing it onto the floor before falling flat on her stomach across the bed, daring herself to rest.

In spite of the air conditioner humming in the window, her nightgown felt hot and stuck to her skin in limp persistence. She untwisted it, then flopped around some more, trying to find a comfortable spot.

Before she knew it, she'd rolled from her bed and torn the offending gown over her head, sending it to the same place that she'd sent her sheet. The floor. But the moment cool air hit her skin, she shuddered. It was too much like a man's breath upon her body to bear.

"Damn you, Lane Monday," she groaned, and threw herself back onto the bed, naked as the day she was born. "Damn you for not being worthless enough to use me. Damn you for having morals. Any other man would have been at this door days ago, whether he liked me or not, just because he could."

She closed her eyes, doubled her fists and resisted the urge to cross the hall on her own. But she would not stand naked before a man who did not want her, no matter what. Bearing the rejection from that encounter—and she was certain that there was bound to be one—would be impossible for her to endure.

And so she lay, and finally slept while Lane fought devils of his own.

Since the crash, his body had healed in so many ways. Seven days had passed and he was almost as good as new. And yet the scars he still bore from his first wife's death were as sore as they'd been five years ago. He couldn't get past the thought of loving like that, then losing again. It had nearly destroyed him. Lane knew himself well enough to realize that he would not survive a similar loss a second time.

And while common sense might dictate that falling in love

did not go hand in hand with dying, Lane's heart was too scarred to trust what his mind might say. All he could do was hope to hell that morning came before he lost all sense of reason and took what he knew Toni would give.

The sun was up, which was more than could be said for Lane or Toni. It was the telephone that woke them, and sent them dashing into the hall on reflex to answer.

It was hard to say who was more stunned, Lane for seeing her wearing nothing more than a robe that she held together with the clutch of one hand, or Toni for having to endure one last sight of all that man wearing nothing but a pair of white cotton briefs.

"The phone's ringing," Lane said as he realized that answering a phone in a house that didn't belong to him was overstepping his bounds.

Toni's voice shook as she turned away. "I hear it," she muttered, and yanked the receiver on the fifth ring.

"Hello!"

"Toni, this is Dan Holley. Did I wake you?"

She didn't answer, couldn't answer, because Lane was on his way back into his room, probably to get a pair of pants, and she was too busy watching him leave.

"Toni?"

She jerked, and then stared at the receiver. She'd forgotten that it was in her hand. "What?" she asked.

"If Lane is up, I would like to speak to him. I have some news he's been waiting for."

Toni pressed a finger across her lips to keep them from trembling before she spoke. She took a deep breath, and when she was certain that she had her emotions well under control, she spoke. "He's up. Hang on." She let the phone drop on the table without saying goodbye to Dan.

"It's for you," she shouted in the direction of Lane's room, and then went back into her room, slamming the door behind her.

Lane left his room and grabbed the phone, then balanced it against his ear with his shoulder as he finished buttoning his jeans. He didn't have the guts to get caught that near-naked around Toni Hatfield again. The next time, he would not be able to walk away.

"This is Monday," he said.

Dan Holley spoke. "They pulled a rather badly decomposed body out of the Pigeon River right after daylight this morning."

Lane felt a grin coming. He'd waited a week to hear this news. And the fear that he'd refused to name began to disappear. At least this part of his worry was over.

"Thank God," Lane said, and leaned against the wall.

"They're doing an autopsy as soon as possible," Dan told him. "Although down here, that may take anywhere from a week to a month. But it was a white male, and he was big. Really big."

"It's Rice. It has to be. He's the only whale we have on the missing-persons list."

Dan laughed aloud. "There sure wasn't any love lost between you two, was there?"

Lane closed his eyes, and thought of the hatred that he'd seen on Rice's face. "No. He was bad all the way through. I can't say I'm sorry he's dead." He paused, pushing himself away from the wall to stare at the door between him and Toni before he thought to add, "Sheriff, thank you for calling. And when you get it, I'd like a copy of the autopsy report to close out my file."

"It's already yours," Dan said. "Have a safe flight."

Lane nodded as the line went dead. The sheriff hadn't needed a response to his request for Lane to have a safe flight. They both knew all too well how difficult it would be for Lane to take that first step onto a plane, and how much Lane was counting on a smooth, uneventful trip.

And then Toni's door opened. She stood, waiting for him to confirm the bits and pieces of what she'd overheard. But he was looking at her too intently for her peace of mind, and so she spoke first.

"They found him, didn't they?"

Lane nodded. "It looks like it," he replied.

"That's good," Toni said. "It's been bothering you, hasn't it?" And when she saw the way he was studying her face and the way her clothes fit her body, she prodded him back to the conversation at hand. "Not finding Emmit Rice, I mean."

Lane nodded again, and thought that if he looked hard enough, he would remember how long her legs were, hidden beneath her well-worn jeans, or how the fullness of her breasts coerced the knit on her shirt to give way.

The nervous swipe of her hand across her hair made him remember how thick and soft the curls were to the touch. And when she gave him a nervous look, he got the full force of eyes so dark that they seemed black.

"A lot of things have been bothering me since the crash. That was one of them."

Now! Say something now! But Toni couldn't find the words. Lane walked back into his room to finish dressing, and the moment was lost.

"Stupid," she muttered beneath her breath, and stalked toward the kitchen to prepare breakfast. "It was a stupid thought. I can't ask it, and that's that."

But the idea wouldn't go away, and Toni had to face the fact that her dream hadn't died a full death. It was still lingering in her mind. Obviously, she was reluctant to give up what life it still had.

Lane was halfway through his second cup of coffee when Toni put down her spoon, replaced the lid on the jelly and pinned him with a bottomless gaze and a question he couldn't ignore.

"Are you packed?" she asked.

He froze with the cup against his lip. It hurt to hear the words, but the look on her face was more difficult to bear. He set the cup down without taking a drink, then folded his hands in his lap to hide the fact that they shook. It was nearly time to leave and he hadn't reconciled himself with the knowledge that when he awoke tomorrow, he would be thousands of miles away from Toni Hatfield and Chaney Creek.

"No," he said.

"You don't want to miss your plane," she reminded him, and began stacking dishes into the sink.

Oh, yes, I do. But he didn't say it. Instead, he stood and walked from the room without further comment. He didn't have it in him to debate.

When she could no longer hear his footsteps, she went limp and grabbed on to the sink for support.

"Oh, God," she pleaded. "Just get me through this."

Half an hour later, she was still saying prayers and begging for a reprieve that hadn't come. And Lane was walking toward the door with suitcase in hand, a well and whole man compared to the one she'd dragged into her house during the night of the storm.

"Take care," she said. "Drive safely."

He turned at the doorway, almost hating her for being able to maintain composure now when his was nearly nonexistent. And then he looked into her eyes and saw that her misery so nearly matched his own that it made no difference.

"Come here," he said, and held out his arms.

She didn't mean to, but resisting his offer was too difficult. With a soft sob, and then a quiet sigh, she walked into his embrace and settled her cheek against his chest. It was like being wrapped in steel, then cushioned by the promise of gentleness waiting.

"I will miss you, even though you are one bossy man," Toni said, trying to make a joke out of it, but failing miserably.

Lane tightened his embrace and felt her willingly readjust herself to the lack of space. Just as with everything else she did, she gave without asking for anything in return. And yet, if she were to ask a favor, he knew what it would be. *Just don't say it, love. Don't say what I see in your eyes.*

"I'll miss you, too," he told her. "More than you'll ever know. And I don't know how I'll ever be able to thank you for saving my life."

Toni went still. Even her heart forgot to beat. This was it. He'd given her an opportunity that she couldn't ignore. What he did when she asked was another thing entirely. But at least, she told herself, she would have made the effort.

"I do," she said.

He grinned and moved back far enough to see her expression. He should have known that she would still be trying to take control. It was the Toni he knew and loved.

Loved? Impossible! Where had that thought come from? *I haven't fallen in love with her, damn it!* he thought. But the shock of his realization was nothing compared to what she said next.

"You could make love to me. Just once. Just for fun."

Chapter 9

She kept talking because she knew that the silence that was bound to ensue would destroy her. She'd seen the shock on his face and felt the tension in his body increase tenfold.

"It's no big deal," she said, trying to smile. "Everyone does it, all the time. It's what they call recreational sex, right?"

Oh, hell, Lane thought. *How do I answer and not lie? My God, I would like nothing more than to take you to bed, woman. But walking away afterward might kill us both.* He heard himself mouthing a platitude that even he didn't believe.

"Now, Toni, you haven't thought this through. You're not the kind of woman to have casual sex."

"Oh, but I have thought it through," she said brightly. "And I'm not a virgin, you know. I've already tried it. Sex, I mean. Twice. In high school. It wasn't much, but I thought I might give it another chance."

There was too much effervescence in her voice. She could hear it and hated that it almost sounded like begging. *Damn you, Lane. Either tell me no, or shut the door.*

My God! She tried it twice? Lane pondered in awe.

The implications were nearly staggering. She was as near to a virgin as a woman could be and still call herself experienced. Lane fought the urge to take her in his arms. As badly as he wanted to comply with her wishes, doing so would only end up hurting them both. And then something occurred to Lane that he figured would end this conversation before it brought them to their knees.

"I don't have any protection with me."

Toni swallowed a lump in her throat. The last obstacle in the conversation had just been broached. It was up to her to get past it without giving away her intentions.

"Oh, that! I'm prepared to handle that on my own." She held her breath, hoping that he would assume what most men would, that she was taking, or using, something that would prevent pregnancy. What she'd meant, though, was that she was prepared to handle whatever came of their union on her own.

Damn you, woman. When will you stop? I haven't got it in me anymore to say no.

"I don't think I've ever had a better offer," Lane said, and cupped her face with his hands, branding her cheeks and mouth with short but gentle kisses that said what he could not.

Toni laughed through her tears. She knew it had been a long shot, but she'd been willing to give it a try. Now there was only one thing she could do to save face—for herself as well as for him.

"But you'll pass, right?" She laughed again, and spun out of his arms, certain that if he touched her again, she would start screaming and never stop. "It's no big deal," she said. "It was just an idea. I thought if you were willing, I would get in a little practice for the next man I fish out of Chaney Creek. But…" She shrugged. "As my daddy used to say, 'that's life.'"

Lane hurt for her in so many places that he wasn't sure he would be able to walk away. The tears in her eyes were vivid. The laughter on her lips was a sham and he knew it. How had he let this happen?

"You aren't a woman for one-night stands, Antonette. You

deserve better, and you deserve a better man than me. Don't give up on yourself. You're a hell of a woman.''

"Thank you, Mr. Monday. You're the first man to say so, but I'm sure you won't be the last. Take care, and drive safely.''

She shut the door in his face before it was too late to hide her shame, and did not watch as he drove away.

As Lane drove, the miles passed without notice. He was vaguely aware of obeying traffic signals and the laws of the road, but all he kept seeing was the pain on Toni's face. And all he could feel was the way she'd spun out of his arms with a smile on her face that he didn't believe.

That memory blended with the past into a collage of the days and nights that he'd spent under her roof and under her care and attention, until he couldn't separate the good from the bad. He couldn't remember her laughter, for seeing the tears he'd left in her eyes. He couldn't remember a single thing that had given her joy, for thinking of what had hurt her.

Sick with guilt, he kept remembering the way her brother had belittled her womanly traits, as well as the times that Lane, himself, had told her no, or turned her away, when every indication she'd given had said that she wanted more. What must she think of herself if every man who knew her took and took, but was unwilling to give?

"That was damned noble of me," Lane muttered as he continued driving toward the Knoxville airport and the airplane that would ultimately take him home. "But just what did I prove? And worse yet, what did my behavior prove to her?''

He swerved to miss a dog that had run across the road, swearing as he came to a shaky halt at the side of the road. Either he got his focus back on the trip, or he would wind up going home the same way that Bob Tell and the rest of the passengers and crew of the plane had done. In a body bag.

Just once. Just for fun.

With one eye on the time and the other on the intermittent cars on the road, Lane tried to ignore the haunting voice and pulled back into the traffic flow, doing everything that he knew how to do to concentrate on driving, not on the woman he'd left behind.

I've tried it twice. It wasn't much.

He groaned. How could a woman get to be twenty-nine years old and stay that…the only word that came to mind was *untouched?* And as soon as he thought it, he knew the answer. He'd been a witness to the reason more than once himself.

She'd been the baby of her family, the one who had stayed behind to care for the aging parent while everyone else had moved away, married and set up separate households of their own. She'd been insulated from social contact by life itself. Add to that the constant feedback from one brother, maybe more, who'd reminded her continuously that it was her size and her capability that were the worthy traits, not the fact that she smelled good, had soft skin and a pretty face.

"Then I come along, after God knows how many other men who'd shunned her," Lane mumbled, "full of myself and with all the right answers for all the wrong reasons and finished the job that they'd started."

He laughed bitterly, then stopped, startled by the ugliness of the sound within the quiet interior of the car.

Practice for the next man who comes along.

"Like hell!"

It was hard for a man like Lane to face the fact that he didn't want her practicing on anyone but him. Then how did he reconcile his decision to remain unfettered by emotional relationships to the fact that he wanted to make love to Toni Hatfield in the worst possible way?

In his mind there was only one logical answer. He owed her. The least he could do was pay his damned debt. And maybe in so doing, get her out of his mind once and for all. With that thought fixed firmly in his mind, he drove onto the shoulder of the road, and when the way was clear, headed back the same way that he'd come. Back to Chaney.

Back to Antonette.

It was nearly dusk when he turned down the long, winding road leading to her house. A red haze hung over the treetops,

and the sun was all but hidden by the gathering clouds. It was
fitting. He'd arrived on the day of a storm. He'd come back
to her in the same fashion.

His stomach twisted, a nervous reaction to the fact that she
just might pull that mud-dauber-packed shotgun on him again
and this time pull the trigger. Why hadn't he thought about
what this could do to her before returning to the scene of what
might be a crime?

But he was too close to walk away, and too much in need
to ignore the pull of knowing that the woman he wanted was
only yards away on the other side of four walls.

He parked, then headed for the house with single-minded
intent. He was as hard eyed and focused as he'd been on the
day that they'd loaded three federal prisoners into a plane on
a runway in Tallahassee, and almost as nervous as he'd been
until he'd learned of Emmit Rice's demise.

He cleared both steps in one leap and made it to the front
door in two. Without knocking, he hit the door with the flat
of his hand, relishing the sharp bang it made against the wall
before swinging shut behind him.

The sounds he heard in the back of the house suddenly
stopped. He knew that she'd heard the door. If he'd frightened
her, it was nothing compared to the way that he felt, waiting
for her to appear. But when she came into the room, the expression on her face said it all.

She'd thought that it was Justin. It was always the way he
entered the house. Loudly. Without knocking. So she wasn't
prepared for the shock, or the man who was waiting for her.

"What happened?" she whispered, then started to shake. If
he'd come back because he'd forgotten something, she was
going to make a bigger fool of herself than she already had.
"Did you forget something?"

He took off his jacket, unbuckled his gun and tossed them
both on the chair near the door before he started toward her.

Toni didn't know whether to run backward or into his arms.
The look on his face was one she'd never seen before.

"Yes, lady, I did. Something very important."

Oh, my Lord, Toni thought. *Now I'm going to have to endure this goodbye all over again.*

"Damn you, Lane, why did you come back?" She knew her voice was shaking, but she couldn't have steadied it to save her soul.

Lane stopped just inches away from her face. Even from where he stood, he could see her fear and feel her shaky breaths on his face.

"I came to pay a debt. And I came to make love to a woman. Just once. Just for fun."

Her expression faltered, but her stance never wavered. And when he started to touch her face, she stepped away, then turned, never looking back to see if he would follow.

Lane shook from the top of his head to the toes on his feet. It took all that he had to follow her down the hall. The leggy saunter and easy sway of her body beckoned him as no word ever could. He'd seen her acceptance, and knew that whatever deeper reason she'd had for asking, she would truly be satisfied with what he could give. Just once. Just for fun. If she could live with it, then surely to God, he could, too.

When he entered her room, she was taking off her clothes. From where he stood, he could see her fingers shaking. She was trying so hard to do this right.

"Don't, baby," he said softly. "Let me. It's part of the fun. Remember?"

She sighed, then dropped her hands to her sides. She didn't know beans about fun and remembered little of her other two times. They'd been with a boy; Lane was a man. As she watched him coming toward her from across the room, she wondered if she was woman enough to hold him. Even for one night. Even for fun.

"I'm scared, you know," she said.

Lane grinned and slid his arms around her, for the moment making no move to undress her any further. It was just like Toni to get straight to the point. What other woman would admit her fears as readily—or vocally—as she did? At the thought, he wondered if he had the guts to do the same.

"I know," he said, and kissed her temple, just above her right ear. She shuddered within his embrace and Lane sighed. "So am I, baby. So am I."

It was the best thing he could have said to her. At least on this level, they were even.

"What do I do next?" she asked. "Something for you…or to you? Or do I—?"

"Let's try something new," he said, and felt her stiffen in his arms. "I don't know if you're up to it, but I can guarantee that it'll make things better."

She bit her lip, hoping that he couldn't see her fear. Something new? She didn't even know the old stuff. But she'd been the one to ask, so it was now up to her to play along. And she wouldn't think of her deception. He thought she was protected from pregnancy. He thought it was for fun. Let him think what he wanted. She would take what she got, and be thankful for the chance.

"What is it that you want me to do?" she asked.

Lane lowered his head. Just before his lips centered on hers, he whispered, "Stop talking."

She almost smiled, and then his mouth descended and removed the last sane thought in her head.

Lane knew from the moment his arms went around her that there was no turning back. She was so much woman for a lot of man, and he didn't know where to start. But when he cupped her bottom, pulling her closer against his groin, then deepened the kiss they were sharing, he knew where to start.

She sighed, then shuddered, and leaned against the wall of chest before her, giving him all of her weight and anything else he might want. They'd shared a kiss before, but there had never been the promise or the passion as there was in this one.

His lips were firm, but his touch was tender, and when his hands cupped her hips and ground her against his obvious need, Toni's legs went weak at the thought of being one with this man and then giving him up without complaint. She'd prayed for a man to give her a child; hoping for more would be pushing her luck. So when he rocked against her hips in a beckoning motion, she followed along because she could not resist.

Lane broke the kiss with reluctance, moving his hands from her hips to her waist and then up. When they came to rest beneath the weight of her breasts, she moaned in spite of herself. She wanted more, so much more, and she wanted it now.

"Lane," she whispered. "Touch me, please. Pretend that you—"

"No more talking, remember? And, darlin', whatever I do, whatever we share, there will be no pretense. Not between us. Not ever. I do what I do out of want. I want to make love to you…with you. Never doubt that, or me."

Joy filled her heart. A sob wanted release, but there was no time because Lane had moved from her breasts to her shirt and was finishing what she had begun.

"Sweet," Lane groaned when she spilled from her bra into his hands. "You are so beautiful, lady. So very, very perfect."

His last word was a whisper against her skin as his head descended. When his mouth replaced his hands, and he began to settle small, searching kisses across the curve of her breasts, Toni's legs went out from under her.

"I don't think I can stand," she said, and felt weightless when he lifted her into his arms and laid her upon the bed.

"It doesn't matter," he said. "What we're about to do is better this way."

Her eyes widened as she watched him descend, and she was reminded of their first night together, handcuffed upon the floor. That night, she'd spent on top and then beneath this man with less results and far less pleasure than what she knew she was about to receive.

"You were well worth the wait," she whispered, and lifted her arms to pull him down.

He didn't know what she meant, and was too far-gone to care. Within the space of a minute, their clothes were on the floor. There was no room for anything else on the bed except the man and the woman who occupied it.

Somewhere between the door and the bed, the unhurried pace had gone out of the act. There was nothing left between them but a driving need to complete their union. And as badly as Lane wanted to be inside of her, he would not make the move until he'd watched and felt this woman come apart in his arms. Only then would he take what she'd offered. He'd come back to her in order to give.

Time ceased for Toni. There was nothing and no one in her world except the man who had taken command of her, body and soul. His touch was a plea that he didn't have to voice. When he urged, she followed, giving herself up to his skill and the need that he invoked.

His skin became slick with perspiration, his body hard with want. Yet his hands were strong and sure, skilled and gentle at teasing Toni into a mindless need she could not control. He watched her burn through a blue haze as he shook with desire. He'd seen her eyes grow black from passion, her lips go slack from shock. And when she'd arched uncontrollably beneath his circling fingers, he knew a kind of joy he'd thought he would never feel again. It was the pleasure of giving to some- one special, to someone he loved.

"Oh! What are you...?" Toni gasped, and clutched his arms as something deep within her belly started to coil.

"Shh," Lane whispered, and increased the intensity of his caress. "Let it happen, darlin'."

Toni fought it. This wasn't the way it was supposed to be. She needed him with her. She was afraid to go alone.

"No," she cried. "Please, Lane, no! Not without you."

But it was too late to stop and too sweet to deny. She gave herself up to the fire and lost sight of everything but the spiral of heat that shattered low, then spread throughout her body in a constant, shimmering release.

"Oh, my darling," she moaned, and covered her face with her hands.

"Don't, baby," he said, and moved her hands with a gentle sweep of his arm. "It's not over yet. Make room for me. I need a place to come in."

Tears burned her cheeks as she shifted, and then he went from beside her to inside her, and she thought that she would faint from the joy. When he began to move in a powerful, rocking thrust, she held him fast with her arms and her heart, and took what he gave without promises or love. Because it was just once. Just for fun.

She met him thrust for mindless thrust, kiss for burning kiss. And when he shattered within her, she held him fast and tight and never minded that he saw her cry.

And then it began to rain.

Just once. That had been all that she had hoped for. Yet twice more before morning, Lane took her body, wholly and without reservation, loving her to glorious distraction and leaving more of himself behind than he knew, while storm clouds rumbled overhead. Yet each time they loved, Toni knew in her heart that all they were sharing was passion. There was no future and no whispered lies being said between them in the dark.

It was, for Toni, enough. She'd had him for one night. It was more than she'd ever dreamed. If God was willing, Lane would leave a piece of himself behind when he left. If not, she would survive because she had to.

But for Lane, the night had held a different kind of resignation. He'd given away something he'd never meant to share. He'd not only made love, but he'd fallen the rest of the way in love with a woman he refused to keep.

When the last kiss and the last drop of passion had been spent between them, they slept, wrapped within each other's embrace, and dreamed of things that were not meant to be.

And when morning came, Toni awoke with the knowledge that the earth outside had been replenished, while she'd been drained of everything except despair.

She was alone in the bed and knew the reason why. There would be no reckless search through a house that she already knew would echo with emptiness, no frantic cry for a man who could not answer the call of his name. Lane had done what she'd asked, and more. He'd paid his debt a thousand-fold, and his last thought had still been for her. At least this time, she'd been spared the goodbye.

By noon Lane was boarding his plane in Knoxville, weary in more than body. His steps were slow and heavy like the beat of his heart. The flight attendant smiled, but Lane didn't notice her. The man in the seat next to him spoke, but Lane didn't hear him. When he buckled his seat belt, he realized that his hands were trembling and that he didn't even remember making the drive from Chaney to the airport in Knoxville. All he could see was the way that Toni had looked when he'd walked out of her room.

She'd slept curled on her side, with one arm flung out, as if searching for a man who was already gone, and the tracks of her tears were still drying upon the curve of her cheeks.

"Oh, God," he muttered, and covered his face, wondering if he was going to be haunted by her and that image for the rest of his life.

The attendant paused at Lane's seat. Her hand was soft upon his shoulder, her voice low and pleasant in his ear. And he resented her and every woman present for not being Toni Hatfield, and he hated himself because it was his own fault that it was not so.

"Are you all right?" the attendant asked. "If you're sick or need some assistance, all you need to do is ask."

He shuddered, then closed his eyes and leaned back against the seat. "I'm not sick. I'm fine. I'm as fine as I'm ever going to get," he muttered, and had the satisfaction of hearing her drift away to the next passenger.

Hours later, the plane landed and Lane entered the airport a sadder and wiser man than the one he'd been a week earlier. He'd survived a plane crash only to find that he might not survive crashing into Toni Hatfield's heart.

Two things happened within days of everyone's departure that did nothing but remind Toni of what she'd lost. The first, a bouquet of flowers from Palmer and Reese, came with a knock on her door. It was enormous, the message on the card a sparse opposite. It simply read, "Thanks for everything."

She wanted to laugh, but the corners of her mouth couldn't make the shape.

"You're welcome," she muttered to herself, and set the flowers in the center of her table, trying not to notice the wobbly legs. It reminded her of why they rocked. Lane had broken it, just as he'd broken her heart. Both had survived, but neither would ever be the same.

The next surprise came hours later when it was nearly evening. She watched from the window as a delivery truck, bearing the name of a well-known furniture store in Knoxville, lumbered up her driveway and parked in the yard. She'd watched, unsuspecting of anything except perhaps that she would have to direct them to another residence.

"Is this the Hatfield residence?" the man asked.

Toni nodded. "Yes, but I think you've got the wrong Hatfield. I didn't order any furniture."

The man looked down at his order sheet and frowned. "Are you Antonette Hatfield?"

An odd warning started in the pit of her stomach. He wouldn't. "Yes," she said.

He nodded. "Then we have the right place. Boys, bring it in. And watch the doorway. I don't deliver scratched goods and that's a fact."

All she could do was watch. There were no words to voice what she felt as they started inside her house with their load.

"Lady, where do you want this?" someone asked.

Tears choked her, making speech nearly impossible. All she could do was lead the way. The deliverymen followed her into the kitchen and set their cargo down next to what they were about to replace.

"Want us to put the old one somewhere else, lady?"

She pointed toward the back porch. It would have to do for now. She couldn't think past the sight of the round top and the rich, dark, shiny color of the cherrywood table.

When they carried out the old table, she watched through teary eyes, staring at the patched underside and uneven legs as it cleared the doorway with little room to spare. Its removal was as symbolic of his departure as the actual one had been. The final link with Lane was gone.

When the last of the six new chairs was in place, the men stood back, admiring what Toni could not face.

"Looks real nice in here," the man said. "Hope you enjoy it." He was starting out the door when he patted his pocket in remembrance. "Shoot! I nearly forgot. This came with it."

He handed her the card, then ushered his helpers out the door. Moments later, Toni was alone, suffering the scent of new wood and high gloss and wondering when her life had gotten so off track. She had only to remember that it had begun with a storm…in the night…on the crest of a wave…and in the arms of a man who hadn't looked back when he'd left.

Her fingers trembled as she opened the card. It was the first time that she'd seen Lane's handwriting, but she would have known it anywhere. It was as large and decisive as the man who'd written it. He'd written:

Dear Toni,
    I can't fix everything I broke, but I can try. Take care
of yourself and remember what we shared.

                                                    Lane

Not Love, Lane. Just Lane. It was more than she'd expected and still not enough.

"What I wanted from you, mister, was not tables and chairs."

She sat down, testing the shape of the chair against the curve of her hip and back, then folded her arms upon the shiny surface and hid her face from the sight. She prayed for the day when his loss would be easier to bear, and prayed also that there might possibly be a little something of him within her that he had left behind.

Chapter 10

It had been the longest week of Lane's life. And in those seven days since his return, the perennial tropic beauty of Tallahassee had, for him, lost its appeal. He drove the streets through the maze of traffic, unaware of the sidewalks bounded by elegant, swaying palms, ignoring the constant throng of females of every size, shape and color who were on a constant search for the man of their dreams.

He was in the midst of a single man's paradise, and wished instead for tall green mountains with smoky caps, quiet mornings and narrow country roads, and a tall, independent woman who gave new meaning to blue-jean shorts and old, faded shirts.

Lane Monday was home, but he was homesick for Toni Hatfield and her Tennessee hills. He'd caught himself in the act of calling her number so many times during the past seven days that he had nightmares of doing it in his sleep and not being able to stop until it was too late. He knew that if he heard her voice, if he made a connection one more time, he wasn't certain he had it in him to tell her goodbye again.

She'd claimed a place in his heart that he hadn't meant to

give up. But making love with her had been a far step from happily-ever-after. She was a woman who deserved a husband and a houseful of children. She needed a family as loud as the one in which she'd grown up, not a man haunted by old ghosts and with no hope for a future except one filled with heartache and disappointment.

For her, as well as for himself, he wouldn't let himself care.

"Hey, Monday! You have a call on line three."

Lane frowned at the interruption as he picked up the phone. He was in the middle of a sentence, and halfway through the report on his desk, so changing trains of thought was a distraction he didn't need.

"This is Monday."

"Naw, it's not, boy. It's Thursday, but who am I to quibble about days of the week when I've got myself a hatful of trouble."

Lane grinned when he heard the laconic drawl of Dan Holley coming across the wire. "Hello, Holley. I don't suppose you called me this early in the morning for any good reason," he said. "And what seems to be the trouble?"

"I don't know any easy way to say this, Monday, so here goes. I got the autopsy on the body we fished out of the Pigeon River this morning. It wasn't Emmit Rice."

Lane's gut twisted. This wasn't what he'd expected or wanted to hear, and it set a whole series of what ifs circling in his brain.

"Who the hell was it?" Lane asked.

"Samuel Sumter."

The skin crawled on the back of Lane's neck. "Then that means…"

"That's not all," Holley said. "The pawnshop in town was robbed sometime last night."

Lane didn't want to hear this sitting down. Something told him that if he did, his legs might not be able to hold him up when he left, and he'd already made a mental plan for departure before Holley had finished talking. The chair squeaked, then rolled backward as he ejected himself to an upright position.

"What was stolen?" he asked, and he could hear the disgust in the sheriff's voice as he answered.

"Guns and ammunition. Not a good way to start a day, is it?"

Lane closed his eyes against the news, but there was no way to deny what he suspected. "Damn."

"That about summed up my opinion, too, boy. I don't suppose I have to ask if—"

"Notify every law enforcement agency in the area to be on the lookout for a man answering Emmit Rice's description. I'll handle the fax information from here." As he spoke, he thought of Toni alone on her farm and got sick to his stomach. "Every resident within a ten-mile radius of Chaney should be notified to be on the alert. Set up checkpoints on all the roads and highways leading out of the area. It sounds to me like someone is planning to make a move."

"That's just about what I expected you to say," Holley replied. "It's already in the works. I'll let you know what—"

"You won't have to let me know anything. I should be there in three or four hours, give or take a few."

"What are you gonna do, hitch a ride with Superman?"

"Something like that," Lane said. "Look for me when you see me coming."

Three and a half hours later, a helicopter set down in the field behind the Chaney city hall. A big, long-legged man emerged from the cockpit, ducking when he ran beneath the spinning rotor.

Lane Monday was back.

Toni walked the length of fence that stretched up the back pasture, placing the last of the metal clasps on the angle-iron posts that would hold her new four-strand barbed-wire fence in place. Down the hill, she could hear the clank of metal against metal as Justin loaded the fencing equipment into the back of his truck.

Working side by side with her brother had been an odd

experience. She didn't know whether or not she was going to be able to deal with being told, once again, what to do and how to do it, but she knew who she had to thank for Justin's help. It was Lane. And it had all begun the day that she'd gone out to repair her mailbox.

She could still remember the high flush of color on Justin's cheeks as he'd yanked the posthole digger from her hands and sent her back to the house, when only moments earlier it had been his suggestion that she repair the broken mailbox post herself.

She sighed, and mentally shut herself off from the pain of thinking about the man she'd pulled out of Chaney Creek. It did no good to dwell on what might have been. For Toni, her might-have-been had come and gone and she was right where she'd been before the crash had occurred.

Sweat ran beneath Toni's shirt, tunneling along her spinal column in a sticky, persistent track. But she didn't notice, or if she did, she didn't care. The job was over. The fence was complete. She dropped the sack of leftover clips in the toolbox and slid into the passenger seat of Justin's truck without comment, then let her head fall back with a weary thump.

"Hot one, isn't it, Toni?" Justin asked.

She nodded. "It's been hotter," she said softly, and rolled down the window as Justin started to move.

"Want me to turn on the air conditioner?" he asked.

She shook her head. "No need. I'll just get hot all over again when we get out to unload."

He sighed. "Judy said for me to bring you home for lunch when we were through."

Toni smiled and then did what was, for her, an unusual thing. She patted her brother on the leg and then leaned over and kissed him on the cheek as he pulled up to the barn.

"I appreciate your help, Justin. Really I do. But tell Judy thanks, but no, thanks. As soon as I clean up, I've got to go into Chaney. The cows are out of salt, and I want to pick up some cubes and sweet feed for the steers."

Toni noticed Justin's shock. She couldn't remember the last time that she'd done something so out of character as to kiss her brother. It was such a female move that obviously he didn't know how to respond.

They exited the truck and began to unload.

"Just so you know," he muttered, "you're always welcome."

She paused in the act of lifting a near-empty spool of wire and rested her arms upon the fender as she gazed across the truck bed at Justin. A Madonna-like smile changed her features from intense to introspective.

"I know that, Justin. It's late. Go on home and get your food before Judy throws it, and you, out to the hogs."

He did as he was told, and minutes later, Toni made the hot, dusty walk from the barn to her house alone. Within the hour, she was clean, cool and on the way to Chaney when she remembered that she still hadn't eaten.

"I'll get something in town," she told herself, and kept driving, her eyes on the road before her, because concentrating on what was going on inside her head might make her insane.

When Toni drove into Chaney and parked her pickup in the alley near the loading dock of Dobbler's Feed and Seed rather than on the street, she missed seeing a big man exit the sheriff's office with Dan Holley and then get into Dan's car.

After leaving the store, Toni went to the café downtown, and was patiently waiting for her order to arrive, unaware of the chain of events that had already taken place that morning in town. If she had paid attention to the babble around her, she would have heard all sorts of comments flying fast and furious about the theft at the pawnshop. But she wasn't listening to the murmurs around her, as much as to the replay of memories inside her head.

The echo of Lane's voice in her ear as they'd made love had not gone away. Neither had the feel of his lips upon hers, or his hands tracing the shape of her body before he took control of her mind. All she had to do to bring the memories back was simply close her eyes and let go of everything but the sound of his name.

Lane.

The blaze of blue from his eyes and the breadth of his shoulders as he lowered himself inside her would be forever in her heart. For a giant, he'd been gentle beyond belief. His first and last thought had been for her. She sighed, and bit her lip to keep her chin from trembling. Crying in front of the customers of the Inn and Out Café would not be smart.

"Do you want catsup with your fries?"

Toni jerked to attention, brought rudely back to the present by the food that the waitress had slid under her nose. She looked down. The hamburger was thick, hot and shiny with grease, as were the fries.

"Catsup?"

Toni couldn't think what to say. It was impossible to go from making love to Lane to an overdose of cholesterol and not be confused.

The waitress sighed. Obviously, the woman was too weary from the noon rush to be patient any longer. She repeated her question in a short staccato chain of words.

"Catsup, Toni! Do you want catsup?"

"No. No, thanks. I don't want any catsup." *I want Lane Monday.*

Toni kept her last request to herself.

Four farms and thirty minutes later, the sheriff turned from the main road onto the driveway leading up the hill to Toni Hatfield's farm. The residents that they'd been notifying had reacted with varying degrees of alarm and alternating decisions. One man had even started packing up his wife and children to take them into Knoxville to his mother's home until the problem in the area was solved. But Lane knew that when Toni was notified, she wouldn't be going anywhere. He could already imagine how her chin would jut, and her eyes flash.

"Hmm," Holley said as he pulled into the yard and parked in the front of Toni's house. "I don't think she's home."

Lane got out and started toward the porch, although he'd already come to the same conclusion. Her red-and-white pickup was missing from its parking place in the hallway of the barn.

Lane knocked on the front door, and then turned the knob. He cursed when the door swung open to his touch.

"Damn it," he muttered as Dan followed him onto the porch. "She doesn't even lock the door when she leaves."

Dan shrugged. "Not many do out here. Haven't had much reason to... before now, that is."

"I'm going to leave her a note," Lane said. "I'll tell her to call the station for details, but for now, I don't want her in the dark about what's going on."

Holley nodded, then dropped into the porch swing while Lane entered the house. He was struck by the realization that the essence of Toni was everywhere. A pair of her tennis shoes was sitting beside the living room couch. Her hairbrush was on the hall table, and one dirty sock was in the hall, as if she'd dropped it on the way to the wash.

He bent down and picked it up. At least he knew where that went, he thought, then tried to focus on his mission as he headed for the kitchen where he knew she kept a notepad and pen for making grocery lists. He tossed the sock onto the washer and tried to think of what to write. But he kept seeing her alone in this house, and then remembered the calf that she'd found and her nephew's dog with a broken neck. The mischief had gone from missing chickens to stolen guns and ammunition. The way Lane saw it, someone had been holed up in these hills, stealing from the land and the people who lived on it, recuperating and readying himself to make a run. With the theft of the guns and ammunition, all clues led him to believe that the person was ready to move out. Although the thought was repugnant, gut instinct told him that it was Emmit Rice.

"If I could live through the crash, then, by God, so could he," he muttered, and started writing his note.

The message was brief. He could imagine Toni's shock when she read it, especially since he'd signed his name. But it was for her own good, and the good of the people, that he'd come back. Not, he kept reminding himself, because he wanted to see her one more time. Not because he couldn't get the feel of her body and the memory of her scent out of his mind. He was a U.S. marshal doing his duty. Nothing more. Nothing less.

When he stepped onto the porch, it was just in time to see a familiar pickup pulling into the driveway. He stifled a grin at the glare of the man who crawled out from behind the wheel and stalked toward the house.

"What the hell are you doing back?" Justin demanded.

Lane grinned. "Good to see you, too, Justin."

Justin flushed, then glared.

"We were on our way to your place next," the sheriff said. "Just as well we caught you. It'll save us some time."

Justin looked startled, as if realizing that someone else was with Lane Monday. "What's going on, Dan?" Then he looked around at the yard, staring intently toward the barn where Toni's truck ought to be. "And where the hell is my sister? It's nearly four o'clock. She should be back from town. Has something happened? Has she had a wreck? Is that why you're all—"

"Whoa," Dan said, and started off the porch. "It's nothing like that, boy. Settle down."

He quickly proceeded to tell Justin exactly what they had been telling everyone in the area regarding the thefts and who they believed was perpetrating them.

Justin went pale. He thrust his hands into his pockets, then yanked them out and combed them through his hair instead, giving him a slightly startled appearance when the strands stuck up in all directions.

"She wouldn't come eat lunch with me and Judy," he said. "She said she needed to get stuff in town. She was leaving for Chaney as soon as she cleaned up."

Lane hated the way his gut twisted. It was too reminiscent of the instinct he had that something was already wrong and he had yet to find out what.

"Go call," he ordered, and had the satisfaction of seeing Justin react toward him in a positive manner. "You know where she was going. Find out when she left, okay?"

Justin bolted into the house while Lane and Dan waited on

the porch. A few minutes later, he came back more anxious than when he'd gone in.

"She got feed. I talked to the man who loaded it. They said she was going to the café. I checked. She left there over an hour and a half ago. I even called home on the chance that she'd gone there to see the baby before coming back. She's crazy about kids, you know." Sweat beaded across his upper lip as he seemed to be considering where else she might have gone.

"Did you tell your wife to be on the lookout for strangers and to lock the doors?" Dan asked, and was rewarded with a nod from Justin.

Lane tuned out the thought of Toni and babies and frowned. There was no need dwelling on what could never be when he needed to be focusing on the issues at hand. And while he wasn't one to jump to conclusions, he also wasn't going to waste time waiting to see what happened.

Lane's hand slid beneath his jacket, feeling for his gun. It was an instinctive safety test, a lawman's gesture that he'd performed many times. And then he stepped off the porch and started toward the patrol car.

"Are you coming?" Lane asked the men.

"Where to?" Justin countered.

"To look for Toni. Where else? It takes exactly fifteen minutes to get from here to Chaney. She might have had engine trouble. She might have a flat. Whatever it is, I'm going to see for myself."

He couldn't let himself think of Toni lying beneath him, giving and giving, while he took and took, and then imagine her in danger. They would find her and then they would all have a good laugh.

"Hurry up," Lane muttered as the sheriff opened the door of the patrol car.

Dan obliged by sliding into the driver's seat as Lane began to fold himself inside the small car. Lane didn't have to look back to see if Justin Hatfield followed. Even inside the car, he could hear the gravel flying as the pickup tires spun out on the driveway. He didn't blame Justin for being concerned. The day had started out bad; there was no reason to assume it was going to get better anytime soon.

Toni's meandering thoughts came to an abrupt halt as the familiar *flap, flap, flap* of a flat tire could be heard upon the blacktop road.

"Well, great," she muttered, and pulled her pickup to the side of the road before getting out.

It couldn't have been a worse time or place to have a flat. This was the only stretch on the entire road home that had no shade, and she had a load of feed in the back. It would be hot and heavy work, jacking up the bed and replacing the tire. And, what made it even worse, her spare tire was on a rack underneath the truck bed.

With a muffled curse, Toni grabbed the key from the ignition, flopped flat on her back, then scooted beneath the bed of the truck, quickly unlocking the spare. Moments later, she was hard at work, doing the thing that she knew best how to do. Cope.

Emmit's two-week growth of beard itched. He scratched it and cursed beneath his breath, unwilling to investigate the itch too closely. It could be fleas. It could be poison ivy. It could be both. He'd encountered both during his time in hiding. But it was of no consequence to Emmit Rice. He had needed a place to heal, and he'd found it.

The first day after the crash had been hazy. He remembered waking up in the wreckage, surprised that he was still alive, then staggering up into the hills. He had no idea where he'd gone or how he'd gotten there. And it had been much later before he realized how lucky he'd been to have escaped during the storm. The rain had washed away virtually every trace of his flight from the area.

He hadn't known that the one-room shack he'd found up in the hills was Samuel Sumter's own getaway place until the big man had walked up on him in the yard. Emmit had never considered trying to talk his way out of the encounter, not after he saw the way the man had eyed his bright orange prison coveralls or the remaining leg iron he had yet to remove.

All it had taken was a swing of the hammer that he'd stolen out of a neighboring barn, and the man had dropped like a felled ox. It had been a simple matter to pull the body to the creek and then toss it into the current. He had considered it a point of luck that the creek had still been in flood stage; otherwise, the searchers he'd seen combing the hills might have found the man's body long before, and Emmit would have lost valuable healing time in trying to hide.

Most of his forays for food had centered on the neighboring farms and their livestock, and had taken place during the day, when many were gone on errands or out in the fields at work. His most daring exploit had been into a house while two women were working in a nearby garden. He still laughed, remembering the pie that he'd filched from the back porch while no one was the wiser.

Emmit had known from the first that he was going to get away. He considered it divine intervention that he had survived and then escaped without detection. And he had run, with no thought of his fellow prisoners or the lawmen who might, or might not, have had a chance to live had he stopped to help.

His cuts had healed, leaving an ugly track of scars as serious proof of his injuries. Long gashes that had been in desperate need of stitches had sealed themselves over and then run with infection before finally coming to a halt. The raised scars that were left behind ran the gamut of his face and body like thick red worms, some still bearing scabs. Emmit Rice could have cared less. It was nothing more than an added disguise for him, a man who because of size alone had a difficult time hiding his presence.

But now he considered himself healthy enough to move out of the area. The searchers were long since gone. He'd laughed, watching them drag the flooded creek, as he'd crawled back up the hill to hide.

But he was ready to move. All he needed now was a means of escape. And like everything else that had happened since he'd crawled out of the wrecked plane, it appeared to him like magic in the form of a red-and-white pickup that was parked on the side of the road.

There was only one problem. When he had left the concealment of the trees in which he stood, he had a good hundred yards to cover, without being seen, just to get to where the pickup had stopped. And while he was debating how to accomplish that, the driver solved his problem when she turned her back on his location and began to change a flat.

"Just one more lug nut," Toni muttered to herself, and reached into the hubcap near her knee where she'd tossed them earlier.

Sweat ran into her eyes; her hands were filthy; her nose itched, and she wanted a drink of water. She was miserable.

"Hey there, honey. Are you about done?"

Startled by the sound of a man's voice, her first thought was that he could have at least come a little earlier and helped. And then she stood and turned. She had a vague impression of a huge ham-fist swinging toward her chin, then oblivion.

When the sheriff's car turned the curve, Lane breathed a sigh of relief. Toni's pickup was on the side of the road. Even from here he could see the elevated rear.

"There she is," Dan said. "Looks like she had herself a flat tire."

But Lane's relief died within seconds as he saw a flash of dirty orange and a hulk of a man pulling an unconscious woman to the opposite side of the pickup. Instinctively, his hand went to his gun.

"Call it in," Lane said harshly. "It's Rice. He's got Toni."

Holley's hand was on the radio before the patrol car came to a stop, and by the time he started relaying the message, Lane was already out of the car. He was crouching behind the half-open door, shouting an order to surrender to a man who didn't know the meaning of the word, as the dust they'd outrun slowly caught up and settled upon them.

"No!" Justin screamed as he ground his vehicle to a halt just behind the sheriff's car, then started to get out.

"Stay down, you fool," Dan shouted. "He's armed."

"But he's got my sister," Justin yelled.

And he's got my lady, Lane thought as his finger tightened on the trigger of the gun he had aimed at Emmit Rice's head.

"Give it up, Rice. Let her go," Lane ordered and shifted the sight of his gun to follow the erratic movement of Emmit's upper body.

"Get back, you son of a bitch, or I'll break her neck," Rice yelled, unable to believe who had pulled a gun on him. The last time he'd seen that man, he'd been dead underneath DeVon Randall and a section of seats. What had he done? Resurrected himself?

Lane didn't blink. His arm was rock steady, his finger taut and ready to pull.

"Let her go," Lane repeated, and fought back a wave of fear. He couldn't let himself think about the woman in Rice's arms. She was a hostage, an unknown. He couldn't let himself remember her laugh, and her eyes or the way she'd gone weak at his touch.

"Like hell! You get back, and I mean now! I'm in charge here! You do what I say or the woman dies," Rice roared.

"Let her go!" Lane said once more, swallowing back the bile rising in his throat.

Rice laughed. His head tilted in amusement as he shifted his squeeze hold on the woman's neck just to prove that he could.

A barrage of images flashed through Monday's mind. A dog with a broken neck. A calf with its throat slashed and gaping. Toni, limp and unmoving, as Rice held her to his chest like a shield.

"Toni! Can you hear me?" Lane shouted.

"Help is on the way," Dan told him, and shifted to a less compromising position at the back of the patrol car.

"Help will be too damned late," Lane growled. He knew this man. He'd seen his rap sheet. There were no survivors of encounters with Emmit Rice.

"You get back, and you get back now," Rice shouted, and waved the gun that he was holding toward Toni's head. "Move, or I blow her brains out. It makes no difference to me, Monday, and you damn well know it!"

"Dear God, no!" Justin groaned.

"I'm taking her with me," Emmit shouted, and started toward the door on the passenger side. "You give me safe passage and I promise I'll…"

Lane's thoughts froze on the word *promise*. Emmit Rice didn't know the meaning of the word. Suddenly Lane stood, his decision made as he offered himself as a target to the man with the gun.

Dan Holley saw Lane's movement and followed to cover him.

Lane shouted. "Rice! Let her go!"

Startled by the shout as well as the lawman's unexpected movement, Rice inadvertently jerked, then turned as he aimed at Lane's chest. Just a fraction. Just enough.

The gun bucked in Lane's hands, and a loud, reverberating roar echoed over and over at the once-quiet roadside where a woman had been fixing a flat. The gun in Emmit's hand discharged in return. But it was only a reflex, and the bullet went into the ground, because Emmit Rice had died the moment the bullet from Lane's gun had hit his brain. He went down, taking Toni with him. Within a heartbeat of the shot, three men were running toward the other side of Toni's truck.

Lane reached her first and tore her out of Rice's grasp.

Don't let this be happening, Lane thought as his hands traced her face and body. *Don't let it be too late!*

This was not the first time that he'd touched Toni's body in such an intimate manner, but now he wanted to feel a heartbeat, not the catch in her breath as their bodies joined. And when he found her pulse, coupled with the slow, uneven groan that slipped out of her mouth, he knew a moment of total joy unlike anything that making love could have brought him.

"Thank you, God." It was all he could say.

He lifted her into his arms and carried her away from the remnants of the man who'd nearly ended her life.

"You damn fool!" Justin grabbed at Lane's shoulder, trying to pull his sister from Lane's embrace. "You might have killed her."

"I *might* have," Lane said, and then looked back at the man on the ground. "But he *would* have. Emmit Rice did not take hostages. He took victims, and left them in pieces for their families to bury."

Justin blanched, then watched, unable to move as Lane carried Toni a short distance away.

"Let it go, Justin," Dan said as sirens could be heard coming down the road. "He did the right thing, and it saved Toni's life."

Chapter 11

Toni shifted in Lane's arms.

"What happened?" she mumbled as her hand moved toward her jaw and the pain that she felt there.

What happened? I nearly lost you, lady. But the thought did not fit the decision that Lane had already made. He couldn't lose something that he'd already given away.

Lane caught her fingertips before they centered upon the swiftly darkening bruise and held them to his lips without caring how it might look to the gathering crowd. All he could think of was the living, breathing woman that he held who had survived the ordeal. He had no way of knowing how long she'd been in Rice's clutches, or what she'd had to endure, but at this point, he didn't care. She was alive.

"You're safe, baby," Lane said softly.

Toni's heart thumped erratically as she blinked to clear her vision. She knew that voice. She recognized the touch.

"Lane? Is that you? How did you…" Toni jerked, and started to fight her way out of his arms. "There was a man!" she cried. "He came up from—"

"He's gone. It's over. He can't hurt you again," Lane said, and felt satisfaction from the knowledge.

Justin knelt, and without asking, pulled his sister from the lawman's embrace. "Come here, sis, don't be afraid. You're safe now."

Toni let herself be traded from one man's arms to the other's because it was not in her at the moment to think straight. But when Lane had turned her loose and walked away, she knew a bit of her heart had gone with him.

Lane had given her up to Justin because he had no right to object, but it was a cold, empty feeling that he took with him as he returned to the scene of the crime. There were things to be done that only he could do, and the one that satisfied him the most was giving a positive identification to the man who was lying in a spreading pool of blood.

"Justin, where did you come from, and better yet, where did they?" Toni shuddered, staring around in dismay at the gathering of people and cars.

"God, Toni, I thought you were dead."

Toni vaguely remembered seeing the man's fist and then everything going dark. It could just as easily have been a permanent "lights out" for her. She had never realized before how fast a person could die.

"It seems that Lane Monday wasn't the only man who survived the plane crash," Justin informed her. "The body the authorities fished out of Pigeon River wasn't Emmit Rice, after all. It was old man Sumter. They're speculating that Rice was responsible for the thievery." He shuddered and clutched his sister tightly. "We figured he was trying to steal your pickup for a getaway. He was going to take you with him as a hostage."

"Oh, my God!"

Toni wouldn't let herself think of what might have been. Suddenly, she was very glad that she'd been unconscious. Having to deal with remembering something like this might have taken a while to get over.

"How did they stop him?"

Justin bowed his head. ''Monday did it. He saved your life.''

Toni's heart leapt in her chest. It was a strange and telling thing to know that she now drew breath because of another person's actions. *Now I know how he felt,* she thought.

''Justin, help me up,'' she said, and started to struggle to her feet.

''No, Toni! The ambulance should be here any minute. Let them check you out first and see if—''

''I have a sore jaw. Nothing more. The dirt on me was already there before he came. I was changing a flat. Now damn it, Justin, help me up!''

Justin sighed. ''Just be careful,'' he warned, but she was already gone, walking through the heat and dust toward the tall, dark-haired man who was standing in the center of the nearby crowd.

Toni's legs were shaky, but her need to get to Lane was strong. She hadn't expected to see this man ever again, and now, to have it happen like this was almost too much to bear. When he'd left last week, in her mind, they had been even. She'd saved his life and he'd granted her a last request.

They were an unlikely couple with an impossible situation between them. He had more than made it plain to her that he didn't want entanglements, and as hard as it had been to accept, she'd taken from him what he was willing to give and told herself it was enough. Yet why, she wondered, did fate keep throwing them together? What good could ever come from the pain of continual parting?

But the knowledge that she could see him, be with him, even if it was only for a short space of time, was worth more sleepless nights, because Lane Monday had stolen a piece of her heart.

''Lane.''

In the middle of a crowd, in the middle of a sentence, Lane froze. The soft sound of his name on Toni's lips sent him spinning around as the people surrounding them blurred out of focus. All he could see was her face and those eyes, dark and compelling, asking more of him than he was willing to give.

He looked over the heads of the people around him, searching for Justin, for the paramedics, someone… anyone…to explain why she was not under someone's care. And then she touched his arm and it was too late to stop the flow of feelings that swamped him. He could no more stop himself from touching her than he could have ceased taking his next breath. His palm cupped her cheek, and gentleness was in every nuance of his touch and voice.

"What are you doing up, lady? You should be lying down taking it easy. You've had a hell of a scare."

She covered his hand with her own and shook her head. "I'm not the one who got scared. I got off easy. I don't remember a thing after a swinging fist until I heard your voice."

"Ah, God." He pulled her into his arms and crushed her against his chest. "I was nearly too late," he said, and let himself go as he started to shake.

Toni wrapped her arms around his waist and allowed herself the fantasy that this was where she belonged. His heartbeat was rapid beneath her eardrum. His clutch seemed desperate as he held her fast. She pretended it was more than relief with which they embraced.

"This time it was you who saved my life," Toni said. "I don't know how to say thank you, but I…"

The words died on her lips. A sensation of having already been in this place, saying these words, made her head spin as a wave of embarrassment sent a rapid flush to her cheeks.

Lane went still. Only days ago he'd been saying the same thing to her. And the memory of what she'd asked was uppermost in his mind as he tilted her face to his and stared long and hard into her eyes. Could he? Should he?

"I do," he said, and felt her shock even though she did not move.

Dear Lord, Toni thought. *Please let this be what I think.*

"You do? What?" she asked.

"I know how you can say thank you."

She closed her eyes and swallowed. If she was wrong, there

would be no way to get out of the shame of letting him know that she cared too much. She opened her eyes. When she looked up, she was staring into a wall of blue fire.

"What are you saying?" she whispered.

He tried to smile, but it got lost in his pain. "Once more...just for fun?" he whispered, and kissed the corner of her mouth.

"Toni! The ambulance is here," Justin said, grabbing her arm as he demanded her attention.

Startled by the interruption, Lane stepped back and resisted the urge to punch Justin Hatfield in the nose.

Toni didn't argue. She was too busy trying to assimilate the implications of what Lane had asked. *Oh, God, if I do this again, will I have the strength to pretend it doesn't matter when he leaves?*

She answered her own question when she suddenly stopped, then turned and looked back to Lane, who was still watching her.

"I suppose there will be all kinds of paperwork," she asked, and knew it was the last thing he might have expected her to say.

"A fair amount, I suppose."

She nodded. "It will probably take at least a day or so, won't it?"

Lane's eyes widened. Suddenly he knew where she was leading, but he couldn't help himself, or hide his expression of shock. She was going to say yes.

"At least," Dan Holley added, overhearing and answering for Lane as he walked up. "It's good to see you up and walking, girl," he said, and patted her gently on the arm. Then he grinned. "And you had better believe there'll be paperwork. Local reports, state reports and federal forms that I don't even want to consider. I've already got this man a room at the Smoky Mountain Motel. He's not budging from Chaney until he has dotted the last *i* and crossed the last *t*."

Toni nodded without looking at Lane again, but it hadn't

been necessary. In his mind it was what she hadn't said that counted. She hadn't told him goodbye.

Toni wished that she were in her own home this evening, instead of under the caring, watchful eye of Justin and enduring the noisy romp of family running in and out of the house. Her thoughts were on Lane and what he'd asked. And she knew good and well that she'd complied simply by asking about his location. Inwardly, they read each other all too well. It was what they couldn't say aloud that was making all of this so difficult.

Justin pretended to be reading a paper, but Toni knew that he hadn't missed one of her fidgets since bringing her home. But her family was simply going to have to worry, because there wasn't anything she could say or do to help. It was going to take time for them to learn how to accept that the ugliness of the outside world had come into their small, rural community and changed their perception of safety forever.

As for herself, she'd already come to terms with losing more than a woman deserved to bear. For Toni, all she had left was her life. Her parents were gone. The man she'd foolishly fallen in love with was leaving her again. She had nothing but years stretching ahead of her. Single, lonely years, unless…

She took a deep breath and rose from her chair, unwilling to let hope get in the way of consequences. She and Lane had made love, but for all the wrong reasons. She'd wanted something from him that he wasn't willing to give, and had taken something he didn't know that he'd left. It remained to be seen whether anything would come of their union, but one thing was clear. Baby or not, she would never forget Lane Monday.

A tiny squeak, followed by a rather loud cry, was all the impetus that Toni needed to pick Lucy up from her crib.

She clasped the baby close against her, loving the feel of downy hair brushing against the skin on her neck. "What's wrong, little girl? Is there too much noise for you to rest?"

Judy walked over and gave her baby's rump a comforting pat. "Noise is the last thing that bothers her," she said. "It's probably my fault. I've done nothing but cry all evening. I'm sure she senses the unrest. Here, let me have her. I'll rock her a while. Maybe that will calm her down."

Reluctantly, Toni gave up her niece, and turned toward the door, unwilling to stay inside another moment under her brother's scrutiny.

"Where are you going?" he asked.

Toni sighed, pausing in the doorway. "Outside, Justin. Only outside. I need some space. Okay?" Without waiting for his permission, she walked out, closing the door firmly behind her as indication that company was not invited.

The next morning, when the sun was barely over the horizon, Justin walked out of the house in time to see Toni loading her overnight bag into her pickup.

"Where are you going?" he asked. "You haven't even had breakfast."

Toni hugged her brother's neck. "I'm going home, Justin, where I belong. I want my own bed. I need to check on the livestock. I want to eat a bowl of cereal in peace without looking to see if you're watching me eat."

He flushed. "I didn't mean to...I just wanted to make sure that you were..." He sighed and ran a hand through his hair. "Oh, shoot, Toni. You know what I mean."

She grinned as two of his children burst out the front door in a fit of shrieks and joy at the sight of a new day.

"And you know what I mean," she said.

He looked over his shoulder at the noise, then shrugged and answered her smile with one of his own. "I guess I do," he said. "It *is* hard to get over a headache in this house."

She cried all the way home, thinking of the quiet that awaited her, wishing it were not so.

Lane put down his pen and hung up the phone. There was nothing left to be done but wait for tomorrow and leave the same way that he'd come. It was amazing how well law enforcement agencies could work together when called upon to do so. He'd been through a number of cases where the difficulty in the job came not from the crime itself, but from having to fight for the right to do his job and not step on someone else's territory and toes.

Tomorrow.

The word was, in itself, an abomination. If she didn't come tonight, he wouldn't see her again. He'd promised himself that much. She deserved to be able to make the choice. And while he'd found himself and his thoughts wandering far too often toward a tall, dark-eyed woman and the way she fit in his arms, he couldn't—wouldn't—let himself forget Sharla, or the way that she'd died.

Remember the disbelief on her face. Remember her pain…and the blood. Remember, you fool, that it was all your fault.

Lane shuddered and buried his face in his hands. How could he forget? He didn't need to be reminded that she'd died because of him. What he needed to remember was the vow that he'd made when it had happened. Never again. Never again.

"Are you finished?" Dan asked.

Lane lifted his head. *Probably, and I just don't know it.* But he didn't say it, and thankfully, the sheriff did not remark on the lonely expression in Lane Monday's eyes.

"I am now," Lane said, and handed the stack of files to Dan. "I do reports, but I don't do files." He grinned to soften his remark. "Besides, I don't know where you want them."

Dan took them and tossed them on his desk. "Time enough for filing tomorrow. Come on, man. I'm treating you to the biggest steak dinner Knoxville has to offer."

The thought of food made him sick. "I think I'll pass," he said. "I'd rather grab a sandwich and an early night. The chopper should be here by daybreak tomorrow."

Dan nodded as he extended his hand. "Monday, we've had one hell of a ride the past two weeks, from pulling you out of Chaney Creek to sending Rice home in a body bag. I can't say that I'm sorry this is over. My fishing is way behind schedule as it is."

Lane smiled back and took the handshake that the sheriff offered. "Take care, Holley, and remember my invitation."

"Yeah, right. Palm trees. Cold long-necks." He grinned as he walked away.

And I would trade every damn one of them for a long night with a sweet woman named Antonette, Lane thought.

Moments later he was gone, retracing the path that he'd worn between the Smoky Mountain Motel and the sheriff's office in Chaney. Hours later, he was inside the room with his back to the wall, watching a door that he feared wouldn't open.

It was almost dark. Toni paced her living room floor, telling herself that she was simply asking for heartache, and then reminding herself what she would get in return. What was a little heartache compared to the joy of making love with Lane? How could it hurt to give it one more try?

"All right, mister. It can't possibly hurt me any more than it has already," she muttered as she grabbed her purse on the way out the door. "Besides, I pay what I owe." And she owed him her life.

Minutes later, the silence of the night was broken by the sound of her truck as she drove away, and then all was quiet on the hill above Chaney Creek.

Four cabins sat in a neat, straight row, facing away from the main street of Chaney. Four distinct little bungalows that had been built during the late fifties when it was "cute" to have awnings on every window. Little, white, one-room houses with green shingles and shutters and small picket fences.

The Smoky Mountain Motel was not doing a booming business. Three of the bungalows were dark and shuttered. It was the one on the far end with the light that drew Toni like a moth to a flame, pulling her closer to a fire that she knew could destroy her, if she let it.

Her truck's engine was barely running above idle as she coasted to a quiet stop near the edge of the mini-picket fence in front of Lane's bungalow. When she killed the engine and slipped the key into her pocket, she had a moment of anxiety, wondering if she was making a mistake, and then knew that the only mistake would be in leaving. For her, the decision had already been made.

But having come, it did not stop her legs from shaking, or make her heartbeat slow down. It didn't make it any easier to knock, and then stand and wait for him to appear.

But when he opened the door, blocking the opening with his size and intensity, the look on his face was of such overwhelming relief that she knew she had not been the only one in fear. When Lane stepped silently aside to allow her to enter, she did so with a graceful finality that was not lost on the watching man.

Toni took his silence as what it was intended to be, filling her mind with the sight of this man to remember when he would be gone.

"Ah, God, lady. You know how to make a man weak. I didn't think you would come."

Moments later, she was in his arms. *I didn't know how to stay away,* she thought, and then thought became impossible.

Lane couldn't get past the fear of yesterday when they had come around the curve in the road and he'd seen her in Emmit Rice's arms. So limp. So still. The experience made her presence here now that more precious.

"Are you all right?" he asked as his hands traced the path of her spine down to the curve of her hips. "Maybe we shouldn't be doing this after what you went through yesterday."

Toni smiled through her tears. "Oh, no, Lane. That's exactly why we should. Yesterday, I realized how easy it was to die. Tonight, I want to remember what it feels like to live."

How easy it is to die. My God, my lady, if you only knew.

"I want you to make love to me again, Lane Monday. One more time."

Her chin quivered and she hid her face against his chest when he whispered against her cheek, "And just for fun."

If that was all it was to him, so be it.

But when their clothes fell away, and they met in each other's arms, what came next was not in the name of fun. Their clasp was as urgent as the heat between their bodies, their breaths as short as the fuse on Lane's control. Gentleness and foreplay had no part in the fierceness with which he took her to his bed and buried himself inside her. There was nothing left but an overwhelming need to forget everything and everybody except the now in which they lived.

Cognizant thought had come and gone, leaving Toni weak and helpless to everything but the need to meet Lane's every demand. His weight came hot and heavy upon her as he thrust between her legs, using the skill of his sex to tell her what he could not say. That he wanted. That he needed. That he loved. That he would leave.

And when the wild, unfettered spiral of pleasure began to unwind low in her belly, and when his mouth was on her lips and his hands beneath her hips, she felt a splintering joy and at the same time a rage that this was over before it had ever begun.

Lane thrust a final time, then shook from the effort as he died a slow death in her arms. It would be justice if he did, he thought, and a fitting place in which to go.

"Ah, lady. You take my breath away," he whispered, and rained kisses across her face and neck, tasting her tears upon his lips.

Their foreheads touched in mutual understanding and agreement for what had transpired. Their bodies had joined, but it was their souls that had met. Yet, for Lane, there were no words to be said to change what was.

Twice more before morning, they awoke. Once it was Lane who turned to her in desperation. And once it was Toni who rolled over and on top of him, taking him into her before he'd opened his eyes. But the pleasure was too brief and the ending incomplete. They had made love, but could not say the words, leaving Toni feeling cheated and Lane with a burden of guilt.

But it was only one more time…and just for fun.

The sky outside was turning gray, losing the shadows of night at an alarming rate. Toni had only a matter of minutes in which to leave before the early risers of Chaney caught her in the act.

She dressed without conscious thought, pulling on clothes simply because leaving this room naked was against the law. But in effect, she had already stripped herself, heart and soul, for the world to see. Loving a man who made no promises was as revealing as it got.

She turned at the doorway. Her lips twisted bitterly as she faced the pain of losing this man once again to a life in which she had no place or part.

"We're even, Lane Monday. Fly safe and fly high. I won't be around next time to save you."

Moments later, she was gone, unaware that he had been awake from the start, listening to the careful, quiet manner in which she'd dressed, absorbing every breath she'd taken and each step that she'd made away from him. But it had been her parting remark that he knew he might not survive.

"Next time, sweet lady, I won't even care," he muttered, and rolled himself out of the bed.

Within the hour he was airborne, up in a flurry of dust and dry grass, above the green cover from the treetops below, back to a place where there were no foggy-top mountains or narrow dirt roads leading to a quiet country farm above a place called Chaney Creek.

Chapter 12

First you get mad, then you get even.

Toni had heard that old saying all of her life. But how, she wondered, could she be mad with anyone except herself? Not once during the two weeks that she'd known Lane Monday had he ever misled her, or given her reason to believe he would do anything other than what he'd done, and that was to leave.

As for getting even, they had more or less parted on that note. She'd saved his life. He'd saved hers. He'd sent her a new dining room set to replace the one that he'd broken. Everything was as nearly normal in her life as it had been before he came. Now there was nothing left for Toni to do but get on with the business of living. How to do that without the tender presence of her towering giant would remain to be seen. She didn't really have a plan. It was going to have to be dealt with one day at a time.

By the time the first letter came, she had numbed herself with a mindless routine of constant, daily work after which, each night, she would fall into an exhausted, dreamless sleep. So when she saw the Florida postmark, and the broad, even strokes on the envelope spelling her name, she wasn't prepared for the pain that came from reconnecting with him, even if it was long-distance and through the mail.

"Just let me out at the mailbox," Toni said as her brother David slowed down to make the turn into the driveway.

"Surely not here?" her sister-in-law Laura asked. "You'll have to carry your groceries up the hill to the house."

Toni unwound herself from the seat, unloading a niece and nephew from each knee as she exited the car. "It's just one sack, and I can always use the exercise. Thanks for the lift," she added, and waved goodbye to the rambunctious crew who had given her a ride home from town.

Thanks to a blown gasket, her pickup would be in the garage for at least another week. She was at the mercy of whichever family member was heading her way and would be willing to take her with them. This morning it had been David and his wife, Laura, as well as all four of their children. The ride had not been monotonous.

She hefted the sack of groceries to her hip and retrieved the handful of mail from the box, absently sorting through the stack before starting toward home.

The serenity of the Tennessee hills should have been balm to an empty heart. Towering pines, thick stands of oak, elm and hickory abounded. Along the road, clumps of brown-eyed Susan and wild white daisies grew, adding a splash of color to the green-and-brown palette that was the setting for her home.

With each step that she took, the dust poofed softly around her shoes, coating the clean white canvas with a dusty red shadow. Her blue jeans were nearly new and swished sharply with each stride. Her white shirt had started out crisp and freshly ironed, but now bore the brunt of a morning in town, and wrestling children from front seat to back during the ride home.

Butterflies danced above the heads of wildflowers, bright, flighty droplets of color that added life and spark to the landscape. But Toni didn't see all this, and even if she had, she would not have been able to appreciate the almost perfect beauty of the land around her. She was too numbed by a Florida postmark and the implications of the letter's arrival.

She didn't know how she got inside the house. It was only after she took the pages out of the envelope that she realized she was in the kitchen and sitting in her daddy's old chair. Holding her breath against the shock of connection, she began to read.

Dear Toni,
    I know that we said it before, but I had to say thank you again. Every day I look at myself in the mirror and realize that I owe my life to you. I hope that you are well. I think of you often and wish you all the happiness in the world. You deserve all that life has to give, and so much more.
    I will never forget you.

                                 Lane

She looked up from the letter, staring blindly out the open doorway as the pages crumpled beneath her fingers. Her face was pale, her lips compressed as her nostrils flared in quick anger.

"So you wish me the best, do you, Lane? Thank you so much for the bland sentimentality. A drugstore greeting card couldn't have said it better!"

Angry with herself for having hoped for something more than a bread-and-butter thank-you note, she wadded the letter and tossed it into the trash.

"That's what I get for getting my hopes up," she muttered, refusing to give way to tears. "Why won't I ever learn?"

She tore into her grocery sack, tossing cans into cabinets and slinging her carton of milk into the refrigerator as she berated herself for the hope that she'd let spring.

"This is it, Toni. Your roll in the hay with a lawman is all you're going to get out of life…and it was more than you expected."

She laughed to keep from crying, but there was no humor, only bitterness, in the sound.

And because she hurt with the days that continued to pass, she lashed out at those around her until everyone, including Justin, began to give her a wide, careful berth. She rarely answered her phone, and when she did, was short to the point of rudeness, no longer willing to listen endlessly to Laura's latest tale of the children's antics. The shopping trips that Judy offered were quickly turned down without explanation. Toni hadn't retreated from life, but she had taken a serious look into regrouping. Rearranging her attitude had to help her get through the pain. It just had to.

Lane's days were long, but his nights were longer, endless, hot summer nights in a cool bed with nothing but a pillow to hold. No sweet sigh in his ear. No soft gasp of breath against his lips as he dreamed of making love to Toni.

He had believed that the letter he'd written thanking her for everything one last time would put a knot in the line connecting him to Toni Hatfield. It should have, but it did not.

Foolishly, he'd watched his own mail for days and then weeks, hoping for a simple return note that might echo his own sentiments. Something—anything—that would bind them together again.

But it hadn't happened, and he tried to accept that it was all for the best. He didn't need to prolong something that had no hope of growing. In his mind, he'd already ruined Sharla's life to the point that it had caused her death. He wasn't about to risk his sanity and another woman's life, not even for love.

And then one day he picked up the phone at work and found himself dialing Toni's number. By the time it rang seven times, he'd regained enough control of himself to disconnect, and thanked his lucky stars that she hadn't been in the house to answer.

What, he thought, would he have said if she'd answered? He had no idea, but the question wouldn't go away, and he couldn't let go of wondering what might have been.

But, he'd done it! It *had* happened. He'd dialed her number and the world had not come to an end. He'd made an attempt to contact her that hadn't interrupted the flow of traffic or initiated another impasse between heads of state. For that reason, it made calling the second time that much easier. And that time, when he still did not get an answer, he told himself it was just as well.

Two days later, without considering his reasons, he bought an answering machine and had it sent Federal Express to Chaney, Tennessee, before he could change his mind. By the time the package was on its way to Toni, he'd convinced himself that what he'd done was only for her own good. In this day and time it only stood to reason that she needed to stay in communication with other people. She was a woman alone in a fairly secluded area. Emmit Rice hadn't been the only bad man in the world.

Convinced that he'd done nothing out of turn, he settled back into a routine and waited. He didn't realize that what he'd done, he'd done to stay in touch with her. It was, quite literally, a "reach out and touch someone" gesture that would have made the phone companies proud.

If Toni's Hereford bull hadn't gotten out and into old man Warner's pasture and serviced four of Warner's purebred Angus cows before it was removed, Toni might have been in a better frame of mind when the delivery van came up her driveway. But she'd already had to apologize to Silas Warner and commiserate with him about the loss of money he might suffer from having calves born of something other than their registered Angus status.

And this morning, for the second time in a week, she'd overslept. Add to that the worn-out, run-down feeling that had dogged her every step for the past few days, and you had a woman who was not in a receptive frame of mind for the deliveryman or the package that he carried to her door.

"Now what?" Toni muttered as she raced to answer the abrupt knocking on her front door.

"Miss Antonette Hatfield?"

She sighed, then slumped against the doorframe at the sight

of the uniformed man bearing a small, but suspicious-looking package.

Her fourteen-year-old nephew Harry, who was her brother Arnie's son, and who lived in Nashville, had taken it upon himself to give the names of every member of his family to a computer company in the hopes of winning some fly-by-night video prize. Harry was already in trouble with his father and two of his uncles because of the stunt. And while Toni had heard of this only through the family grapevine, she wondered if she was about to become victim number three. If this was a free-for-ten-days-or-send-it-back-with-no-charge deal, she was not going to be happy knowing that she was now on some con artist's mailing list, and Harry would probably be grounded for life.

"Miss Hatfield? You are Antonette Hatfield, aren't you?"

She peered over his clipboard to the package in his hand, but couldn't see anything other than a bunch of upside-down labels and codes that she wouldn't have been able to understand had she seen them upright.

"Yes, I'm Toni Hatfield."

"Package for you," he said, and handed her the clipboard. "Sign here, please."

She did as he asked, and watched the dust in the driveway settle long after he was gone, realizing as she closed the door how suspicious she'd become since nearly losing her life. Emmit Rice may have missed his target when he'd failed in taking her hostage, but he'd taken something precious just the same when he had died. She no longer assumed that she was safe, and *trust* wasn't just a word, but a thing to be treasured.

"So, Harry. What wonderful prize have I just won, and how much is it going to cost me to claim it?"

The small smile she'd been wearing as she tore into the wrapping died on her lips with the card that fell on the floor at her feet. Once again, the shock of seeing that broad, dark slash of handwriting bearing her name seemed a mockery in the face of his absence.

"What now?" she muttered, and then stared at the obvious.

"An answering machine? What on earth can he be thinking…?"

The card said it all.

Dear Toni,

    Just to make sure you are still all right, I tried several times to call you. You kept missing my calls and I realized how isolated you are out there. The instructions for hooking this up are simple. Take care and maybe we will make a connection another time. My address and phone number are enclosed.

                                           Lane

"He tried to call?" She let out a shout of anger, but no one heard. "What, pray tell, could he possibly have to say to me that he hasn't already said?"

She glared down at the answering machine, still packaged inside its box, then headed for the kitchen, muttering beneath her breath with every step that she took.

"I don't need to be checked up on, and if I'd wanted one of these…these…things, I would have bought it myself. My God! The nerve of the man! He's worse than Justin. Next thing I know, he'll be sending me a pager so that he can keep track of my whereabouts!"

She scribbled a scathing retort that she chose not to reread, afraid that if she did, she might relent and be nicer to him than he had a right to expect, then stuck it to the outside of the box. Paper flew and string knotted as she wrapped and taped and cursed all manner of men for their hard heads and small minds.

"When he left, he gave up any right he might have had to worry about me," she said, walking to the bathroom where she washed her face and yanked a brush and then a comb through her hair. "And why would I want to call him? What on earth would I possibly say?" She snorted and ignored the furious glaze of tears shimmering across her eyes. "Maybe he's expecting a 'next time you're in the neighborhood come on by' invitation. I suppose he's ready to have a little more *fun.*''

Although it was nearly suppertime, and the cows would be coming down the lane anytime now to be fed, Toni hauled herself and her ''gift'' out to her pickup, thankful that her vehicle was now in good repair, and tore down the driveway in a flurry of drying leaves and red dust. If she hurried, she would just about make it to the post office before it closed for the day.

Having had one hellish day at work had done nothing for Lane's peace of mind. Traffic was snarled, the weather was hot and he'd had dreams last night that he couldn't forget. They had ranged from the first moment he'd opened his eyes and found himself face-to-face with a dark-eyed angry woman to seeing her unconscious in Emmit Rice's arms. During what was supposed to have been a good night of rest, his emotions had run the gamut to the point of exhaustion. He'd gotten up tired, gone to work mad and was now coming home to a lonely, solitary apartment.

But, he reminded himself, it was what he wanted, and then reworded that message within his own mind. No, he didn't necessarily want it, but it was what he had to do, for her sake as well as his own.

When he saw the Tennessee postmark on the package in his apartment mailbox, he realized that the response he'd been hoping to get wasn't coming. This one was as unorthodox as the woman who'd sent it. Not only did he get his answering machine back, but the note that came with it set him back on his heels.

I kept the table you sent because you broke mine. After all, fair is fair. But frankly, Mr. Monday, I believe that we've traded about all there is to trade between us. Like lives, a roll in the sack, etc. You get the picture.

Unless you have something more to say to me than what's already been said, I don't see the need for further communi-

cation. You came and went through my life like the flood that
went down Chaney Creek.

We owe each other exactly nothing, which under the circumstances, is probably for the best. I do not need a man who
does not need me.

What totally irked Lane was the fact that she'd referred to
him as "Mr. Monday," and the way that she'd signed the
note.

Sincerely. She'd signed the damned letter, Sincerely, Toni
Hatfield.

He was all but shouting as he dropped the answering machine into a trash can and tossed the note in after it, then
pivoted and picked it up again, rereading the last two sen-
tences, trying to make sense out of the ambiguous remark.

"What the hell does she mean…under the circumstances…probably for the best…do not need a man who does
not need me? I never said she needed a man. Hellfire! All I
did was send her a damned answering machine!"

And then all the anger in him died. He had just answered
his own questions. "Under the circumstances" was simple.
He was here. She was there. Whatever happened to her from
now on was none of his business, and he'd made that point
perfectly clear by leaving her. After all, it had been "just for
fun" between them. It was what she'd wanted, wasn't it?

As for the "doesn't need a man who didn't need her," she
was right. What possible good could he do her? He'd shown
her what he needed and wanted by walking out on her after
the first time they had made love without so much as a goodbye. And he'd let her go the second time with more of the
same. What Toni needed was a man who was able to stand
by her, not an emotional cripple like him.

"Ah, God, lady," he said softly as he folded her letter and
put it in a drawer. "I didn't mean to…"

He couldn't even finish his own sentence, because Lane
himself didn't know what he'd meant. All he knew was that
his days and nights were being haunted by two women. One
that he'd killed, the other that he'd left behind.

That night, for the first time in more than five years, he shut himself in his apartment with a fifth of whiskey and drank himself into oblivion, because facing what he had done was an impossible, unbearable task.

The same night, many miles and mountains away, Toni felt pain and knew that it was not all her own. And when morning came, bringing a bright, new day, she could not find it anywhere within herself to care.

That came later, on the morning that she'd overslept for the umpteenth time in as many weeks and then rolled out of bed just in time to throw up. Only after the calm in her belly had resumed did it occur to her to wonder why she'd been sick. And when realization dawned, so did Toni Hatfield's hope for salvation. She'd lost her man, but if she was right, she would be having his child.

"No, Justin, I don't need company just to drive into Knoxville," she argued, and wished for the hundredth time that she hadn't bothered to tell him that she was going. She shifted the phone to her other ear as she gauged the time against driving distance. If she hurried, she would just about make her appointment, and the last thing she needed was her eldest brother at her side when she found out for sure that she was about to become an unwed mother.

"Look, I've made the drive a jillion times before and you never cared. What's the big deal now?"

Justin sighed heavily. "I didn't mean to imply that you needed help, sis. I was just remembering…" He stopped suddenly. "Never mind. If you want to, you can call before you leave Knoxville. That way, you'll simply be safeguarding yourself. Understand?"

Toni relented. He was right. And she was being too touchy only because she didn't want or need anyone's advice about what she'd learn.

"I'm the one who should be saying I'm sorry," she said. "I appreciate knowing someone is around who cares whether I live or die. It may as well be you. I'll call you before I leave Knoxville. I promise."

Every breath that Toni took as she drove toward Knoxville was a prayer that what she suspected would be so. And although she could have bought a pregnancy test kit in Chaney, it would not have been wise to do so. The inevitable would be revealed in time. For now, keeping the secret to herself seemed the best possible option.

She didn't even mind as much as she usually did when the doctor's nurse asked her to disrobe for her examination. What was a little embarrassment compared to what she could gain?

"Well, Mrs. Hatfield, I believe congratulations are in order. You are going to be a mother," Dr. Cross told her a scant fifteen minutes later.

"Miss." Toni corrected him absently.

Her heart was too full to care that his face had reddened slightly.

"I'm sorry," he said, and glanced at her chart, noting her age and that this would be her first. "I didn't mean to imply—"

Toni smiled. "Don't be sorry," she said, and clasped her hands in her lap to keep them from shaking. "This baby is nothing less than an answer to a prayer."

He smiled. "Is the father going to be in the baby's life at all?" he asked.

The smile froze on her face. "Not likely," she said shortly. "But I have seven brothers. If I need a male role model, I have more than enough."

He laughed. "I'm a member of a rather large family myself. I think I know what you mean. A little can go a long way, right?"

"Right," Toni echoed, and tried not to think of Lane Monday. Not now. He didn't belong in this joy, because he hadn't wanted to belong in her life.

"At first I'll need to see you only on a monthly basis. The closer you come to term, the closer your checkups will be. My nurse will give you a handful of literature. Read it all. Ask me questions next month. If you have any problems, and I do mean *any*, call me, day or night. Got that?"

She nodded.

"I don't know what you do for a living, but I want you to get plenty of rest, eat right and give up any strenuous activities. Exercise is good. Overdoing it is not."

"Since my father's death, I rent out my farmland, but I still raise cattle," Toni said. "From time to time, I do lift heavy things. Bales of hay, sacks of feed...that sort of stuff."

He frowned. "I don't recommend you push yourself so hard anymore."

She shrugged. "So I'll hire help."

"Good girl," he said. "Ask my nurse to make your next appointment, and I'll see you next month. Okay?"

Toni stood, and then impulsively hugged him just because she could.

"Thank you, Doctor," she said, and grinned when he blushed again.

"Don't thank me," he said. "I'm just the bearer of the news. Thank the man who made you this happy."

That, my dear doctor, is impossible. We've burned more than bridges between us.

"Then that would have to be God for answering my prayer."

The doctor grinned. "You're not going to try and convince me that this was an immaculate conception or anything like that?" he teased.

"Hardly," Toni responded. *I would say it was closer to a careful deception.* "See you next month," she said, trying not to let her elation show as she left.

But it was impossible to ignore her joy. It had lasted all the way home, and she was halfway through her evening meal when the phone rang and she remembered that she hadn't called Justin to tell him she was leaving Knoxville.

Certain of the caller's identity, she answered on the second ring and was apologizing before she'd given him a chance to speak.

"I'm sorry. I'm sorry. I'm sorry," she said, her voice light and full of laughter, waiting to hear her brother's disgusted remark.

Lane forgot what he'd been about to say. He hadn't expected to hear such happiness from her. He closed his eyes, picturing the expression on her face and trying not to think of who had put such joy in her voice.

"No, Toni, I'm the one who's sorry," he said softly. "I overstepped so damned many boundaries with you that it makes me sick. Forgive me, lady. Then maybe I can forgive myself."

Toni froze, and before she could think, before she could react to the shock of hearing his voice, he hung up the phone.

"Oh, my God," she whispered, feeling behind her for a seat before she fell to the floor instead. "Lane? Lane, is that you?"

There was nothing but a dull buzz and an empty silence, and she heard it clear through to her soul. She hung up the phone, then buried her face in her hands. Fate had to be laughing up its sleeve at this coincidence.

On the day that she'd learned she was pregnant, the father of the child called and expressed regret for everything that had passed between them. If she had needed a sign to let her know she'd made the right decision to keep her news to herself, then she'd just gotten it. In big, loud, clear tones and compliments of the telephone.

Chapter 13

A new peace settled within Toni's heart. It came with the acceptance of what life had given her, and from knowing that she had the will to endure whatever negative response she might suffer. The happiness she felt for the forthcoming child far outweighed whatever else might occur.

Her family saw her change and she knew they did not understand. They only knew that the angry, semireclusive woman that she'd been was gone, and for that they seemed grateful. Toni realized that they would never have imagined, not even in their wildest dreams, that independent, do-it-myself Toni was going to become a mother. Or that she had done so under the grayest of circumstances. Deliberate deception was not something they would have ever associated with straightforward Antonette.

As for herself, Toni didn't care or worry about anything except her health and the welfare of the baby that she carried inside of her. She let the hot, lazy days of summer pass her by with little fuss, and she did what she needed to do without pushing the limits of her endurance.

Hiring a semiretired widower named Abel Morris to help

her with the heavy work had been a stroke of genius. He was so thankful for the chance to be busy again, he nearly begged her for chores.

It was a time of passage that was doomed to an all-too-brief sojourn in her life. Inevitably, her family would have to be told, preferably before they saw for themselves the changes that her body was already undergoing. But for now, she waited, and cherished the life that was growing within her, and tried not to care that the man who was responsible for it all was unaware of what he'd done.

All fall Toni had put off the inevitable. The telling of her blessed event was going to produce a family uproar and she knew it. She'd practiced her speech so many times in so many different ways that it had gotten to be her own private joke.

Once, Justin had even teased her by commenting on the fact that in her old age and solitary state, she had started talking to herself, and recommended that she get a house cat rather than the barnful of half-wild felines that roamed the hay rafters. She had laughed in his face. A cat? The joke was almost too good to keep to herself, but she'd done it just the same.

But in her fifth month, and on the latest trip to her obstetrician, she'd done something that she couldn't hide with loose clothing and jackets. She bought a baby bed, and then a high chair and a stroller. Before she knew it, the bed of her pickup was fully loaded with cardboard boxes and packing crates, all marked "Some Assembly Required."

Not only was she going to need expert help, but someone was going to have to help her unload.

"Maybe I should just call everyone and ask them to bring a screwdriver and come over," Toni muttered, arguing with herself as she exited the highway from Knoxville onto the county road leading to Chaney. "Sort of let them figure it all out for themselves."

She glanced over her shoulder, peering through the window to make sure that her load was still safely intact behind her.

"Or, maybe I could just show up in their front yards for a sisterly visit and let each brother draw his own conclusions as to what I'm hauling."

Then she groaned and shifted uncomfortably on the seat, reminding herself that she was being silly. Something this monumental could not be told in such a cavalier fashion.

"Goodness, baby," she whispered, and patted the gentle swell of her belly to apologize for complaining. "Who would have thought that carrying a little thing like you would make everything else in my body ache?"

Yet her sense of fair play and unwillingness to deal with an all-out brawl within the family warned her that she had only one outlet.

"I'll tell Justin and let him deal with everyone else," she decided aloud, and waved at the sheriff as she sailed through town, hoping that Dan Holley was thinking about fishing and not what she had in the back of the truck.

Seeing the sheriff brought another lawman to mind, one she kept trying to forget. The memory of Lane should have faded. It had been almost five months since she'd seen him, and in those five months the Smoky Mountains had undergone as drastic a change as she had. But her memories of him were as vivid as the night she'd dragged him from the flood.

Sometimes during the day when she was lost in some mundane job, with her mind on one thing, her hands on another, the old farmhouse would creak and she would turn, expecting to see Lane come walking into the room. The disappointment that came next was always startling, and she hated herself for being so weak.

And late at night, when finding a comfortable place in her bed was next to impossible, she would remember the feel of his arms cradling her and the solid thud of his heartbeat against her ear, and she would cry from the loss of it all.

Lost in thought, she turned into her driveway in a cloud of dust, scattering the covering of autumn-hued leaves that had fallen near the road. She drove the pickup like a red-and-white arrow, streaking up the driveway and moving aside all that lay in her path.

And that was how Justin saw her as he came out of the barn, her pickup racing just ahead of the dirt and the leaves. He grinned and dumped the tools in the back of his truck, and started toward the house to help her unload.

"Oh, God," Toni groaned. Whether she liked it or not, her Waterloo was at hand.

She crawled out of the pickup and stood, leaving the cab between them as Justin neared the front yard. From where she stood, she could see the expressions on his face as they changed. He'd went from greeting to gawking, and when he leaned over the truck bed and shifted one box to read what was written on the side, then another, then another, he looked up at his sister with an expression that she didn't want to face.

"What in the world have you done, Toni? Lucy doesn't need any of this stuff. The stuff we already have is going to last through her baby years just fine."

Toni exhaled slowly, then counted to ten. He thought that she'd bought these things as a gift for his own baby. It figured. He would never expect her to need anything like this for herself.

"They aren't for Lucy," she said. "They're for me."

The look in his eyes said it all. Shock turned to disbelief and then to overwhelming rage. He dropped the box that he'd been holding and walked around the truck like a man in a daze. His eyes never left her face until he turned the corner of the truck bed. At that point his gaze went straight to her belly. Toni watched his eyebrows arch and his mouth go slack.

He cleared his throat several times before he spoke. "I don't believe it!"

"Believe what, Justin? That I could possibly be pregnant, or that I didn't tell you?"

"Why didn't you say something to me sooner, sis? No matter what the son of a bitch said to deny it, I would have made damn sure he owned up to what he did to you!"

Toni felt weak. This was exactly the attitude that she'd expected Justin to have. And when he saw her sway, he grabbed her to keep her from falling and led her to the house.

"Come inside, honey," he said as he opened the door and

led her into the living room. "Sit down before you fall down. We'll decide what to do as soon as you're feeling better."

Toni sighed and stifled a smile as she sat down. It was so like Justin to assume that she needed someone to tell her what to do.

"I've already decided what I'm doing, Justin. I would think that it was fairly obvious. I made my decision the day I found out I was pregnant. I'm having my baby and thanking God that I can."

"I'm not going to insult you by asking who the father is, because this is nothing more than what I feared might happen when you took that bastard Monday in. I told Judy he would take advantage of you. I'll break his damned neck if he doesn't get himself down here and marry you."

This was where it was going to get rough. But Toni didn't have it in her to lie, or to let Justin keep maligning a man who was as ignorant of the facts as he himself had been until only moments ago.

"He did not take advantage of me, Justin. In fact, it was just the opposite. He was nothing but a gentleman the whole time he was here."

Justin frowned and threw up his hands in frustration. "Don't try to protect him. You didn't get like this by yourself. He lied to you, and now you're paying the consequences." He headed for the telephone in the hall.

"No!"

She was shouting as she bolted from her chair and yanked Justin's hand from the phone before he could make the call.

Toni's mouth was grim, her eyes dark with fury. For the moment, she had her brother's full attention.

"Now you listen to me, and you listen good! You aren't going to like this, but it's the truth. And so help me God, if you do something without my consent, I'll never, and I mean *never,* speak to you again!"

Justin went pale. "But, sis, why would you—?"

"Shut up and listen to me! Just once, will you listen?"

He bowed his head and waited. He seemed to understand that he had no other choice.

"Lane Monday never said he loved me. He never told me a thing to lead me to believe he would do anything other than leave when he was well enough to travel. He did not make unwanted advances. Why should he? I'm not the kind of woman a man wants to marry."

"What do you mean...you're not the kind of woman a man would marry?"

She spun toward him, her laughter as sharp and brittle as the lines around her mouth.

"Do you see any men lined up at my door? Have you *ever* seen them standing in line for a date with me? No! I don't think so. It's fairly obvious to me that men don't want some big moose to take to bed when they could have a beautiful, feminine lady instead."

"Oh, my God." He buried his face in his hands. "I'm sorry, so sorry. We did this to you. We didn't mean it, Toni. I swear to God. You're as pretty as any girl I've ever seen. I can't believe you think that you're not."

Her laughter was short and just below a snort of disbelief.

"I will be thirty years old before this baby is born. I have never been proposed to. I have never even had someone try to take advantage of me. How do you think that makes me feel?" And before he could answer, she told him. "It makes me feel like a failure, Justin. In fact, as a woman, I *am* a failure. But by God, as a mother, I will be just about perfect. So don't you dare go and ruin what has happened to me. As far as I'm concerned, it's a gift from heaven, not something of which I should be ashamed."

"I don't get it," he persisted. "If the man was such a gentleman, then how did this happen?"

Toni's chin went up. Her eyes blazed with a light that Justin didn't dare dispute.

"Because I asked him to sleep with me. And I got pregnant because I took no precautions...on purpose." She leaned closer until they were eye to eye. "Do you understand what I mean? Is that plain enough for you?"

"I can't believe that in this day and time a man with his

background would just blindly sleep with a woman without taking precautions of his own, or at least ask about them.''

Toni's voice faltered, but her gaze did not. "He didn't ignore it. He asked me if I was protected. I didn't exactly lie to him, but I also didn't tell him the truth. I purposely let him believe it was safe.''

She'd said all she was going to say about an incident that was her own painful, personal memory, then spun toward the door.

''Where are you going?'' he asked.

''To the pickup. I have things to unload. I'm hiring painters next week and redoing the bedroom next to mine. I think I'll paint the walls green like my Tennessee hills, and have Marcy Simmons, the high school art teacher, do a mural. Maybe I'll have her add some trees and birds to it, too, sort of like an American jungle, if you know what I mean. What do you think?''

Justin's mood was a shadow of its former belligerence. ''I think you don't need to hire the painters. David and I will paint the damned walls green. We'll paint them black and blue if it will make you happy. Just let me help.'' And then he added, ''Damn it, sis, I need to help.''

Tension slipped out of her stance as quickly as it had come. She smiled, then stood aside to hold back the door.

''Okay,'' she said. ''And just because I love you, I'm going to let you have the privilege of dealing with 'some assembly required.' ''

She heard him groan as he passed, but it didn't matter. The worst was over. Saying it aloud hadn't been easy, but not nearly as difficult as she'd expected it to be. And as for the rest of the family, the grapevine and the telephone would do the rest. They could think what they chose, and say what they must, as long as they kept the news to themselves. The last thing she needed was for someone to mind her business and tell Lane Monday that he was going to be a father. She knew her brothers. They would all bow to Justin's decisions, just as they had during their growing-up years.

That is, all of them except Wyatt. The youngest Hatfield

male and only four years older than Toni, he'd been a rebel
from the day he'd learned how to walk. If anyone would interfere, it would be Wyatt. But Toni knew her younger brother
would never get the chance to put in his two cents. He'd
walked off the family farm on his eighteenth birthday, joined
the marines and went off to ''see the world,'' as the poster at
the recruiting station had promised.

Yes, Toni didn't know when they'd be seeing Wyatt Hatfield again.

''Is the turkey about done, Aunt Toni?''

Bobby Hatfield's plaintive cry was nothing more than an
echo of the same lament that she'd heard from every other
hungry mouth awaiting the arrival of ''the bird.''

''Almost, sweetie,'' she said, softly. ''Go wash, and tell
your cousins to do the same.'' She ruffled his short, dark hair
before sending him scooting with a pat on the rear.

The heat from the old, roomy kitchen was near to intense,
Just like the marathon baking it had just endured. Pies in sun-
dry shapes and scents lined the sideboard while hot rolls, fresh
from the oven, mounded the breadbaskets at either end of the
table.

Toni eyed the feast critically and knew that she would be
glad when this day was over. Volunteering to hostess this annual event had been done without thinking of the backbreaking
chores that would accompany it. Thankfully, the army of able
sisters-in-law had done more than their fair share of adding to
the Thanksgiving repast, but the effort had taken its toll on
her.

''Is it done?''

Toni turned and grinned at Justin, who hovered at her elbow
with a hungry look that matched the one his son had been
wearing.

''Like father, like son. And yes, it's done.''

''I'll lift it out for you,'' he said, taking the pot holders
from her hands.

She willingly gave up the chore. Bending was difficult

enough these days without bringing a twenty-five-pound turkey, hot from the oven, up with her as she stood.

"Let me finish for you," Judy offered as she sidestepped two other helpers to get to the bird that needed to be transferred to the platter.

Toni sighed, smiled and moved aside for the time being, allowing them to interfere because it made her family feel as if they were helping her cope. But the truth be known, she was coping pretty well on her own.

She wandered to the kitchen window overlooking the front yard, and smiled to herself as she watched the yardful of children at play.

Next year...or maybe the next when the baby is a little older, he, or she, will be out there, too.

Her vision blurred as she looked into the future, imagining that she could almost see the dark little head and the short, baby steps of a toddler wobbling about, investigating every rock and leaf in its path.

And then her world and everything in it suddenly came back into focus as she saw a black sports car pull up and park among all the other vehicles and the tall, dark-haired driver start toward the house.

His stride was laconic. She knew if she were closer, she would be able to see devils dancing in the soft brown depths of eyes just like her own.

"Oh, my God," she gasped, and headed for the door.

"What is it? Did one of the children get hurt?" Justin was right behind her before she got out the door.

"It's Wyatt!" she cried. "Wyatt came home for Thanksgiving!"

Toni, still graceful even in the latter stages of pregnancy, bounded from the back porch and started toward him across the yard, dodging kids and footballs with every other step. "Wyatt! Wyatt! Welcome home!"

"Well, well," he muttered, grinning. "My, how things have changed."

He caught her in midflight and swung her off of her feet

and up into the air, completely disregarding her condition as well as the shock on everyone else's face.

"Be careful, Wyatt!" Justin shouted, then breathed a sigh of relief when his brother finally put Toni's feet back on earth.

One after the other, Wyatt hugged and greeted, pounded backs and kissed cheeks.

"Come back inside," Toni finally said. "You're just in time to carve the turkey."

Everyone began filing back into the house, but Wyatt caught Toni's hand and tugged it in a teasing gesture, speaking softly to her alone.

"Honey, I think you should let your husband carve the turkey. I haven't had the pleasure yet, but if I were the man of the house, I would be expecting to do the honors myself, especially on Thanksgiving."

Toni stopped. When she turned to face him, the shock had all but disappeared from her eyes.

"Justin didn't tell you, did he?" she asked.

Wyatt frowned. "Tell me what?"

Toni sighed, unaware that she absently rubbed her belly in a protective gesture, then started to explain. "There is no man of the house, Wyatt. I'm what you might call an unwed mother. And before you get all indignant, you need to know that it's by choice. That's also all you need to know. Get it?"

It was hard to explain the rage that settled deep in his belly. It didn't even make sense for him to care when he'd all but abandoned the entire family for the better part of twenty years. But something about the way that Toni held herself apart from the words, as if she had faced the truth of her condition without facing the pain, told him that it wasn't all right, and he wasn't about to put up and shut up as she expected.

He pulled her into his arms and hugged her. "You always were a hardheaded, prissy little thing," he said gruffly. "I can see some things never change." He stepped back. "So where's that bird in need of a trim? I'm hungry as hell, and so glad to be home that I don't even care if I eat off the tail."

Toni grinned. "I was never prissy, not one day in my entire life. If I had been, I would have been better off."

Wyatt pondered the oddity of her remark all during dinner and long into the night after everyone else had gone home. What Toni didn't know, and what Wyatt hadn't decided until he'd set foot back on Tennessee soil and seen the condition his family was in, was that he wasn't going anywhere. At least not yet.

His life had gone to hell in a hand basket, but there was no reason for his sister to wind up the same way. He would find out what he needed to know and then fix it.

Living through holidays had always been rough for Lane, and this year had been no different. A child of foster homes and faceless pretend-parents, he'd only truly known family life after marrying Sharla. The short time that they had been together, he'd gotten a taste of what it meant to have someone else who cared. When she died, the hole it had left in his life was even bigger and emptier than the one he'd had before they'd met.

On the job he was always the man who volunteered to do holiday duty. It was no sacrifice on his part to show up at work because he had no one at home. In fact, it had helped him to get through the loneliest parts of the year.

But when Thanksgiving rolled around this year, he found himself thinking of Toni and that wild brood of Hatfields he'd met, and he could only imagine what dinner would be like in that household. It would be full of laughter and love, leaving a warmth deep inside a man that had nothing to do with the heat from a fire.

The want that came with the sound of her name and the memory of her face still amazed him. He should have been over a woman who he had never really claimed. The memory of the passion that they had shared should have faded.

Should have, but had not.

And yet when the need to reconnect with her came, it was always followed by a silent warning to himself that he couldn't get involved with another woman. All he had to do was think of what he'd done to Sharla and then transpose that horror and fear onto Toni's face. It was enough to put a damper on the fiercest of needs.

"Monday! Phone for you! Line two!"

The voice snapped him out of his reverie. Lane spun in his chair and picked up the phone. "This is Monday."

"This is Wyatt Hatfield. We haven't had the pleasure, but I'm—"

Lane sat upright. "You're one of Toni's brothers, aren't you? I remember her talking about you." And then a shot of adrenaline surged. Why should this man be calling? "What's wrong? Has something happened to Antonette?" he asked, unaware that his voice had come out sounding like a growl.

"Yes, you could say that," Wyatt drawled.

"What happened? Damn it, man, get it said!" *Oh, God,* Lane thought. *I didn't know it would hurt this bad to say her name.*

"It's a little hard to explain over the phone," Wyatt said. "And if the truth was told, she would take the hide off of me for calling you. But if you're half the man everyone said you are, you'll come out and see for yourself."

"Lord! Don't call me long-distance and then give me some mystic bull. What the hell is wrong with Toni?"

"I've said more than I should. But no one made *me* promise not to tell."

"Tell what?" Lane asked, and knew when every man in the office turned and looked at him that he'd just shouted into the phone at the top of his lungs.

The line went dead in his ear.

"Son of a bitch!"

He slammed the receiver onto the cradle and bolted up from the desk.

"Damn it to hell!"

He stuffed a stack of papers into a file and then tossed them on Palmer's desk as he stomped past.

"What's wrong?" Palmer asked, and then held up his hands to ward off the blow he felt coming. "Don't mind me," he muttered, and picked up the file Lane had tossed. "I'd be more than happy to finish it for you. Thank you so much for asking me first.''

The door banged behind Lane, and then all was silent in the room as the officers stared at one another in shock.

Chapter 14

Lane left Tallahassee in a blaze of sunlight and arrived in Tennessee on a cold winter chill. It was the first snow of the season. Two weeks before Christmas and the light dusting on the ground was still not enough to make a decent-size snowball, although to give them credit, every child in Chaney that Lane had passed seemed bent on trying to do just that.

"Chaney hasn't changed. I just pray to God that neither has anything or anyone else."

Lane wouldn't even pretend to guess what the phone call from Toni's brother had been about. There were too many ominous implications to wonder. But the fear was real that had carried him from his apartment to the airport, and then across miles and through states on the road back to her.

And all he could feel was the cold sweat that came with the sound of her name, and the memory of a line going dead in his ear. If this was nothing serious, he was going to punch Wyatt Hatfield in the nose. But if it mattered...

He took a turn in the road, passing the place where he'd killed Emmit Rice and in so doing had saved Toni's life; he didn't even remember to look.

"When I see her face, then it will be all right," he reassured himself, and had to be satisfied with that thought.

The driveway loomed. He took the curve high and fast, his eyes on the rooftop visible above the treetops, and on the silly rooster weather vane that marked the spot where Toni lived.

Toni spun at the knock on the front door, then rolled her eyes as she wiped her hands on a towel. Wyatt must have locked himself out, although she couldn't imagine how or why. She smoothed her hands down the front of her plaid shirt and brushed a smear of flour off the leg of her jeans.

Carrying a baby hadn't changed what she wore, only the style. She'd traded her 501 Blues for maternity denim, but she was still the same dark-haired, chocolate-eyed woman with more hair than she could manage. Older but wiser, and only a little bit rounder, she wore her pregnancy with grace.

"What did you do, lock yourself out?"

The laughter died on her lips as she stared in openmouthed shock at the man across the threshold. She had the intense urge to slam the door in his face before it was too late, but knew that it already was.

She looked into his eyes, saw the shock and a stark wave of horror slide across his expression, and wished Wyatt to hell and back for what he had done. And she knew it was Wyatt who had caused this from the look he wore as he came up the steps behind him.

"Oh, my God," Lane muttered.

He stepped across the threshold unaware of the man behind him and started backing Toni across the room, his arms reaching out to her in a beseeching manner that she kept trying to elude.

"Oh, Lord! Toni, baby...you shouldn't have...you don't understand, you can't..."

He couldn't think past praying, nor could he find the words to say what needed to be said. And when he did, they came out all wrong.

I shouldn't have? I can't? Toni needed to scream, but she

settled for a sarcastic remark instead. "What do you mean, I can't? I already have, Mr. Monday."

"Toni, Toni, what in hell have you done?"

The accusation was as sharp as a knife thrust beneath her heart. It rang in her ears long after Wyatt had entered the room and closed the door after him.

"Nothing that concerns you," Toni said. "And why, may I ask, have you come at this late date in our…association?"

Lane shook his head and wiped a hand across his face. "I got a call. Someone said you were…I thought you'd been hurt or worse. I came as quick as I…" He spun, suddenly aware of someone standing there.

Wyatt leaned against the wall with the nonchalance of a man who knew he was in the right. "You would be Lane Monday, am I right?"

"You son of a bitch," Lane muttered. "You scared me half to death."

Wyatt grinned. "You came, didn't you?"

Toni shook from shock and rage. At that moment she hated both men. Wyatt for interfering, and Lane for reacting exactly as she'd feared and not as she'd dreamed.

"Why don't you two take your disagreement outside," Toni said. "I don't feel like mopping up blood."

Lane turned to face her, completely blocking out every thought except what he'd just learned.

"Why didn't you tell me?" he groaned, and tried once again to take her into his arms.

Toni pushed his hands away and glared through her tears. "Probably because it was none of your business, and because I knew you would react exactly as you did. I don't need pity. Thanks to an interfering family, I have all that I need."

Lane paled. His hands shook, and the room tilted. He had a momentary vision of Sharla's face contorted in excruciating pain, and then he remembered the blood and the way in which life had drained from her eyes. He groaned.

"Oh, God, not again. Not again."

Wyatt frowned. "What do you mean, not again? Are you trying to tell us you've done this before? Gotten some woman pregnant and then walked out on her without so much as a thank you, ma'am?''

Toni gasped. "Wyatt, I told you it was all my doing! You shouldn't have interfered. He didn't make promises, and I didn't ask for any.''

"You can't have this baby," Lane said quietly, and wondered if he could die from a broken heart.

Toni thought that she was prepared for everything, but to hear this man telling her that she should terminate a pregnancy she had prayed for made her weak with shock.

"How dare you?" she accused, and cradled her belly as if to protect the child from the sudden appearance of a demon. "How dare you ask me to kill my own—"

"Oh, God," Lane groaned, grabbing her hands from her stomach and pulling her fiercely into his arms. "That's not what I meant, honey! That's not what I meant! I meant, you won't *physically* be able to have it. If you try, it will kill you. It happened before. It will happen again.'' Ignoring her protests, he buried his face against the heat on her cheek and wished that he'd drowned in the flood. "I can't be responsible for another woman's death. So help me God, I just can't.''

Toni froze. She heard what he said, but it didn't make sense. The only thing certain was the true depth of Lane Monday's fear, because he was coming apart in her arms.

"You're crazy," she said, and tried to tear herself away. "I'm fine. The baby is due in a couple of months. Everything is, or was, perfect until you showed up. I'm sorry Wyatt frightened you, but you need not worry that I'll make any demands on you. I know you didn't want me, and I learned to accept that, but I want this baby. It's mine," she said, and finally succeeded in pushing him away.

Didn't want you? How did our signals get so messed up? he wondered. Yet listening to her talk, he felt that he knew. What he'd meant as caution, she'd felt as rejection. He groaned beneath his breath. It was time for explanations.

"I weighed eleven pounds when I was born," Lane said.

Wyatt whistled softly between his teeth, eyeing his sister's belly. "Damn."

"After my wife, Sharla, got pregnant, they told her she would have to have a cesarean delivery because the baby was going to be so big."

"Lots of women have those," Toni said.

"She went into labor at seven and a half months while I was out of town. All sorts of complications happened before they found her. I got to the hospital in time to watch her die in my arms."

"That's not your fault," Toni argued.

But Lane couldn't—wouldn't—hear the truth in what she said, even though it was an echo of what the doctor had told him that fateful day. If he'd been a different man…a normal-size man…his wife and baby would not have died, and that was a fact. The memories were making him shake, but he couldn't seem to stop. He took Toni by the arms and all but shook her as he spoke.

"I stood in her blood, watching her trying to have a baby that was too damned big for her, and you stand here telling me it's none of my business! Like hell, lady! Like hell!"

"Oh Lord," Toni whispered, and unintentionally cradled herself again. "I'm sorry, Lane. I didn't know. I swear I didn't know."

She inhaled slowly, choosing her words carefully, hoping that she could make him understand. "You don't realize it, but you aren't thinking clearly. You're letting something that happened a long time ago color your judgment of an entirely different situation. Look at me! I'm as big as a horse, and as healthy, remember? That won't happen to me. I'll be fine. You don't have to worry."

Lane glared at her. *She would be fine!* He'd just spilled his guts about something that had haunted him every day of his life since it had happened, and she'd brushed it aside as old news.

"I don't intend to worry, because I'm not letting you out of my sight until this child is born," he said. And then he leaned forward, trying not to glare at the woman who was carrying his child. "And maybe not even then."

Toni's eyebrows arched. Her chin jutted. And in that moment, Lane knew how much he loved her, and how impossible it would be to make her believe it.

"You will marry me," he said.

"I will not."

"I'll find a judge. Being a lawman has its perks, and bypassing waiting periods is one of them. If you want anyone besides me present, you'd better start calling. As soon as the license is in my hands, you're mine, lady."

"I'm not yours," Toni retorted. "You didn't want me, remember? And I won't marry a man who doesn't love me!"

"Why the hell not?" Lane shouted back at her. "According to you, you went to bed with one!"

As it turned out, she had called no one to come and witness her humiliation other than the brother who had caused it all. Wyatt was present in a dishonorable position, relegated to the sidelines by a look from Toni that would have wilted a lesser man's nerve.

The minister shifted his Bible to a position nearer his eyeglasses and cleared his throat as he began the ceremony. "Dearly beloved, we are gathered here today to join this man and woman in holy matrimony. If there be anyone present who objects, speak now or forever hold your peace."

Lane increased the pressure of his hold on Toni's wrist and stared down into her eyes with a warning that she didn't dare ignore.

But her chin jutted just the same as she stared at him without blinking, daring him to utter one kind, sentimental word about this farce of a marriage.

Everything floated in and out of Toni's consciousness. Words were traded with little emotion. Feelings were hidden well-deep inside, where no one could tell how moved she was by the moment, and how desperately she wished that this had been done in the name of love, not duty and fear. She kept reminding herself that this was for the baby's sake. That now, her child would know its father.

Lane's hand was strong and firm upon Toni's arm as he repeated his vows, but his thoughts kept jumping in and out of the past. And then his attention ricocheted sharply from the past to the present as he heard the preacher repeat his question.

"Mr. Monday, do you have a ring?"

Before Lane could answer, he heard Toni take a deep breath, and when she yanked her hand out of his, obviously overwhelmed by the entire ceremony, he took it as an indication that she was ready to bolt. Before he had time to think, the handcuffs that normally hung from his belt were in his hand. For a lawman used to restraints that corralled the unwilling, it had been an instinctive gesture. And considering their history, the move was highly appropriate. He popped one bracelet across her wrist, then calmly fastened the other one to his own.

"It's symbolic," he said shortly, ignoring the preacher's bugged eyes and Toni's shocked gasp. "Please continue."

The preacher nodded.

Wyatt started to laugh, but the look of disbelief on Toni's face and the warning that Lane gave him stifled his mirth.

"In lieu of the traditional giving of rings—" the preacher cast one last glance at the metallic binding upon their wrists "—I now pronounce that you are husband and wife. Mr. Monday, you may kiss your bride."

Lane exhaled on a slow, weary breath and looked at his new wife.

"You have no right," Toni said, hating herself for the tears running down her cheeks.

"I do now, Mrs. Monday," he said softly, and cupped her face with his hands and tasted the tears on her mouth.

Toni froze. Tenderness had no part in this day or the farce that they had enacted. But resisting this man had been impossible for her from the start. Today, in spite of her disappointment that it had all come to this, she could not resist the tug of his lips against her own, and her resolve softened just enough to return the kiss.

"My turn," Wyatt said, and started to swoop his sister into his arms when the handcuffs binding the pair together clanged against his waist and got in his way. "Do you mind?" he asked Lane, pointing to the cuffs.

Lane shrugged and unlocked the cuff. Toni's hand came loose at the same moment Wyatt took her in his arms.

"Congratulations, baby sister. You make a beautiful bride."

"I will hate you forever, Wyatt Hatfield," Toni muttered, and suffered his kiss.

"No, you won't," he said softly, and then turned back to the glowering groom. There was no jest in his voice as he spoke. "Monday, you are now in possession of the only sister we Hatfield boys have. We care for her greatly. If you hurt her, I will kill you, and that is a promise."

Lane wasn't impressed by the man or his threat. He saw past it all, but felt compelled to add a warning of his own. "Yeah, and if you ever scare me again like you did yesterday, there won't be enough left of you to do the deed."

Wyatt grinned. "Fair enough, brother," he said with a grin, and reached out to shake Lane's hand. "Welcome to the family."

Toni wouldn't let herself care about the pleasure that she saw on Lane's face when Wyatt embraced him, or the joy in his eyes when Wyatt had said, "Welcome to the family." Wyatt didn't have to live with the man. Her brother hadn't deliberately deceived someone for the chance to have a baby.

"I'll be leaving now," Wyatt said. "Take care, Toni. Have a great honeymoon."

She snorted lightly beneath her breath and then had to suffer the echo of his laughter long after he had gone.

"Where to now?" Toni asked.

"Home. I'm taking you home."

"To Florida?" Dismay was deep in her voice.

Lane shook his head and gently brushed a curl away from her face. "No, baby. You're the one with roots, not me. I'm taking you back where you belong."

It was the first good news that she'd had all day.

The house echoed with their footsteps as they entered, two silent people caught up in a web of their own doing, uncertain how to fix the situation that they now found themselves in.

Lane stood near the doorway, his gaze never wavering from

Toni's face, gauging the pale line around her mouth against the flush across her cheeks.

"Do you want to lie down?"

She sighed. "Do you want something to eat?"

Lane tried a smile. "I asked you first."

Toni walked past him on her way to her room. She didn't have the energy to fight. Not today. Not anymore. She'd just gotten married to the father of her child, and knew that they were the least happy couple she'd ever seen.

Lane watched her go without venturing another word. What could he say that hadn't already been said? He picked up his bag, and followed.

Toni was sitting on the side of the bed about to pull off her shoes when Lane walked into her room and headed for the closet.

"What do you think you're doing?" she asked.

"Hanging up my clothes."

"Not in there!" she cried.

"Why not? I see no need in getting out of bed each morning, and then having to go to another room to dress." He unzipped the bag as if there were no argument and proceeded to unpack.

She'd never felt so helpless or frustrated in her life. It didn't seem to matter what she said to this man, he just kept bulldozing his way through her business as if she weren't there.

"You're not sleeping in here, either," she said, and resisted the urge to stomp her feet. They were too swollen for fits of pique.

"Yes, I am," Lane said. "This is marriage, Toni, not a horse trade where one tries to outdo the other." He dropped his bag and sat down beside her. "It may have happened for all the wrong reasons, but it's not going to continue that way. I made love to you because I wanted to, not because you think you talked me into it. All you did by getting pregnant was give me a damned good reason to break an old promise I'd made to myself. The mistake was not in making love. My mistake was that I did not take precautions with you. If I had been as responsible as you tried to be, this might not have happened to you.''

"I don't believe you, you know. You did not love me then. You do not love me now." She bit her lip and told herself it wouldn't matter if she lied just this once. "Just like I don't love you," she said.

Even to her own ears, she knew that the lie didn't sound right, but she couldn't find it within herself to admit to him that she'd loved him ever since she'd found him in the flooded creek. It was humiliating to be the only one who cared.

"I don't care what you believe," Lane argued. "The truth is, I let you take all the responsibility of precautions and obviously they failed.''

Oh, Lord, Toni thought. *They say that confession is good for the soul. I can't live with a man under these circumstances and let him think this baby was an accident.*

She took a deep breath.

"I did it on purpose," she said, staring at a corner of the carpet design to keep from looking at his face.

Lane didn't move—couldn't move. What she'd said had absolutely dumbfounded him. She couldn't possibly mean what he thought that she meant.

"Exactly *what* did you do on purpose, Toni?"

"Got pregnant.''

"My God," he muttered, and got to his feet with a jerk, staring at her as if she'd lost her mind. "Why? Why would you do that?"

She shrugged. "I wanted a family. But I knew no man would ever want to marry me. It was the only way I knew how to make one by myself.''

"Bull!" He tilted her chin to his gaze. "I'm sick and tired of hearing you put yourself down.''

"It's true, and we both know it. I wasn't pretty enough or woman enough, not even for you. You didn't want to make love to me. You only agreed to it after I asked.''

"You still don't get it, do you?" Lane shouted. He was angry. With her, the situation, and even himself. He leaned toward her until they were nearly nose to nose. "My wife died because of me. Our child died because of me."

Toni felt his breath on her cheek. His voice shook with each word that he spoke. "And now there's you. I'm living through this hell all over again when I swore never to put another woman—or myself—in this position."

Toni pushed him away and stood. "You are obsessed with something that was never your fault," she argued. "And as for putting yourself through this again, remember this, mister. I didn't ask you to marry me. You brought *that* upon yourself."

She stomped out of the room, leaving anger in her wake.

It was nearly midnight. The floorboards creaked beneath Toni's feet as she rolled out of bed and headed for another trip to the bathroom. Being pregnant had its annoying drawbacks.

Minutes later, she was still up and wandering through the house, taking comfort in the familiar darkness and the safety within these walls. The baby turned within her belly, rolling so distinctly that she cradled herself and tried not to grunt as it settled with a plop.

"You can't sleep, either, can you, baby?" she whispered, and absently rubbed the mound of her stomach as she went to get a drink.

"Are you all right?"

The sound of Lane's voice startled her. She spun at the sink, clutching the glass between them like a talisman against something that she couldn't name as she peered through the shadows to the dark, bulky shape of the man in the doorway.

"I came to get a drink," she said shortly, and turned her back to him, afraid that he could see too much of what was in her heart.

He moved silently across the room on bare feet, wearing nothing but a pair of cotton briefs, and then stood behind her.

"Let me," he said, taking the glass from her hands and running the water long enough to let it cool in the pipes before filling the glass. He handed it to her, and as he did, traced the side of her arm, testing the surface of her skin. "Are you cold? I could turn up the heat."

Toni set down the glass with a thump. "Lane, if we're going to get through this together, you are going to have to get over this," she said. "I can get my own drink of water. If I'm cold, I have enough sense to do something about it. I do not bend, and I will not break."

He watched her like a hawk eyeing its prey, but did not speak. Toni glared through the shadows and then took a drink too quickly, coughing on the last gulp and hating him for making her appear so inept. She set the glass down on the counter with another thump.

"I'm going back to bed." When he started through the house behind her like a silent but persistent shadow, she couldn't resist a final dig. "I will be glad when this is over, and you can get back to your own business and leave me to get on with mine."

Lane stopped short. It was the first time since they had started this travesty of a marriage that he realized she thought it was going to come and go.

"No way, lady," he said shortly. "That's not the way this is going to work. I'm not here just until the baby is born. I'm here forever. The sooner you get used to that, the better off we'll both be."

Toni's heart raced. The surface of her skin suddenly felt cold and clammy as shock slid into her system. And while she tried to think of something to say, Lane walked past her and crawled back into the bed. But he wasn't alone long.

She ripped back the covers on her side of the bed and then crawled in on her knees. "What do you mean, you're here forever?"

"It's late. We'll talk tomorrow," he said, then reached up and pulled her down against him, moving her without her permission until she was safe and snug beneath the covers.

"Be still," he mumbled, when she would have resisted his embrace, and shifted his hand from her arm, letting it slide over her belly, then cupping the mound beneath with a tenderness that brought tears to her eyes.

"I hate you," Toni whispered, and knew that she lied.

"No, you don't, Antonette," he said softly. "It's yourself that you hate."

She lay still beneath his touch because she knew she had no choice. And she heard what he'd said because it was the truth. She did hate herself. For being less than a woman. And for practicing a deliberate deception.

Chapter 15

Within the first week of their marriage, Lane had tied up nearly every loose end of his life prior to Toni. His request for an extended leave of absence from his job had been received with shock by all who knew him, but granted nevertheless. He had sublet his apartment, transferred his bank accounts, both savings and checking, to the bank in Chaney, and yesterday his car and the rest of his clothes had arrived via two lawmen who had volunteered to bring it all out on the way to their annual hunting trip in Kentucky.

But he had yet to confront the balance of Toni's family or the doctor in charge of her care. The family would have to wait. Lane was determined that Dr. Cross tell him to his face that she was not in danger. Accompanying her to her next appointment was high on his list of things to do.

The phone rang sharply in the hall, breaking the quiet with a persistence that sent Toni scrambling to answer. She picked up on the fourth ring and was gasping for breath when she lifted the receiver to her ear. "Hello?"

"What's wrong?" Justin asked. "You sound like you're out of breath."

Toni leaned against the wall and pressed her hand to her chest, trying to slow down the rapid thump of her heartbeat.

"I am, you dolt," she said lightly. "I can't even walk without puffing, never mind running for the phone."

"You shouldn't be running," Justin said shortly. "You might fall."

Toni sighed. "Justin, for once, have pity on me and give it a rest. I hear caution on a daily basis now, you know."

"No, I don't know anything about what's going on over there anymore," he said, sounding slightly aggrieved.

"It's probably just as well that you don't," she muttered, and didn't realize that she'd spoken aloud.

She saw Lane out of the corner of her eye and tried not to stare. If he would only put on more clothes after his shower, she would be able to cope with his presence in a more dignified fashion. In her mind it wasn't seemly to be so ungainly with child, and still so in lust for the man who had fathered it. She kept waiting for her nesting instincts to replace the ones that had gotten her into this mess, but they were lost somewhere in the memory of making love to a gentle giant.

Lane watched her from the hallway, and thought that she grew more beautiful with every day. Hiding his feelings was difficult, but imperative. Telling her that she was loved before she believed that she was worthy was not a wise move. Not after all that had come and gone between them during the past week.

After a lifetime in sunny Florida, the shock of a Tennessee winter and the warm woman he held each night without possibility of loving was making him slightly insane. Coupled with that, each day he was reliving a hell on earth just by watching her body grow bigger with a child that he'd caused, a child that he still believed might kill her. He was not a happy man.

Toni turned away from the intensity of Lane's gaze and realized that Justin had stopped talking. She hoped that he had not been waiting for an answer to a question that she hadn't heard.

"So, Justin, other than a small dose of guilt, which, by the way, remind me to thank you for later, was there anything else you wanted me to know?"

"I was just making sure you had someone to take you to your doctor's appointment today. And," he added, "Judy wanted me to invite you…and the lawman…to come to dinner this weekend after church. Everyone will be here."

Toni wanted to say no, but there was really no point in delaying the inevitable. Her family already knew Lane as the man she'd saved from the flood, and who later had saved her life. But they had yet to meet him on personal ground as the newest member of the Hatfield clan. The implications of what might happen when they got together boggled, but she knew the time had come.

"I suppose we could," she said.

Lane paused in the doorway, wearing nothing but a towel and giving her a look that she didn't want to interpret. He was her husband in name only, but she still felt obligated to inform him of the invitation.

"Justin has invited us to dinner the day after tomorrow. Is there a reason why we can't go?"

Lane grinned at the flush on her face, letting his gaze rake her lush, pregnant curves from top to bottom, then shook his head slowly from side to side.

"Not one I can do anything about," he whispered for her ears alone.

Toni inhaled sharply and spun away from his taunting look. Why he kept flirting with her while she was in this…condition was beyond her comprehension. She'd always imagined that men would be turned off at the thought of hugging a whale. She hated pretense, and she was convinced that he was only being nice to her because he was a nice man, not because he really cared a damn about her. She had, after all, deceived him four ways from Sunday.

"We'll be there," she said. "And Lane's going to the doctor with me, so I don't need you to ride sidesaddle anymore."

"Well, if you ever need me, Judy and I are just a phone call away," he muttered, and hung up the phone.

Toni replaced the receiver with a sigh. Her brother was feeling rejected, but she didn't have time to pamper his ego, not when Lane kept putting himself in her direct line of vision.

"Aren't you ever going to get dressed?" she grumbled. "We'll be late for my appointment."

Lane grinned. "No, we won't. But just to make you happy…" He came so close to her that she could smell the scent of soap still fresh on his skin. "I'll go put on some clothes. I wouldn't want to make you mad." He leaned down and kissed the tip of her ear. "I like to keep my women happy."

"And you're very good at it, too, aren't you? Comes from extreme amounts of practice, I would assume."

She glared at him, almost begging him to deny what she'd implied, that he'd had so many women that he was highly adept at keeping them satisfied. But he did nothing but arch an eyebrow and stare intently at the curve of her lower lip.

"You're very beautiful when you're angry, did you know that?" He tilted her chin just enough to catch the light from the window behind him and knew that she was in shock by what he'd said. "It makes those little gold flecks in your eyes almost burn. And your nostrils flare, just like they do when you make love. It's a sexy thing to see, Antonette. I hope you know you're making me hurt all over."

Oh, my God. I can almost…almost believe he means that.

She slapped his hand away and pushed him toward the bedroom door. "Just put on some clothes and quit lying through your teeth. I don't need to hear all of this, and I damn sure don't believe it."

Lane groaned softly with want. Ignoring the pout on her mouth, he leaned down and kissed her, savoring the connection as deeply as if it had been their bodies and not their lips that had joined.

"But you will," he whispered as he reluctantly released her from the kiss. "One of these days you will believe everything

I tell you." *If it isn't too late,* he thought. *If I haven't already killed you and we just don't know it.*

"I'll be ready in a few minutes." He ran a finger down the straight of her nose. "You know what? You don't have any more lipstick on, honey." He winked as he walked away.

Toni held the memory of that kiss and his wink long after they had ended, and reminded herself not to make so much of the lust that she'd seen in his eyes. It had to have been her imagination.

As usual, the doctor's office was crowded. Women in various stages of pregnancy sat or sprawled, as their conditions demanded, upon the waiting room chairs while herding their other offspring with weary eyes.

Lane tried to find a place for himself among this all-female show, but considering the location, and his size, it wasn't easy. His legs stuck out in the aisle, and his shoulders bunched as he tried to make himself as small as possible.

At this point in their lives, no matter what their marital status, these women were almost past appreciating the male of the species. But Lane Monday was a hard man to ignore, and so he suffered more than one speculative glance.

Toni checked in, quietly giving the receptionist the new information regarding her name change. But a half hour later when the nurse announced the name of Toni Monday, and the woman everyone had known during the past few months as Toni Hatfield stood, the women grinned.

"Way to go, girl," one woman said, and wiggled her eyebrows at Toni and appreciatively eyed Lane's long legs and backside as they passed.

"Good grief," Lane muttered, and sighed with relief as they bypassed the waiting room for an examining room instead.

Toni hid a grin. It was the first time in their entire relationship that she'd seen him ill at ease. She wanted to laugh at it all. At his unwarranted fears regarding the child. At the way fate had intervened with her plans. But she wouldn't laugh in the face of fate. Not anymore. She'd come to realize that she was no good at playing God with people's lives. She'd tried to have a child without the father's knowledge and look what had happened. She'd ruined his future as well as her future plans. She'd planned on being a mother, not a wife. In her mind the two had still not mixed.

"Just have a seat," the nurse said. "Dr. Cross will be with you shortly."

The moment that they entered the confines of the sterile-looking room, Lane started to sweat. There were too many ugly memories associated with baby doctors and hospitals for him to relax.

Toni recognized his agitation and suspected its cause. Instinctively, she sought a way to make his fears a little easier to bear.

"It will be fine," she said softly, and patted his arm without thinking that she'd initiated a contact she'd sworn not to make.

Lane covered her hand with his own, and then caught it to his lips, pressing a kiss on the palm of her hand before pulling his chair as close to hers as it could get.

"God, Toni, you just don't understand. You keep saying that I should look at you and know that you can handle anything. Well, look at me for a change. See me and know the truth. I'm so big, Toni. Maybe too big. I sire children just like me."

She shuddered and wanted to throw her arms around him. But that would be admitting to herself, as well as to him, that she couldn't do this alone.

"I certainly hope so," she said. "I always wanted a child with blue eyes."

Lane's eyes widened, and a slight smile spread across his face. "You are so damned hardheaded, aren't you?"

She shrugged, trying to think of an answer that was close to the truth; then the doctor entered the room and saved her from lying.

"Miss Hatfield, I see you're—"

"Mrs. Monday," Toni said, correcting him at the same instant that the doctor noticed Lane. "Dr. Cross, this is my husband, Lane Monday. And he seems to believe that I will die having this child."

The shock of her statement stayed with Dr. Cross as he watched the man unfold himself from the chair and then stand to shake his hand. He looked up, then up some more.

"Mr. Monday, it's a pleasure," he said, and waved for them to sit as he dropped onto his stool. "And what exactly is it that causes such fears? Your wife is as healthy a patient as I've ever had."

"I've already lost one woman I got in this condition, that's why," Lane growled. "Now, you tell me that it's not going to happen again."

"I don't understand," the doctor said.

"His first wife died trying to give birth. The baby was too big, and she didn't survive the shock of other complications. Because of his size, Lane blames himself."

"A common, but unfortunate, misconception," the doctor said. He smiled at Lane as if to ease his words. "You are definitely a big man. But all big men start out as small babies."

"Not always so small. I weighed eleven pounds when I was born," Lane said. "My first wife wife died trying to give birth to a seven-and-a-half-month preemie that weighed nearly ten pounds. Talk me out of this. I need to believe you," Lane said.

The doctor's eyebrows rose as he listened to the big man's shaky voice. "Look, Mr. Monday, during a woman's pregnancy and the ultimate act of birth, the only real thing a man can take credit for is the sex of the child. Whatever else happens during the pregnancy and birth process is the mother's and the doctor's business. You just sit back and wait for it all to happen. If there should be a complication, thanks to your warnings, we'll be well prepared. But I do appreciate knowing your family history. It will help me prepare for things I might not have foreseen."

"I told you it would be fine," Toni said, and tried not to think of another woman dying without being able to give life to the baby that she and Lane had created.

"I will believe it when I see that baby and know that my wife is fine and not before then," Lane said stubbornly.

"I take it you wish to be in the delivery room," the doctor said.

"I have to be," Lane replied, taking Toni's hand as he spoke. "I need to see for myself that she will be all right."

He doesn't mean that the way it sounded, Toni told herself. *He doesn't really care about me on that level. It's just fear, and not love, that I hear in his voice.*

But the notion had still been set, and when the checkup was over and they were on their way home, Toni dozed with her head against his shoulder, and dreamed of a man and a baby and matching eyes of blue.

"You sure are big," a young Hatfield announced. "Are you a giant?"

Lane eyed the stair-stepped brood of children surrounding his chair, and tried not to grin. They were so serious that he felt they at least deserved his full attention.

"Nope," he said, and ruffled the dark brown hair of the nearest child. "Do I look like one?"

"Yes," they chorused, and then giggled.

"Well, you all look like little squirts to me. Are you?"

A small blond girl giggled. She was David and Laura's youngest, and the Sunday dinner that Lane was given to endure seemed destined to be a series of questions and answers. First from the grown-ups, now from their children.

"I'm not a squirt," the child said. "I'm Chelsea."

Lane laughed, and lifted the tiny child onto his lap. "Hello there, Chelsea. You sure are pretty. Just like your aunt Toni."

She nodded, apparently well aware of her worth in her family. "Did you really marry my aunt Toni?"

"Yes. Is that okay?"

"I guess so," she said, giving his face and hands special consideration. "You don't even have to stand on a chair to do the tree, do you?"

Even the adults who were trying not to listen laughed along with Lane at the little girl's reference to decorating the Christmas trees that stood in every Hatfield home. And it was fairly obvious, even to the babies, that Lane Monday did not stand on chairs to do anything.

Toni watched from across the room, wishing she believed Lane when he said that she was pretty, and wanting desperately to be the one sitting in Lane's lap, and not her niece. She was tired and aching, and sleepy beyond belief, and she could have used that broad strong shoulder to lean on.

Her spirit was still willing, but her body was giving out on her on a daily basis. At eight months pregnant, she completed daily tasks with slow deliberation, not wasting a motion or wanting to retrace a step.

She shifted in her seat, and then stood, bracing her back with her hand as she slipped from the room. Maybe if she could just find a quiet place to lie down for a minute, she would feel better.

It was instinctive, but the moment Toni left the room, Lane seemed to know it. It was as if she'd turned out a light behind her. The sense of loss was physical as his gaze lifted from the child in his lap to the people sitting and standing around the room.

He stood, making a game out of dumping the little girl on her head in the chair that he had just vacated, while he searched the room for a sign of his wife.

"Where did Toni go?" Lane asked.

Both Justin and David looked startled at Lane's obvious concern. "Why, she's right over…"

The chair was empty.

Lane walked out of the room without waiting for an answer. He would see for himself.

There were no empty beds. They were full of napping babies in various stages of development, from toddlers to crawlers. The youngest baby, Lucy, claimed the baby bed for her own.

Toni sighed and then smiled at the sight of the babies in slumber. "I should have known better," she said, and then turned and walked straight into Lane's outstretched arms.

"Oh!" she gasped, and would have staggered but for the

strong clasp of his hands upon her arms. "I didn't see you there."

"But I saw you," he whispered, aware of sleeping children and his weary woman, and held out his arms again. He groaned beneath his breath when she walked into the hug without complaint. Little by little, she was coming around. He just had to have faith that she would finally realize what she meant to him.

"Are you ready to go home?" he asked as he stroked the back of her neck with a gentle, massaging touch. "You look tired."

Toni leaned sideways against him, remembering a time when their bodies fit much closer, and tried not to cry, although it was something that happened often these days.

"Yes, I am. Thank you for asking."

He frowned. "I don't need to be thanked for taking care of what's mine."

Oh, Lane, if only I believed that you meant that. But the only sign that she gave of how moved she was by his words was to lay her head a little closer to the middle of his chest. It felt safest to be closest to his heart.

She entered the living room beneath the shelter of his arm, although from Toni's point of view, Lane was simply helping her stay on her feet.

"What's wrong?" Justin asked when he saw how Toni was leaning.

Lane answered for the both of them. "She's tired. We're going home. Thank you for dinner and the family welcome. She will call."

Toni didn't even bother adding to his comments other than sending a smile and a couple of kisses to a niece who demanded what she called "bye-bye sugars."

She wondered as they drove home if she dared let herself get used to someone making decisions for her. Having a broad shoulder and a warm body to lean on was a luxury she could get used to fast.

It was almost dark when Lane burst through the kitchen door, slamming it shut behind him, trying to outrun the cold gust of air that had been on his heels.

"I wondered where you had gone," Toni said nonchalantly, trying not to let him know that she even cared. She'd awakened from her nap to an empty house and realized how much she'd come to depend upon his presence for comfort.

"I was helping Abel feed the livestock," he said, stuffing his gloves into the pocket of his coat before hanging it on a peg by the door. "He says it's going to snow before morning."

Toni shrugged. The man that she'd hired months earlier to help her with the heavy work had taken a definite liking to Lane.

"If Abel says it will snow, then it wouldn't surprise me." And then she smiled at the thought of the Christmas tree in the living room and the presents tucked far underneath the spreading branches. "In six more days, it will be Christmas. It would be nice if we could have a white one."

Lane frowned at the thought of snow and ice. "I don't want to be stranded up here," he muttered, unaware that he'd thought out loud.

Tears stung Toni's eyes, and she turned away, unwilling to let him see that he could hurt her this badly, simply by admitting that he didn't want to be around her.

"I know I'm not the best company, but you asked for every bit of this, you know."

Lane groaned, caught her in his arms, then turned her to face him. "I didn't mean I didn't want to be stranded *with* you. I meant I didn't want *you* to be stranded, honey. When are you going to get it through your head that I want you safe?"

"And when are you going to stop making me crazy talking like I'm a doomed woman? How do you think that makes me feel, Lane? I've never had a baby before. I want this to be a positive experience, not one where I go in expecting to breathe my last gasp on a delivery table while you stand there pointing and saying 'I told you so.'"

Shame made him acknowledge the truth of her words, although he couldn't let go of his fear.

"You're right," he said quietly, and tilted her chin with his fingertip. "I'm sorry. I'm a jerk."

"I already knew that," Toni said, then looked away so that he would not see her smile.

"How can I make it up to you?" Lane asked, and nipped the lobe of her ear with his teeth before cupping her hips with the palms of his hands.

"Don't," Toni said, trying to twist out of his arms. "I'm ugly. You don't want to—"

"My God," Lane said, and shook from the need to make love to her. "How can you say that? Better yet, how can you think it, lady? Do you feel this?"

He grabbed her hand and slid it down the front of his jeans. It wasn't the zipper that bulged against her palm. Her eyes widened as he wrapped her in his arms and whispered against her cheek.

"I lie beside you and watch you sleep and think I've never seen a woman as beautiful. You smile and my damned legs get weak in the knees. I've loved you far longer than I had a right to. And I don't care anymore whether you believe me or not. I had what I thought was a really good reason to leave you behind. You, my hardheaded woman, have proved me wrong."

"I don't believe you, you know," Toni whispered, and let his hands wander across her body because it felt too good to make him stop.

"Oh, hell, I know that," he muttered, and picked her up into his arms as if she didn't weigh an ounce.

"Where are we going?" she asked.

"To bed. I want to show you something."

"What?" she asked.

"How many ways there are to make love without rocking the boat…and our baby."

She gasped and unconsciously covered her belly with her hands. "You can't actually mean you want to…that we can…" She ducked her head and then closed her eyes when he laid her gently in the middle of the bed. She heard the rustling of clothing being removed and moaned softly. "I don't want you to see me like this."

"Why not, love, why not?" he whispered. "I'm willing to let you see me like this."

Toni opened her eyes and couldn't tear her gaze away. He wore nothing but the jutting proof of his desire and a fire in his eyes that burned white-hot.

Her voice shook, but her gaze never wavered as she made a place for him on the bed.

"Oh, Lane, what was I thinking when I pulled you out of that flood?"

"If you weren't out of your mind then, I can assure you that before we're through tonight, you will be."

"It snowed."

"Good morning, love," Lane whispered as he walked up behind her, kissing the back of her neck before peering over her shoulder and out the window. "Of course it snowed. Abel said it would, remember?"

Toni remembered a whole lot more about last night than Abel's predictions. She'd never known a body could soar when weighed down with a burgeoning anchor.

"Oh!" she gasped, laughing when the baby kicked and rolled inside her like a tumbling pup. "Feel that! We're not the only ones awake."

Lane's eyes turned dark with emotion as Toni grabbed his hands and held them flat against the skin on her belly. But old memories got in the way of new joy, and he dropped his hands and turned away. As badly as he wanted to share Toni's joy, he was unable to let himself care. If he cared too much, it might jinx them all.

"Don't," Toni urged, pulling him back around and then stepping into his arms. "Don't be afraid for me or for your child. We're going to be fine."

And if you're not, I will not survive twice.

Chapter 16

The days rolled one into the other until finally Christmas arrived, bringing a false frivolity with it that had little place in the reality of their lives. The intensity of Toni's fears increased on a daily basis. Facing the fact that she loved Lane without hope of a lifetime together was unbearable. But she wouldn't let herself pretend that he would stay after the baby's birth. Once he saw that they were safe and that he had not been responsible for another woman's death, she fully expected him to leave.

And Lane watched her coming closer and closer to her time, and spent countless nights awake, watching for a sign of impending danger, praying that he would be able to prevent another tragedy from occurring. Life without the child that she carried would be heartbreaking, but life without Toni would be impossible to bear. All he could do was hope for the best and pray that they both survived.

And so they existed, day after day, not saying what was in their hearts, and pretending that nearly all was well.

Lane propped himself onto one elbow as he played with the tousled curls that lay across Toni's forehead, careful not to wake her as he kept watch. She slept without moving, weary from daylight to dusk from the burden of the child that grew bigger with each passing day.

It was instinct that made him feather his fingers across the swell of her belly, desperate for some kind of assurance that all was well within. But when the tiny kick of little feet and bumping elbows vibrated beneath his palm, he buried his face against her shoulder and shook with fear. So much life. So much danger.

Toni sighed, and rolled over on her back, unaware that the man with whom she lay was on sentry duty at her side.

Lane watched her eyelids flutter and knew that she was near to waking. When her arms stretched high above her head and she arched her back like a slumberous cat, he rolled over, grabbed the small box from the bedside table that he'd put there earlier, and leaned down and kissed her the rest of the way awake.

"Merry Christmas, love."

Unaware of the turmoil with which he'd spent the night, Toni rolled over in bed and then sat up, rubbing sleep from her eyes as Lane dropped a small package in what was left of her lap.

"What is this?" she asked.

"Your Christmas present. Open it."

"My hair," she muttered, and started swiping at the curls that had escaped their tie.

"Lady, you would drive a man crazy just to prove that you could," he growled. "I love your hair. I like it in knots. Open the damned present."

"I need to go to the…"

Lane groaned and rolled over onto his back. "Go," he said, and pointed toward the bathroom door. "I should have known better than to try to compete with Mother Nature."

Unable to wait for her return, he tore into the wrapping himself, and when she came out, hair combed, face washed, ready to open her gift, Lane met her at the door with it already in his hand. He spread her fingers and then slipped the ring onto her finger and didn't know that he was shaking until he took a breath.

"It's a sight better than handcuffs, don't you think?"

Tears blurred all but the glimmer of stones from her vision.

"Does this mean you're going to keep me?" she asked.

He groaned and then held her. "You don't listen very well, do you? I already told you I'm here forever."

"I don't know why you still care," Toni said. Guilt pricked her conscience on a daily basis, and this show of affection only made it worse. "I begged you to make love to me. Then I lied to you. I tricked you. I used you, Lane. You should hate me…why don't you?"

He sighed, and rubbed the small of her back where he knew that she always hurt.

"Beats the hell out of me, woman," he said softly. "All I know is I don't want to let you out of my sight."

"What about when this waiting is all over and I've had the baby?" Toni asked. "What will you do with your life then, Lane?" *What will you do with mine?*

"It will never be over for me," he whispered. "I'm always going to be waiting for you to come into a room and light up my life."

Toni sighed. She'd heard it before, but she needed to hear it again. Maybe if she heard it enough, she would really begin to believe.

"And you really don't mind that you had to transfer your job location?"

He grinned. "Naw…I'm sort of looking forward to it," he said. "For a lawman, one place is just about as good as another. I like the business and don't much care where it's done. Besides, I'm enjoying this time off. I've even learned enough about farming and ranching that Abel has stopped laughing at me."

She leaned against his chest and lifted her hand, tilting her fingers so that the brilliance from the circlet of gold and diamonds caught the rays of early-morning sun coming through the bedroom window and reflected it back into her eyes.

"Do you like it?" Lane asked anxiously.

Toni smiled through her tears. "I love it." *And you. Maybe one day I'll be able to say so without making a fool of myself.*

His grin said it all. Impulsively, Toni threw her arms around his neck and did something he wasn't expecting. She kissed him. Hard. With something close to desperation.

Their lips met. His were firm and slightly shocked; hers were soft and warm, begging for an acceptance that she already had and just wouldn't believe.

"Ah, Toni girl, I love you so much." He wrapped her in his arms. "How did I ever exist without you?"

She took his words to heart and pretended that it was so. "Want some breakfast, or do you want to wait for lunch?"

They were going to Justin's for the holiday meal, and Toni knew from experience that the feast would be endless.

"I don't want to wait for anything," he whispered, and feathered kisses down the side of her neck.

She blushed. "Would you like your present now?"

"Please," he groaned, and took her back to bed.

It was only later that he opened his gift that she had hidden beneath the tree. Compared to what they had shared in their bed, it came in a distant second, but he would never tell her so. Her joy in finding him a sweater that actually fit his long arms and broad shoulders went a long way toward getting him through the day with in-laws who watched his every move, and the multitude of children who reminded him that he and Toni would soon have one of their own.

Several inches of snow covered the ground. Icy spears clung to the eaves of the house as well as to the tree branches in the surrounding yard. New Year's Day had arrived with a blast of fresh winter weather that they were just now coming out from under. Two days earlier the roads had been nearly impassable.

It was with relief that they had awakened this morning and seen that things were starting to melt. Lane had gone to town for groceries, leaving Toni safely inside where it was warm, with no danger of slipping and falling and a promise to be back within the hour.

Only moments ago she'd heard the pickup pulling into the

barn and breathed a sigh of thanksgiving that he was back. She felt off center, as if something approached from an unseen angle. And then the quiet within her erupted as her nephew, Bobby, burst through the back door in tears.

"Aunt Toni! Aunt Toni! You've got to come quick!"

The child's frantic cry was thick with fear. And the shock of seeing Justin's ten-year-old son come running into the kitchen with blood on his hands and face made her sick.

"Oh, my God! Bobby! You're bleeding! What happened? Did someone have an accident?"

And then everything faded out of focus. She saw the little boy talking, but she couldn't hear his words. Staggered by the shock of what was happening, she braced herself and leaned against the cabinet while a sharp pain rippled low across her back. "Oh," she groaned, and cradled her belly. It suddenly felt as if it had doubled in weight.

Lane jumped the steps and entered the house on a run, unaware that the shock on Toni's face was from pain, and not the sight of her nephew covered in blood. From the barn he'd seen Bobby coming through the trees and knew from the way he was running that something was wrong.

"What happened, son?" he asked, catching the child just as the child spun around and flung himself into Lane's arms.

"It's my daddy," he cried. "You've got to come. A tree fell on him. I can't get it off!"

"Dear God," Toni moaned, and pushed herself away from the cabinet. "Where is he?"

"We were cutting firewood down in the hollow beside the old spring. Daddy slipped on the ice just as the tree started to fall. He slid under it. I couldn't get it off of him. I tried and I tried to pull him out, but I couldn't."

"Bobby! Listen to me," Lane said. "You've got to calm down so we can help your daddy. How long ago did this happen?"

Bobby choked, swallowing his sobs as he swiped at his face with both hands, streaking the blood even worse. Toni tried not to think of her brother and death in the same breath, but it was impossible.

"Just a little while ago," Bobby said. "Maybe fifteen minutes."

"Good," Lane said. "Now, was your daddy talking to you?"

"No," Bobby groaned. "He's all pale and I know he's cold. There's snow all over him."

Lane hugged the child and then knelt. "Can you show me where your daddy is?"

Bobby nodded.

Lane stood abruptly and turned to Toni, unaware that she bore the burden of two fears. He was all business.

"Honey, call the sheriff. Tell Dan that we need an ambulance and whatever rescue equipment the volunteer fire department has. I'm going with Bobby now. When the men get to the farm, tell them how to get to the spring."

She nodded, and bit her lower lip to keep from moaning. She was scared to death to be here alone. What if they were gone a long time? The baby was coming. She knew it. And then she looked at Bobby's face and her decision was instantly made. She could not sacrifice her brother's welfare for her own safety. If Lane knew what was happening to her, he wouldn't go and she knew it. He would wait for the sheriff to arrive and that might be the difference between Justin living and dying. Whatever was happening to her she would deal with after they were gone.

"Take the tractor and a log chain," she said. "There should be several in that empty granary next to the feed bin, and you should probably take the first-aid kit. I don't know what's in it, but you might be able to use something."

"I'll get it, Aunt Toni," Bobby cried. "I know where it is."

Toni clutched at Lane, willing some of his strength into herself as she wrapped her arms around his waist.

"Be careful," she whispered. "I don't know what I would do if anything happened to you, too."

Lane's heart leapt. He'd been waiting for weeks to hear her say something like this, and now to be unable to stay and pursue this declaration was painful. But for Justin's sake, it would have to wait.

"That goes double for me, lady," he said, and pressed a hard, hungry kiss against her mouth. "You take care of yourself and our baby. Don't do anything stupid, honey. Call Judy and tell her what happened, then call the rest of your family. Some of them will probably go to her, but make sure that someone comes to stay with you. I don't want you here worrying alone."

She nodded, and then they were gone. Her fingers shook as she dialed the phone. But it was not from fear. It was pain. Another spasm rolled across the muscles of her back, ripping through her senses as a reminder that this was only just starting.

When Dan Holley answered the phone, his voice was music to her ears.

"Chaney Sheriff's Office."

"Dan, this is Toni Monday. I need an ambulance out here fast."

Dan grinned. "Is it time, girl?"

She gritted her teeth. "You have no idea," she groaned, and leaned against the wall to brace herself for what she felt coming.

"Where's that big ol' husband of yours? I expected him to be the one making the call," he teased.

"Listen to me, Dan. I don't have much time," she gasped, and let the pain roll across her senses. "Justin's been hurt. I don't know how badly. All we know is that a tree fell on him while he and Bobby were cutting wood. Lane's gone back to the old spring below our place to try to help. We need an ambulance and all the rescue equipment you have."

"Oh, my God," Dan muttered. "Hang on, honey. We'll be there in a whistle."

She bit her lip to keep from crying. "And would you send a second ambulance for me while you're at it?"

Dan nearly dropped the phone. "Are you saying what I think you're saying?"

"I'm in labor. Lane doesn't know it. It just started, but it seems like the pains are already pretty severe."

"How far apart?"

"Maybe five minutes," Toni said, and hugged herself to keep from shaking. Doing this alone was scary business.

"I'm calling for a mediflight helicopter. Lane already told me about the difficulties you might face during delivery. There's no way an ambulance will get you safely to Knoxville in time, not if your pains are already that close."

"I don't care what you do," she cried, then doubled over. "Just hurry!"

"For once, make that big family of yours useful and get someone over there with you now!" he said, and hung up in her ear.

Seconds later she'd dialed another number. "Laura, this is Toni. We need help."

By the time she was through, Hatfields were in motion, but she didn't care. She was trying to get to a bed. Standing had become an impossible feat.

"There he is!" Bobby cried, and pointed toward the slough on the opposite side of the creek from where they stood.

Without wasted motion Lane shifted the tractor into low gear and proceeded across the frozen streambed. He stopped on the last level space of ground, aware that if he got any closer, he would be sliding down the incline and right into Justin's lap, which was exactly what they didn't need.

"Now if only we'd brought enough chain," he muttered.

They had not.

"What are we going to do?" Bobby said, and started to cry. "We can't pull the tree off of him. The chain's too short."

"Damn it," Lane said, then dumped the log chain, and slid down into the slough without giving himself time to think.

The snow felt like ground glass. It was icy and hard, and packed to the point that standing was next to impossible. Lane made the last few yards to the fallen tree on his rear. He knelt beside Justin, then felt on his brother-in-law's neck for a pulse.

"Thank God," Lane muttered when he felt the faint beat,

then cupped Justin's face in his hand. "Justin! Can you hear me?"

Justin's eyelids fluttered. It was all the answer that Lane was going to get. He looked at his watch, gauging the time from when they'd left the house against the time that it would take the rescue squad to arrive, and he knew that they were looking at another thirty minutes at least.

He won't last.

Lane knew it as surely as he knew his own name. Justin was already in shock. And from what he could see of the wound on his leg, it was a wonder that he hadn't already bled to death. The cold was probably what had saved him, but it could ultimately be what killed him, too.

Lane stood up, then looked to the hill where the ten-year-old stood, frozen in horror by what had happened to his daddy.

"Bobby, get down here."

The child quickly obeyed.

"Here's what we're going to do," he said. "When I lift this tree up off of your daddy's legs, I want you to grab him by the boots and pull. Do you think you can do that? It's downhill enough that I think his own weight will help him slide out from under the tree if you can get him started."

Bobby's eyes grew round. He stared down at the immensity of the tree pinning his father to the ground, and then back up at the man towering above him.

"Can you do that?" Bobby whispered.

Lane's lips thinned with determination. "I hope to hell I can, son. Now come on. Say a prayer for your daddy, and one for me while you're at it. We're both going to need some extra help today."

Bobby gritted his teeth and sniffed back the last of his sobs.

"Yes, sir," he muttered, and bent down.

Lane cursed beneath his breath when he saw that Bobby Hatfield's hands spanned less than half the circumference of his father's work boots.

"Maybe you could get a better grip on his blue jeans instead," he offered, and nodded when he saw Bobby get a good, solid handful of denim in each fist.

"Good boy," he said, bending toward the fallen tree. "Now get ready. When I say pull, you give it all you've got."

The boy nodded, and when he looked up at Lane with all the trust in the world written upon his face, Lane recognized it as a look that Toni had given him more than once. The thought of what he had to lose gave him the courage to continue. But he was going to need more than courage to move the tree.

The bark was rough against his palms, the snow cold against his knees as he knelt. He had already decided that lifting the tree from a dead squat would be impossible, even for him. It left him with one option that involved great risk for him, as well.

There was just enough space near the root end for a man to crawl under. And if he was lucky, and didn't slip on the ice and the snow himself, there might be a way for him to lever the tree up enough for Bobby to pull his father out. To do it he would have to use the broad surface and great strength of his size and the back that God had given him.

Lane dropped to his knees.

"What are you doing, Uncle Lane?"

The quaver in the boy's voice was all the reminder that he needed to hurry, but it was what Bobby had called him that he would never forget. He didn't want to lose that respect...ever.

And then Justin moaned, and his eyelids fluttered open just as Lane centered the tree directly across the strongest part of his back.

"What the hell do you think you're trying to do?" he groaned, and pushed weakly at Lane's arm.

"Don't bite the hand that's about to free you," Lane ordered; then he grinned and winked at Justin, trying to alleviate some of the terrible tension of the moment.

"You're a stupid, crazy son of a bitch," Justin mumbled. "If it slips, we're both dead."

"Daddy, try not to move," Bobby said as tears rolled down his face. "It makes your leg bleed worse."

"Shut up and help your son when he starts pulling you

out,'' Lane ordered. ''Remember, Bobby, when I say pull, you yank for all you're worth.''

''Yes, sir,'' Bobby said, and reaffirmed his grip on his father's jeans.

Before he could talk himself out of what he intended to do, Lane started to lift. The weight was at once unbearable and impossible to budge. He shifted his body lower down the trunk and closer to where Justin was pinned, then repeated the lift, letting most of the weight rest upon the broadest portion of his shoulders.

In spite of the cold, in spite of the ice and snow down the tops of his boots and inside his pockets, he started to sweat. He groaned and lifted himself a little bit higher, using his leg muscles now, as well as his arms, to lever himself higher and higher off of the ground.

A twig on a limb down the trunk snapped. And then another and another, and Lane knew that he must be moving something other than the snow beneath his hand and feet for the branches at the other end of the tree to start breaking.

''You're doing it! You're doing it!'' Bobby shouted. ''A little more, Uncle Lane. Just a little bit more.''

Lane groaned again, and moved his knees a little closer to his chest, now using his full body weight as a lever against the end of the fallen tree. His muscles bunched, then tightened, then burned, and he knew he was nearly at the end of his strength. He couldn't look over at Justin and see the fear on his face. But he desperately needed to concentrate on something other than the ground slipping beneath his feet.

He cursed, shifted his weight once again and closed his eyes and thought of Toni.

''Damn it, move!'' he cursed, and bunched every muscle in his body toward the weight upon his back, then tried to stand.

The branches that were holding it off the ground at the other end suddenly snapped, and Lane felt the tree beginning to give.

''Now, Bobby!'' he shouted, readjusting his position so that the tree would not move with the pull of Justin's body. ''Pull, son! Pull with everything you've got.''

At first nothing happened. He heard the child's frantic sobs and desperate gasps for breath. He heard the scrape of snow as Bobby slipped and fell backward upon his rear. And then suddenly Justin was sliding out of his line of vision, and Lane blinked rapidly to clear his sight as sweat ran and burned into his eyes.

"He's out! He's out!" Bobby cried.

"Keep pulling him," Lane urged. "The tree might slide back over him when I let it go!"

Justin did what he could to help, digging his fingers into the snowpacked ground, trying to pull himself along. Then a miracle occurred. He started to slide.

"Let me go," he yelled, and waved his son aside as he tried to get as far away from the tree as possible.

"Let it go, Uncle Lane," Bobby cried, and ran in front of the tree until he was eye to eye with the big man who had just saved his father's life. "He's sliding down the hill by himself. The tree can't hurt him now."

"Get back," Lane groaned, and knew that he had nothing more than a few seconds in which to clear himself from the danger of being trapped as Justin had been.

With his last ounce of strength, he moved the bulk of his lift from an upward motion to a backward one instead, then propelled himself forward, falling facedown onto the icy ground. Snow spewed up into the air as the tree belly flopped only inches from his heels, and Lane moaned, then rolled over on his back, gasping for breath, and staring up into the gray, winter sky, never so glad to feel cold in his entire life.

When he could breathe without pain, he lifted his head and looked over the tree and down the hill. Justin lifted his arm and waved. Lane started to return the favor, when he realized that Justin was not waving at him. He looked up at the crest of the hill. Help had arrived. And from the trail of blood Justin had left behind him in the snow when he'd slid out from under the tree, it was none too soon.

Dan Holley was first on the scene, followed closely behind by paramedics and a couple of men with chain saws.

"Doesn't look like we'll be needing the saws, boys," Dan

said, and left Justin's care to the experts, while he knelt at Lane's side. He looked down at Lane and shook his head. "I have a feeling I just missed a hell of a show."

Bobby Hatfield appeared out of the crowd and threw his arms around Lane's neck. "You did it! You did it! You're the strongest man in the whole world, Uncle Lane."

Lane grinned and wrapped the boy in a warm but shaky hug. "You helped, Bobby. I couldn't have done it alone, and don't you ever forget it."

"You should have seen him, Sheriff Holley," Bobby said. "He just lifted that big ol' tree off of Daddy like it was nothing."

Lane fell back onto the snow with a weak laugh. "Had one of them faked out, didn't I, Dan? Did you hear him? Like it was nothing." He covered his face with his hands and moaned before rolling to a sitting position.

"Help me up," he said, lifting his hand for Dan to pull. "I've just about used up all there is in me."

Dan frowned.

"I sure hope you've got a little bit left, old son, because if things are still going like they were when I left your place, you're in the process of becoming a father."

Lane was on his feet without aid in seconds. "Lord," he muttered as he headed for the ridge where he'd left the tractor. "Turn my back on her and look what she does."

"I already called for a mediflight helicopter. I didn't think she could make the run to Knoxville, considering the facts."

Lane stopped in midstride and turned. The look on his face was colder than the ground on which he was walking.

"What do you mean...considering the facts?"

Dan shrugged. "She was already having pains five minutes apart when she called for an ambulance. If you hurry, you just might get to kiss her goodbye before the chopper lifts off."

Lane was already running up the hill.

Chapter 17

Lane was coming through the trees below the house when the chopper set down in the backyard where the garden had been. He shoved the tractor into high gear and spun up the slippery slope and into the yard just as they carried Toni out the back door.

Running on legs that felt like rubber, he made it around the house and caught the stretcher just as the flight crew was about to lift it into the belly of the aircraft.

"Wait!" he shouted, and felt the air being sucked out of his body by the impact of the spinning rotor above their heads.

"Mister, there isn't any time left to wait," the paramedic shouted. "And there's no room for passengers."

Lane looked down into Toni's face, expecting to see fear, even accusations of abandonment flowing from her lips. She was gritting her teeth, but she was smiling through tears.

"Race you," she said, trying to laugh at the fact that she was going to beat him to the hospital by nearly an hour, and then caught her breath upon another pain.

"This is it, buddy. Kiss her bye-bye. We're gone."

Lane grabbed the man by the arm, pinning him to the spot with the intensity of his gaze as well as his brute strength.

"If it comes down to it," Lane shouted, "you tell that doctor to save my wife. No matter what else happens, you save her…for me."

Toni's pulse rocketed on a pain and a joy, all at the same time. *Save her for me. No matter what.*

And then his mouth was on her lips, and he swallowed her moan of pain and wanted to scream. When they pushed him away and the helicopter lifted off, he felt incomplete, bereft. Everything that mattered to him in this world was out of his hands and swiftly moving out of his sight.

Seconds later she was gone, and Lane was running back into the house for dry clothes and the keys to his car, scattering Hatfields in his wake like chickens.

"Here comes another one, Toni. Now push."

Dr. Cross's order came on the heels of a pain that had lifted Toni off of the bed. She hadn't needed his warning that the pain was on its way. She'd felt it coming a long time before he had.

"I'm pushing," she groaned, and gripped the sides of the bed to brace herself.

"More. More. Just a little bit more," he urged.

"No more," she said hoarsely, then shuddered and moaned and fell back onto the bed, weak and spent.

Time, for Toni, had ceased upon her arrival at the Knoxville hospital. There were no seconds ticking, minutes passing or hours flowing in the birthing room, only wave after mind-bending wave of pain that seemed to have no end. No matter how hard she'd tried during the past hour, the baby hadn't budged. She could tell by the expression on Dr. Cross's face that he was beginning to be concerned. And while she couldn't read the monitors to which she was hooked up, even she knew when the numbers began to fall.

"We're losing pressure, Doctor."

The nurse's whisper was soft, but Toni heard the warning, anyway. She moaned weakly as she felt the arrival of another wave of pain, then lifted herself onto her elbows and bit her lip to keep from screaming. There was no energy left in her to react to the pain, only what it took to survive the next spasm.

"This is it, girl," Dr. Cross urged, and pressed his hand in the middle of Toni's abdomen. "Come on, honey. You can do it."

It was the tiny blip registering a fading pulse and a waning heartbeat that gave her the impetus to give it one last try. She'd done the unforgivable in order to bear this child; she would do the impossible to keep it.

She gritted her teeth, braced herself and closed her eyes, concentrating on the contraction and the pressure, trying to follow it with her body. She would have this baby or die trying. Lane flashed into her mind with the thought, and in that moment, Toni knew that she couldn't afford to die. He would never forgive her.

"Oh, God," she groaned, and let herself go with the pain.

She never even heard the doctor's shout of approval, or her baby's first cry. She was out of hearing distance, lost in the blackness between unconsciousness and exhaustion.

And then she felt a weight upon her belly and instinctively clutched it in her arms. She opened her eyes and looked down just as the baby's head turned. Their eyes met, and for a fraction of a second, Toni swore that recognition passed between them...mother to child.

"Well, hello, sweet baby," she whispered, and ran her finger across the tiny face, feature by feature, unwilling to wait for the nurse to even clean the infant up. She'd waited entirely too long as it was to meet this child.

"It's a girl," the doctor said.

"Is she perfect?" Toni asked, cradling the tiny head within the palms of her hands as the doctor did a quick inspection.

Dr. Cross grinned. "Now if I say she's not, will you give me a head start before you take off my head?" And then he relented. "From the looks of things, I would say so." He lifted her from Toni's arms. "She needs to take a little trip, to get weighed in, blood-typed and such. And you need a breather, too. By the time you're both changed, you can have one hell of a conversation for all I care."

Toni frowned when the baby was lifted from her arms. "Do you promise to bring her right back?"

"I swear," he said. "But first things first."

Moments later the sounds of a baby's loud cry could be heard down the hall in the nursery.

"She's fine," the doctor cautioned. "It sounds like she just doesn't like having her face washed."

Toni frowned and then started to cry.

"Here now," Dr. Cross said. "You're supposed to be happy."

"I've just had a baby, and I don't know if my brother is alive or dead," she said, and sobbed a little bit harder.

"If you promise not to cry, I'll get you your answers. What do you say?"

Toni hiccuped and closed her eyes. She was too tired to argue. "I promise. Especially if you can find my husband in the process."

"That might take some doing, but I'll give it my best shot," the doctor said. Moments later she was alone except for the nurse who was quietly cleaning up.

Lane came off of the elevator on a run and met Dr. Cross coming down the hall. Their expressions were of mutual surprise.

"Just the man I was sent to find," Dr. Cross said with a grin.

Lane grabbed the doctor by the shoulders and tried not to shout.

"Where is my wife?"

"Room 301. They haven't moved her out of the birthing room yet, but…"

Lane left him standing there.

"As I was about to say, feel free to go in," Dr. Cross muttered, then continued on his way.

Lane was inside the room before it dawned on him that he hadn't even asked the doctor what had happened. And then he saw Toni, rolled over on her side away from him, her shoulders shaking with sobs, and he felt the floor going out from under his feet.

Oh, my God. Something bad happened. It was all he could think of to explain why she was crying.

"I'm sorry, sir," the nurse said. "She's not ready for visitors. Please wait outside."

"Toni? Sweetheart," he said, ignoring the nurse's behest.

Toni rolled over onto her back and held out her arms.

"I didn't think you would get here this soon."

He sat down on the side of the bed, and when her arms slid around his neck and she began sobbing against his chest, his heart froze. Breathing constricted until words became impossible to form.

"My God, sweetheart, I'm sorry. I didn't know. I didn't know. I wouldn't have left you if I had."

"Justin! How is Justin?"

"It's all my fault. Whatever happened, we'll get through it together. I love you, lady. With all my heart. Don't give up on me now. I couldn't make it without you in my life."

Toni tightened her hold around his neck. He wasn't making sense, but it felt so good to be holding him that she almost didn't care.

"Lane, what happened? Did Justin…is he okay?" Her voice trembled as she waited anxiously for him to answer.

"We can adopt a baby if you want. Hell, we can adopt ten. Just don't send me away."

"Have you lost your mind?" Toni sighed, and snuggled her nose a little deeper in the breadth of his chest. He smelled of after-shave and the starch that she'd used on his shirt and cold, fresh air, and she'd never been so glad to feel a man's arms around her in her life.

Her words finally penetrated. He leaned back enough to be able to see her face, then kissed the corner of each of her eyes before moving to her mouth.

"I love you, Toni. I'm sorry I—"

"Lane, listen to me!"

He jerked. "What is it?"

"How is my brother? Is he okay?"

He leaned his forehead against her shoulder and sighed.
"Oh, hell, I'm sorry," he muttered. "Yes, honey. We got him
out. His leg didn't look good, but he's alive."

"Thank God," she said, and hugged him tight. "I knew
that you could do it."

He cradled her face in his hands, searching for signs of
despair that he could not see.

"Are you all right?"

"I need to sleep for a week, but I fear my sleeping days
are over," she said.

"The baby…was it…did they have to…?"

Toni's eyes widened. Obviously he still didn't know that
she'd safely delivered their child. And then the door opened
behind him.

"See for yourself," she said, and pointed toward the nurse
who was entering with a wiggling bundle in her arms.

Lane's head turned toward the door. He stood, a look of
wonder upon his face, then stared in disbelief at the baby.

"You did it," he muttered.

"I suspect you helped," the nurse said sweetly, eyeing the
mass of man before her. "Hold out your arms."

Lane did as he was told, and then staggered backward, using
Toni's bed for a seat to avoid dropping them both onto the
floor.

"Oh, my God," he whispered, and parted the tightly
wrapped blanket.

"Now you've done it," the nurse admonished as the baby's
hands began to flail in the air. "This one's a real live wire.
She doesn't like to be still." She gave Toni a look of admiration. "And if she'd weighed a whit more than the ten
pounds, two ounces that she came in at, she wouldn't be
here."

For Toni the details and what ifs were over. She was too
lost in the joy on Lane's face as the nurse walked out of the
room.

"Say hello to your daughter."

He turned to Toni with tears shimmering across his eyes and shook his head, unable to speak.

The baby's mouth pursed, and just when she would have puckered and yelped, Lane's finger stroked the side of her cheek. Her mouth turned like a magnet toward the touch, instantly open in an instinctive search for sustenance.

"Wrong parent," Lane whispered, and bent down and kissed the baby's soft cheek.

Toni was moved to a fresh set of tears. "Do you want to name her?" she asked.

He nodded, then lifted the baby close, cradling her in arms so big against a chest so broad that she was almost lost in the vast amount of space. He looked down at the woman who'd given him the world.

"Since the day that we met, you have given me joy. Constantly...without asking for anything in return. Would you care if I named her Joy?"

Toni held out her arms for the baby. "Let me see if she looks like a Joy," she teased. She ran her hands lightly over the baby's head, loving the feel of soft hair and tender skin beneath her palm. "You look like a Joy. Do you feel like a Joy, little girl?"

The baby squeaked and wiggled. Toni grinned. "She says yes, thank you, she believes that she does."

Lane grinned through tears. "My days are numbered," he muttered, to hide his emotion. "I will be forever outvoted in a house full of women. What is a man to do?"

"Love us?"

Lane heard the uncertainty in her voice. Even now, after all they had been through together, she still doubted her ability to hold a man's love.

"I already do," he said solemnly. "You should know that by now, Antonette. Don't ever, and I mean ever, ask me that in such a doubting fashion again."

Toni sighed and lay back on the pillow, snuggling the baby closely against her side. She closed her eyes and thought of answered prayers and a future that she never thought she would have, and looked up to find Lane staring intently at her face.

"Lane?"

"What, sweetheart?"

"I don't know the words to thank you for all that you've done…for what you've given me."

Lane's eyes narrowed until Toni could see only slits of blue fire.

"I do," he said quietly.

Her eyes widened. Suddenly this conversation had a very familiar ring.

"You could tell me that you love me. Just once. Just for fun."

Emotions overwhelmed her. Of what he had given and given without hope of return. "I love you."

Lane sighed. He was so certain she wouldn't say it that he was already talking before her words sank in. "I'm not asking for much, you understand. It's no more than a man has a right to expect from the woman he expects to spend the rest of his life with."

"I love you very much."

"I've told *you* countless times that I love you. You can't…" He quit in the middle of a sentence. For a moment he couldn't think past the wonder of what he'd just heard. And then she smiled and patted the bed beside her, and he lay his head in the bare space between baby and breast and let her love encompass them all.

Toni threaded her fingers through his hair, loving the way the silky, dark strands parted at her touch.

"I hope Joy has your hair and eyes," she whispered, and felt his shoulders shaking beneath her hands.

Lane lifted his head. "Say it again, Toni. Tell me you love me."

"Of course I love you," she whispered. "I had to love the man before I would consider having his child. I just couldn't believe that he would love me back."

Lane's eyes widened in disbelief. "Are you telling me that you've been in love with me all along?"

Toni smiled, and lifted the baby into her arms. "Lesson number one, little girl. Men are dense."

Lane laughed aloud. "But we float pretty damned good," he said, reminding her of how they had met.

Toni grinned in return. "With absolutely no sense of direction," she added, her own reminder of how she'd saved him from the flood.

"That's what women are for," Lane whispered, his mouth aiming for her lips. "To keep us on the straight and narrow... forever and ever, till death do us part. Remember?"

The kiss was sweet, with a promise of years to come. When Lane broke the connection between them, he whispered one word that she instantly understood.

"Deal?"

Toni smiled. "Deal."

Epilogue

The morning glory that hung over the front-porch roof swung back and forth in the easy breeze like small blue bells with no sound. Sunshine dappled the yard between the spaces of shade where children ran, shrieking with excitement as they searched out the brightly colored eggs hidden earlier. Baskets already overflowing with chocolate bunnies and yellow marshmallow chicks had to make room for the Easter eggs that were being found.

It was Easter at the Monday homestead, and the Hatfields had come to dinner. But no one was eating. Those who weren't watching the frivolity in action were busy snapping pictures of the event, trying desperately to capture the expression of joy on each child's face when a new egg was discovered.

And Toni was right in the middle of it all with her baby on one hip and a basket full of eggs on the other, while the persistent breeze molded the skirt of her white cotton dress to her body.

"Smile for Daddy," she said, and jiggled Joy into a wide,

toothless smile while Lane aimed the camcorder in their direction.

Lane watched it all through the camera's eye, and he knew that if he lived to be a hundred, he would never see a more beautiful sight than what was before his eyes.

Marriage and motherhood had made a beautiful woman out of a pretty lady. Her face creased constantly in smiles, and she was never still. She wouldn't have changed a thing in her world if given the chance and he knew it. The knowledge that he held the hearts of two beautiful females in the palms of his hands was staggering. The baby adored him, and Toni's love bound them all. He was a man twice blessed.

"Uncle Lane, watch this."

In response to the shout, he turned, taking the eye of the camera with him, and found Bobby Hatfield centered within the frame, attempting to juggle three eggs.

Bright pink, brilliant blue and grass green eggs went up, then down, then fell at the boy's feet with a splat as he made a frantic grab for the last one and missed. Lane aimed the camera at the mess, then back up at the look of disgust on Bobby's face.

"You've got to have faster hands than that, boy," Lane teased, then laughed when a couple of barn cats headed for the disaster, already licking their whiskers at the unexpected feast.

While they were watching, the sheriff pulled his car into the driveway and parked.

Lane aimed the camera and caught the look of surprise on Dan Holley's face when he accidentally stepped on an egg hidden in the grass.

"Oh, shoot," Dan said, stopping to clean off his shoe. "These are my new boots."

"What do you suppose he wants?" Justin muttered as he limped up beside Lane.

"Here, you do the honors and I'll go find out," Lane said, handing Justin the camera.

"You're supposed to put them in a basket, not on the sides

of your feet," Lane said, and grinned when the sheriff rolled his eyes and lightly cursed beneath his breath.

"Fine thanks I get for coming out on a holiday," Dan said, handing Lane an envelope. "I found a Western Union man lost as hell on the other side of town. He was looking for your place. It was easier to bring this myself than to try and explain how to get here."

"Thanks," Lane said, then opened up the telegram.

HAPPY EASTER TO EVERYONE. STOP. KISS MY NEWEST NIECE FOR ME AND HUG MY SISTER. STOP. THANKS FOR PROVING ME RIGHT, LAWMAN. STOP. IF I CAN FIX MY WORLD THAT WELL, MAYBE I WILL COME HOME. STOP.

LOVE, WYATT

"Well, I'll be damned," Lane said. "The prodigal son might actually return one of these days."

"Must be from Wyatt," Dan said.

Lane nodded, then looked up at Toni in the middle of it all, and smiled. He had a lot to thank Wyatt Hatfield for. He hoped he *did* come back.

"You're just in time to eat," Lane said, and gave the squashed egg on Dan's boots another glance. "I think the egg hunt is nearly over."

Dan grinned. "No, thanks, but that's my cue to exit. You have a good day, now, you hear?"

Lane waved him off and then turned to see Toni coming toward him across the yard.

"Lane, you have a phone call. It's your boss. He called me darling and praised the latest picture of Joy that he'd seen and told me you never looked better." She made a face. "It sounds to me like it's a good thing I did the laundry yesterday. You'll be needing clean clothes for the trip."

Lane sighed and hugged her. "Maybe not. Here, Dan brought a telegram from Wyatt. You can share it with the clan while I get the phone." Then he held out his hands to the baby who was wearing a miniature bunny suit, complete with long pink ears and a tiny, white powder-puff tail. "Want to come with Daddy to talk to the bad man?"

Toni laughed, and watched with a happy heart as Joy willingly went from her arms to his with a drool and a smile and pink ears flopping. Father and daughter disappeared into the house as Justin walked up.

"What did Dan want?"

Toni handed him the telegram. "It was from Wyatt. You can read it. He said to tell everyone hello."

Justin quickly scanned the page, and handed it back with a rueful smile.

"He's right, you know. He read Lane Monday's intentions better than any of us. Thank God that he interfered. If it wasn't for Lane, you wouldn't be this happy, and I would be less of a man today."

Toni hugged her brother, then whispered softly in his ear. "I don't care what you look like, Justin, or how you walk. You will *never* be less of a man. You're just about the best brother a girl could have."

Justin grinned to hide how moved he was by Toni's praise.

"Well, hell yes, I'm the best. If you don't believe me, you can ask Judy."

Toni grinned and hit him on the arm. "You're awful," she said. "I've got to go see what that darned man wanted with Lane. I suspect duty is about to call."

She hurried across the yard, her long legs moving gracefully beneath the full skirt of her dress, and entered the house on the run. Lane met her at the door empty-handed.

"Where's Joy?" Toni asked.

"Laura took her. The kids wanted to have their picture taken with the Easter bunny. Joy seems to be it."

Toni grinned. The suit had been an inspiration. "When do you have to leave?" she asked, knowing Lane's assistance was needed on another assignment. His duties had been lessened, but her husband's expertise was still essential to some cases.

"Tonight."

Lane slid his hands around her waist and then lowered them until her hips were perfectly cupped in the palms of his hands.

She moaned softly in his ear when he pulled her close against the thrust of his manhood.

"When will you be back?" she gasped, wishing that they were alone.

"Day after tomorrow."

She tried not to let her dismay show, but she hated to sleep alone and he knew it.

"I will miss you like hell," he whispered. "Can't you tell everyone to go home now? I want to make love to my wife."

Toni made a face, and wrapped her arms around his neck. "I don't think so," she whispered, and sighed when his mouth descended.

He tasted of baby powder and soap, and she knew that the last place his mouth must have been was on their baby's face.

"I love you, Lane," she said when his mouth had moved from her lips to her throat.

He stilled, and his arms tightened around her waist, crushing her to him until she found it difficult to breathe, but she did not protest. Being loved this much, by this much man, was something special. She would take all that he had to give her and still want more.

"I love you, too, Antonette," he whispered, and then he grinned. "I'll bet I'm the only man who can claim the luckiest day of his life was the day he nearly died."

Toni smiled, and leaned back in his arms, well aware that it placed their lower bodies in perfect but painful alignment.

"I might know where there's an empty hayloft," she said.

Delight was rich in his voice as he swept her off of her feet and twirled her around the room while the party went on outside without them.

"Are you asking me to take you to the barn and make love to you?"

Toni pursed her lips and cocked her head thoughtfully, giving him a cool, assessing look.

"I might be…but only just this once."

He laughed. "And just for fun?"

She wrapped her arms around his neck and blew lightly in his ear.

"Darling Lane, is there any other way?"

* * * * *

SILHOUETTE
SENSATION ®

AVAILABLE FROM 21ST JANUARY 2000

BRIDGER'S LAST STAND Linda Winstead Jones

Heartbreaker

When two strangers met that cold and lonely night something special whispered in the air... But with their affair ruined before it began, that was so nearly the end of it—except that Frannie could identify a murderer and needed Bridger's protection. Suddenly, only Bridger's arms could make everything better...

THE LADY'S MAN Linda Turner

Elizabeth Davis believed in relying on herself. The last thing she needed was a self-appointed rescuer—even if he was a gorgeous government agent... Close contact with Elizabeth had Zeke forgetting what was so good about the single life!

KEEPING ANNIE SAFE Beverly Barton

The Protectors

Dane Carmichael was the only man who could keep Annie Harden safe. From the moment he laid eyes on stubborn, beautiful Annie, he knew she would be his... But Annie had never encountered a man so strong, so dominating, so absolutely infuriating as Dane. And never had she needed—*or wanted*—a man more!

THE MERCENARY AND THE NEW MUM
Merline Lovelace

Follow That Baby

Sabrina Jensen was prepared to do anything to protect her precious child, but the intruder standing over the baby's crib was the man she'd once loved beyond reason, the father of her daughter. *But Jack Wentworth was supposed to be dead!* What was going on?

AVAILABLE FROM 21ST JANUARY 2000

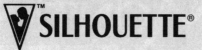

Intrigue
Danger, deception and desire

LOVER, STRANGER Amanda Stevens
RELUCTANT WIFE Carla Cassidy
THE BODYGUARD Sheryl Lynn
TO LANEY, WITH LOVE Joyce Sullivan

Special Edition
Compelling romances packed with emotion

DADDY BY DEFAULT Muriel Jensen
WRANGLER Myrna Temte
DREAM BRIDE Susan Mallery
MARRIED BY ACCIDENT Christine Rimmer
IF I ONLY HAD A...HUSBAND Andrea Edwards
NOT JUST ANOTHER COWBOY Carol Finch

Desire
Provocative, sensual love stories

PRINCE CHARMING'S CHILD Jennifer Greene
JUST MY JOE Joan Elliott Pickart
THE SOLITARY SHEIKH Alexandra Sellers
COLONEL DADDY Maureen Child
THE OUTLAW JESSE JAMES Cindy Gerard
COWBOYS, BABIES AND SHOTGUN VOWS
Shirley Rogers

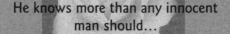

2 FREE

books and a surprise gift!

We would like to take this opportunity to thank you for reading this Silhouette® book by offering you the chance to take TWO more specially selected titles from the Sensation™ series absolutely FREE! We're also making this offer to introduce you to the benefits of the Reader Service™—

- ★ FREE home delivery
- ★ FREE gifts and competitions
- ★ FREE monthly Newsletter
- ★ Exclusive Reader Service discounts
- ★ Books available before they're in the shops

Accepting these FREE books and gift places you under no obligation to buy, you may cancel at any time, even after receiving your free shipment. Simply complete your details below and return the entire page to the address below. *You don't even need a stamp!*

YES! Please send me 2 free Sensation books and a surprise gift. I understand that unless you hear from me, I will receive 4 superb new titles every month for just £2.70 each, postage and packing free. I am under no obligation to purchase any books and may cancel my subscription at any time. The free books and gift will be mine to keep in any case.

S0EA

Ms/Mrs/Miss/Mr ....Initials.............................
                                                                BLOCK CAPITALS PLEASE
Surname ....
Address ....

....

....Postcode................................

Send this whole page to:
UK: FREEPOST CN81, Croydon, CR9 3WZ
EIRE: PO Box 4546, Kilcock, County Kildare (stamp required)